The characters and events portrayed in this book are fictitious. Any similarity to real persons, living or dead, or events, is coincidental and not intended by the author.

Copyright © 2019 by Camille Douglass
All rights reserved.
Curse It
First Publication: January 2019
Dead Mouse on Cheese Publishing
ISBN: 978-1-950163-00-7 (ebook)
ISBN: 978-1-950163-01-4 (paperback)

Cover Art: Deranged Doctor Design

For Weejer, a.k.a. D.J., my favorite brother

ACKNOWLEDGMENTS

It's strange when you realize that despite your strong introvert tendencies that you really do have quite a few people in your corner. First, thank you to my family: Dad, Mom, Danielle, D.J., I am forever grateful to have a family that thinks I'm mildly smart and pretty damn funny, and even likes me when I'm salty.

I would have never gotten this far without the OG EVW group. Particularly Jami Gray who has been my rock in the writer's life storm. Additionally those friends who have read drafts, discussed business-y things, believed in me, my craft, and my ability to become independently wealthy through writing (ha!). A few of those people are Alicia, Sheena, Nicole, Kelly, DeAnna, and Dave. I'm sure I've missed many, but this is a series so I'll get to you.

Finally, thank you to the professionals who have helped make this book better. Jessica Dall from Red Adept Editing did an amazing job with content edits. Tanja from Deranged Doctor Design thank you for making an image out of words that perfectly fits the story.

Finally, to the readers, thank you for taking a chance on a new series.

A PEG DARROW NOVEL

CURSE IT

CAMILLE DOUGLASS

1

I chose the wrong dive bar.

"Well, Jake, how is it justice if you're cursed, and you have to apologize to the witch to have it lifted?"

"I don't know, Jessica." The voices were garbled coming from the cheap speakers.

"Exactly. Why should we suffer them to live? The Bible says it plain and simple: we shouldn't."

"Life isn't fair, you idiot," I yelled at the TV.

The bartender glared at me. He probably hadn't expected a rowdy patron at two in the afternoon on a weekday.

My eyes dropped from his glare as I dug around in my purse looking for change for the jukebox. I would play anything at this point to drone out the daytime talk show. A girl just wanted to be able to sit in a bar and drink away an awful job interview. Not listen to dreck. Sadly, my purse lacked the quarters needed to end my suffering. I could leave, but I'd paid five bucks for the stupid vodka soda and damned if I wasn't going to drink it.

An angel of mercy heard my silent prayers because

another patron in possession of quarters graciously started playing some Janis Joplin. The TV automatically muted in deference to the paid music. I could finish my drink in one song and get the hell out of here. I exhaled deeply.

"Bad day, Sug?"

My head snapped up to the deep feminine voice that I knew from somewhere. My eyes widened when I saw who'd taken a stool next to me. "You could say that."

The girlish giggle that escaped didn't match Pammy's husky voice and broad frame. "I would hope not. If you're drinking in a bar this time of day without a reason, you've got a whole other set of problems."

"Why are you here?" I sipped my drink for a little liquid courage.

"Well, Sug, I take care of everyone's problems, so say something random and I'm probably dealing with it in some form or another."

I set the glass back on the napkin provided as to not cause another ring on the already warped bar top. "I guess being sheriff for the witches isn't all it's cracked up to be."

"Oh no, it is everything it's cracked up to be, but everybody needs some me time. And when your brain won't stop running, sometimes it needs some help." She lifted her drink.

"Amen." I lifted my glass and clinked it to her beer bottle.

"Funny thing is, I came here to get away from witch problems and here I encounter another witch with a problem. I'm guessing divine intervention. So, tell Pammy your problems. I'll try to help you fix them."

Janis stopped singing and Elvis immediately started crooning. Whoever played the first song had blessedly paid for multiple songs.

"How'd you know I was a witch?" I gave my glass a

little swirl, the ice clinking against the glass as I avoided eye contact.

"Hmmph, how'd you know I was one?" She turned in her seat not letting me shy away.

"Uh, being the sheriff of an entire state makes you fairly recognizable."

"Yup, and being sheriff I notice things. You were downright pissed off about that talk show. Got all red and splotchy, could just be a witch sympathizer if it weren't for your tell."

I decided to play along. "Tell?"

She teetered her barstool back on its hind legs holding onto the edge of the bar, rocking a back and forth like a twelve-year-old delinquent asking to break his head open. She wasn't concerned; she let go of the bar with one of her hands to grab her beer and took a swig before smirking at me. "You were scratching your palms. You were so annoyed that your magic was giving you itchy palms. You know that tends to be a sign of a lot of raw power." With that she plopped the stool back down on all four of its legs.

I took another sip of my drink. "I've got a fair bit." Not that it did me much good. The Mesa School District wasn't impressed with the fact that I could take down a predator with one shot of power, help heal a broken arm, or perform magic light shows for children. In fact, all of my magical skills were decidedly frowned upon.

"No need to be modest. It's a good thing."

"One would think so."

"You here because someone didn't think so?"

"Yep, my twenty-third job interview in two years since I finished my master's. Too bad nobody wants a witch for a teacher."

"Psssh, life's a bitch, Sug. You had to have known there wouldn't be a job for you."

Maybe I did know. I just wanted to believe that I was the exception. Rather than answer her I took another large gulp of my drink. There was only a sip left. I needed to head out. I raised my arm to gesture for the check.

Just as the bartender looked up, Pammy called out, "Two reposado shots, and a couple of beers."

"Oh no, I can't. I drove here." I lowered my arm.

"Take a cab, or I'll get one of my girls to drop you off. No sense in going home where you'll be miserable. Drink some tequila and tomorrow you can be miserable for a good reason, but tonight, tonight all your problems won't exist."

A shot glass was set in front of me, overfilled so it ran down the side. My eyes crossed at the fumes coming off of it. *Why the hell not?* I raised the shot and clinked it with Pammy's.

"To poor life choices!"

Pammy laughed before adding, "Peg Darrow, don't be so sure it's a poor life choice. This might the beginning of something wonderful," she said, knocking back her tequila in a single swallow.

I stared at her for a moment, wide eyed. *How did she know my name?*

Pammy set her now empty glass down and stared at mine expectantly. I slammed the shot before I lost my nerve, or maybe to gain some nerve—because I wasn't sure if having the head honcho of the Arizona witches know my name was a good thing or not. She must have read my mind because there was another shot in front of me before I could think too hard on the subject.

I decided to go with the flow and lifted the shot to my lips without argument.

"Atta girl," she smiled wide, her teeth a startling white

against her dark skin. "Since the teaching gig ain't happening, ever think of working for me?"

The tequila went down the wrong pipe, burning as I coughed it out. Pammy gave me a hearty slap on the back. I sputtered as she went on.

"If it's money you need, I could use another Fortune. Think about it."

I grabbed a napkin and continued to wheeze, my mind spinning. I wasn't sure if it was from the booze or the unexpected offer. Once I could breathe again, I looked at Pammy, who arched a brow at me in challenge. Crap, she practically dared me. I never could turn down a dare.

2

T hree weeks later and I still couldn't look at a bottle of tequila. Sometime in that long day that had not ended until the wee hours of the next morning, I'd accepted Pammy's job offer. I'd assumed the offer had been made in pity, but drunk Peg did not believe that pride was a particularly useful trait. Pammy had seemed pleased when I'd made a bottle of vodka explode in protest when the bartender cut us off, five drinks after he should have. Good thing Pammy held her liquor better than I do because someone had needed to calm down the bartender when he'd threatened to call the cops on us. Ironically, Pammy would have been called on herself.

Witches didn't fall under police jurisdiction. Pammy and her Soldiers of Fortune otherwise known as Fortunes took care of policing their own, for a price. The government said they weren't equipped to deal with magical crimes. Truth was they didn't really want to protect witches. Especially since the general public didn't hold much love for us, thanks to an ancient curse, a messy betrayal, and the death of children. I always thought it was the last one that set the humans off. But, if humans knew what else lurked in the dark, they would consider us downright harmless. Unfortunately, that ancient curse also took away our immortality, leaving our kind too low on the totem pole to stir the cauldron, so to speak.

For the past few weeks, I'd played Pammy's errand girl. I dealt with the small-potato gigs, a curse gone bad, a missing familiar, underage drunk witches. All in the minor leagues. Not that I was totally keen on taking on the majors. The state of my bank account argued otherwise. After all, more danger meant more money.

Friday night rolled around and here I stood in front of the house of a Violet Williams. Another easy job. Violet hadn't checked in with her bedridden father in the last twenty-four hours and he was worried. Fifty bucks for a quick welfare check was definitely worth my time.

Pammy texted me the address, along with a photo, and some general info about the missing girl. The drive hadn't been far from my house, which was just a bonus. The city of Mesa was mostly suburban sprawl outside of Phoenix. Some areas, like the one I was driving through, were built in the earlier half of the twentieth century and included large lots with irrigation to flood the water-starved yards. I pulled up to such a house with my turquoise seventies Jeep Grand Cherokee. The secluded house sat at the end of a dead-end street. Citrus trees peeked over the block fence, much like those in my own yard.

Thanks to the big yard, Violet's home remained somewhat isolated, even though it was near downtown Mesa. Since witches were the only supernatural race currently out to the humans, so to speak, we tended to like our privacy. The neighborhood streetlights were sparse, and other than the general outline of the house and trees, there wasn't much to see. The area garnered a sinister feeling but that could be due to the late hour, my tiredness, or both. Grabbing my phone, I got out of the Jeep, not bothering to lock it, despite leaving my purse in the car. This time of night, no one would be wandering by to check cars. Perhaps I was being more trusting than the average person and definitely more trusting than the average witch. A concrete pathway led up to the front porch, and I followed it. As I went to step onto the raised porch, I hit the wards.

The impact knocked me back about a foot and nearly set me on my ass. Not what I expected. Apparently Violet wasn't the trusting type. My own heavy-duty wards were because of my job and a rough family history, but according to Pammy's texted information, Violet was an RN at a local witch clinic. Not the usual type for deluxe warding. Besides, wards were expensive, unless she had the power to do them herself. If Violet was home, her wards would've warned her about my presence. Perhaps she'd come out and see who was visiting. I waited a minute and then put up my hand sending a pulse of non-threatening power through the ward. A simple knock, knock. Again, I waited. No answer.

It didn't look like anyone was home. Unfortunately, that wasn't a good enough answer for a worried father. There weren't any set rules to completing bounties. The main goal was to get the job done without pissing Pammy off. However, different things would piss her off on different days, which meant I seemed to be walking on a tightrope. I was tempted to call and ask if I should break the wards to check the house, but then Pammy's lecture on growing a pair and making my own decisions from a case a few days ago echoed in my head.

I didn't lack assertiveness, but bounty collecting hadn't been my planned career, and the job training for Fortunes seemed shockingly sparse. The Arizona Board of Education had grudgingly granted me a substitute teaching license, but the schools only called me when they were desperate. So here I was, trying out a new job to pay the bills, and trying to "grow a pair" in case this became my permanent bread and butter.

Stepping up to the wards again, I raised my hands and sent out another pulse of power. This time it wasn't a knock but a probe. My magic picked its way over the wards, looking for a weak spot. The wards were stronger than I had first thought. Luckily, what I lacked in finesse I made up for in raw power.

The only weakness was on the corner of the porch roof. Which made sense because it was likely the place the warding had been started and completed. Personally, I would have double-knotted them with a spider web, but I wasn't in the business of creating wards; the insurance premiums were too high on magic-centered security companies.

I put up both my palms and centered my magic. It took a few minutes to pull up the amount of power needed, but once gathered, I pushed it out toward the weak spot with as much force as I could. The bright green light of my power would have woken up the human neighbors if they could see it. But humans lacked witch sight. Or goblin sight, vamp sight, fae sight, or whatever, depending on whom you asked.

When the stream of green hit the weak spot, it met with the wards' own magic, and the impact forced me backwards. My power turned defensive, fighting against the red glow of the wards, then winked out. The wards weren't defeated, but they were weakened. Unfortunately, so was I. I bent over, placing my hands on my knees and took a few wheezing breaths.

Power wasn't infinite; otherwise becoming mortal

wouldn't have mattered to witches. I needed sleep and food and regular practice to maintain my stamina. Since I had two out of the three, I straightened up and released my power again. This time when it hit the wards, I could feel little static pop pops in the air. Despite my exertion, my magic remained bright green whereas the wards became a flickering pink.

When they finally shattered, I took a shaky step back and sat in the middle of the walkway cross-legged. I felt like I'd just run a marathon and noticed the sweat running down my forehead as well as soaking my shirt. *Sexy.* I reached up and touched my hair; sure enough, my sweat had made little wisps stick out at frizzy intervals. All that wasted effort to tame my hair into a French braid. I sighed and pushed myself to my feet before I drew the attention of a nosy neighbor.

After all of the effort I used breaking the wards, I was surprised to find the front door unlocked. The discrepancy of the unsecured door versus the heavy-duty wards made the hairs on the back of my neck stand up. Before stepping into the darkened foyer, I did a quick check on my power reserves. Not much there. If I were attacked, I could cast a quick knock back and run.

Never underestimate the flight in the fight-or-flight mindset. I didn't, and it had saved my ass on many an occasion. I considered doing an aura sweep, but I couldn't justify using the last of my reserve. The last thing I needed was to pass out on the stoop, vulnerable to anyone or anything passing by.

I took a deep breath and forced myself to enter the house.

"Hello? Violet, are you home? Are you hurt? Do you

need assistance?" I called out into the dark space. Receiving no response, I wasn't sure it was a good thing or a bad thing. If Violet was hale and hardy, living it up in Rocky Point, she was going to be pissed to come home to broken wards. Still, she could take that up with her father...or Pammy, if she was feeling suicidal.

Running my hands blindly over the cool stucco wall, I searched for a light switch and was happy to find it without stubbing any toes or bruising any shins. The light illuminated the small foyer and cast shadows to my right into what appeared to be a living room. Reaching around the entry, I did another grope for a light switch, surprised to find the smooth plastic easily yet again. Normally these older home were wired in what could be at best described as a creative fashion, and at worst as a pain in the ass.

The light illuminated the room, and the results were a bit startling. Like Violet, I owned a small older home on a big lot, so I expected something more like my living space. Whereas my home was warm with thrift store finds and antiques, Violet's was jarring, with bold colors and clean sterile lines. Her couches were scarlet and didn't look comfortable. Her end tables and coffee table were chrome, glass, and severe angles. Some would like it; I wasn't one of them. I liked comfy furniture and tables that wouldn't draw blood if I were unlucky enough to bump into them.

Shrugging, I gave myself a mental slap. I was here to look for Violet, not judge her taste in interior decorating. Stepping into the room, my tennis shoes sank into the deep black carpet. It was downright luxurious. *Maybe she could lie on the floor when her couch made her ass fall asleep*. Walking around the small space, I saw no sign of anyone. The room had a connecting walkway to what looked to be a formal dining room. Turning on another light, I reminded myself to ignore the furnishings while scanning the space for possible threats that weren't related to the interior design police. As I continued through the house I found same lack of anything *off* in the dining room, kitchen, and a small spare bedroom doubling as an office.

It wasn't until I opened a door to what I thought would be the master bedroom, based on its size, that confusion set in. The room didn't have any of the bright colors torturing the rest of the house. Instead it was sterile in a whole other sense of the word. The fluorescent lights combined with shiny laminate flooring created an artificial glare. It bounced off the out of place pieces of medical equipment. Yet, since Violet was an RN, what did I know? Maybe nurses liked to keep their work close at hand. Looking around and seeing no signs of foul play, I moved on to the final room in the house.

Opening the door, I finally found the master bedroom. Like all the other rooms, it had clean metal lines and bright colors. Once again, I saw nothing to suggest foul play. But as I turned to leave, one item struck me as…off. Sitting at the foot of the bed was a large metal trunk, too large for the space and not matching any other decor. Rich and warm, it was wrapped in metals of gold and bronze, decorated with elaborate scrollwork, and clashed horribly with the cold, gleaming chrome of the bed frame.

I walked toward it, mesmerized. The chest called to me. Running my hand over the delicate metalwork, I recognized it for what it was. The intricate details and delicate melding of numerous metals was the work of a talented goblin artisan. It felt like finding Renaissance art in the middle of a Modern art exhibit.

It was also strange: goblins were by no means struggling financially and didn't sell their work to outsiders. Not even to witches. Witches once fought beside goblins in wars past, but since losing our immortality, goblins treated us the same way that one would treat a distant relative, with respect but no assistance. How had Violet gotten the trunk? A generous lover who was powerful enough to risk the *faux pas*? Getting down on my knees, I tested the lid to see if it was locked. It wasn't, and despite invading Violet's privacy, I needed to open it.

The pale corpse tucked inside me made me fall back flat onto my ass. Violet lay inside the trunk. I scrambled back to my knees and reached inside checking for a pulse just in case. Her skin was cool to the touch but not completely cold yet. Fear shivered down my spine. I should have checked for auras before entering the house. *Too late now.*

If someone were lurking in a closet, I would need every iota of magical power I could find to keep myself safe. This bounty was turning into a bigger deal than fifty bucks would cover. I needed to call Pammy.

3

Standing up to pull my phone out of my pocket, I did a visual sweep of Violet. Her pale skin had the flawless quality only present on the young. Her medium brown hair was cut into a severe bob in direct contradiction of that youthful appearance. The light frilly pink negligee clashed with her home decor. My gaze drifted down to her hands, and I hissed in a sharp breath while my heart began to race. Willing it to slow, I placed my hand on my chest. If tonight brought me any more surprises, I wouldn't have to worry about unpaid bills because I would have a heart attack.

There, placed in her hand was a poppy flower. To humans, the bloom often brought to mind the fun print used on dishes and bedding. For a witch, a poppy usually meant one thing—vampires. Cold sweat, rancid with fear, made my T-shirt cling to my skin once more. Vampires were the worst of the other supernatural races, and they hated witches with a particular viciousness. Once we became mortal and therefore vulnerable to their glamouring, we were considered fair game.

Witches were addictive like crack to vampires. For a brief time after they drank our blood, they would have a small fraction of our powers. Shifter and fae blood had the same benefits, but those donors were immortal and a lot more likely to retaliate once they shook off the blood loss. Goblins, rumor had it, had skin too thick and only minimal power would travel through their blood, so they weren't considered worth the effort by most vampires.

My hands were shaking as I dialed Pammy. She answered on the first ring, an unintelligible din played in the background.

"What's up, Sug?"

"We have a problem."

"Hmmm." The background noise was silenced.

"Violet is dead, and she's holding a poppy."

"Well, shit on toast." Pammy didn't even pause.

Holding back the inappropriate laugh that bordered on hysterical, I forced out, "Tell me about it."

"Haven't had a vamp murder in a while." She paused. "You ready for your first big gig?"

Not really, but I needed money. The current fee however would not be worth risking my hide for. Callous or not, I went for honest. "Not for fifty bucks."

Pammy laughed. Apparently possible vamp murders didn't phase her much. When her laughter petered out, she continued, "The father can't afford our rates, but we can't let a murder of one of our own go unpunished. I'll call the Benefactor." She hung up without saying goodbye.

She'd call back within a few minutes. I took a deep breath in an attempt to stop my hands from shaking. I slid to the ground next to the metal box to wait. Did I want a bounty murder case? One that involved vamps? Ultimately, what Pammy came back with would be the deciding factor.

The Benefactor was an anonymous donor who paid for

justice when a family couldn't. The whole no-police-assistance thing meant witches paid for our own protection. If we didn't, or humans were involved, vigilante justice happened while the government turned a blind eye. The Wild West mentality of old Arizona had never gone away for non-humans, although the same could be said of those back East, they just didn't have the Tombstone reference.

For the most part witches were considered our own nation. On the bright side, my taxes were minimal. The only reason we paid any taxes at all was because the fire department would still put out our fires, so they wouldn't spread to the human houses, and we still drove on the streets, and we could still go to the library.

Pammy's ringtone startled me.

"Hello?"

"Hon, you sure you're ready for this?"

Nope, not one bit. "It's not so much a case of want, so much as need, depending on the price of course." I felt like a jerk reiterating it.

Pammy grunted. "Fair enough, hopefully the price will help. The Benefactor has agreed to pay three thousand plus expenses at the closing of the case."

I nearly dropped my phone. Violent bounties were lucrative, but I hadn't realized how lucrative.

Pammy spoke into my stunned silence. "The extra thousand is hazard pay; we always get the extra thou when dealing with those fucking sociopaths. You gonna take it, or should I call someone else?"

"I'll take," I squeaked.

The hazard pay made sense. "Should I call Bubble Bubble Toil and Trouble? And do I need to inform her father?"

"Yes, call them, and have them process the body and bill me. I'll call Dusty."

Relief washed over me. I wouldn't have known what to say. I realized I needed to break the silence. "I'll keep you updated." I hoped I sounded more confident than I felt.

Pammy grunted into the phone.

Hanging up, I hit the speed dial for Bubble Bubble Toil and Trouble, the local witch morgue and lab, grateful Pammy had given me a list of numbers to program into my phone when I'd started.

"Big Butts and TaTas, Craig speaking, how can I help you?"

"Huh?" I almost ended the call, thinking I had called the wrong sort of establishment.

"Guy's gotta have a little fun where he can get it." A cheeky voice responded before my thumb made contact with the end-call button.

"Uh okay, I have a body to be picked up that will need an autopsy."

Any remaining trace of humor in his voice vanished. "Sure thing. Who am I speaking to? Also, I'll need the address."

"This is Peg Darrow. I'm a Fortune." It felt weird saying that.

"Oh, the new girl." The sound of typing came over the connection. "Am I billing this to Pammy?"

"Yep."

The exact address escaped me, so I gave him directions about how to get to Violet's, adding that there was an electric-blue Jeep out front, and he wouldn't be able to miss it. I hung up and returned the phone to my pocket, rubbing my clammy palms on my jeans. Knowing that the cavalry was coming, so to speak, made me feel better. Whoever the morgue sent would add two more witches to the picture. My mind would be more at ease if it weren't picturing the murderer hidden somewhere in the house. I took a shuddering breath.

Using the edge of Violet's metal coffin, I pulled myself back to my feet. *Time to earn that hefty paycheck.* I hoped intelligence would trump formal training. Not that anything about my taking the job screamed intelligent.

I bent to examine the body and tried to disassociate the name from what remained. The vampire association had me checking the most obvious spot first. There were no signs of any bites or bruising around her neck. I grabbed her hands, gently turning her wrists out. Full rigor mortis hadn't set in yet: they moved easily. The morgue wouldn't need the poppy, so I plucked it from her hand and set it on the dresser for the time being. I wanted to run an aura trace on it later.

Next, I lifted her nightie and looked at her inner thighs. There was some scarring on her inner thighs, but it had faded to a slight luminescence of spider webs, something that happened when scars were old and properly tended. There were no fresh bite marks, anywhere.

I found it hard to believe a vamp would kill someone and leave behind a free meal with extra-special magic vitamins.

I smoothed down the nightie, allowing Violet a little dignity.

My gaze roamed her body once more looking for clues. Nothing marred her skin. Not a scraped knee, a broken fingernail, or a colorful bruise. My best guess would be poison or possibly asphyxiation. I closed the lid on the chest looking along the edges. The chest appeared to seal completely. If it had been lack of oxygen that had killed her, she had to have been drugged. Otherwise she should have been able to open it or shown signs of trying to claw her way out. I shivered at the thought.

My leg cramped from squatting next to Violet for too long. I stood and looked around the room again, searching for something I'd missed before. When I saw a tea mug perched on the nightstand, I belittled myself for a moment. I should have noticed it right away, but since I was known to have several glasses sitting on my nightstand. It seemed normal. If one took into account Violet's pristine living environment, it didn't make sense for Violet. Had she woken up in the morning, she would have taken her mug to the kitchen and put it in the dishwasher. Everything had a place in this home.

My legs tingled as I walked over to the nightstand to examine the cup, shaking off the cramp. The ceramic was cool against my hands. I lifted the cup to my nose and took a sniff. The overly sweet scent of chamomile made me wince. I would have the guys take the cup as well to see if there were any sleep aids stronger than the botanicals in the tea. That or permanent sleeping pills.

The medical room suddenly came to mind. Setting the cup carefully back on the nightstand, I wandered down the hall to the room in question. I flipped the light switch on in the room. Under the harsh fluorescents, I saw what I missed before. The equipment from the chairs with their side tables, the tubes, and syringes were all related to phlebotomy.

Going over to the large fridge, I opened it. Sure enough, it was filled with bagged blood. Looked like Violet had been running an underground blood bank. I'd have bet money I didn't have on what kind of blood she was supplying—witch.

A witch caught selling blood to a vampire, let alone operating a business doing so, was a pariah to our kind. If this became public knowledge, the memory of her would always be tainted. I hadn't known Violet, but I knew she had a father who loved her.

BBTT would rely on aura trace spells to gather evidence, not the standard physical evidence used by humans. So long as I could keep them out of this room, they'd never catch on to Violet's side business. Turning out the light, I left the room and closed the door firmly behind me. If the time came that the information needed to come out to anyone beyond Pammy, I would make sure it happened.

For now, I believed that desperation forced Violet into something so distasteful. I'd keep her secret, so another witch wouldn't be forced to endure the stigma associated with being an addict. A vampire's bite was addictive to witches. I'd seen it with my aunt. Despite escaping that life she remained a shell of the woman she should have been.

My resolve faltered, and I considered leaving the door open for everyone to see. If Violet turned out to be an enabler for the vampires without good reason, I wouldn't be happy with my choice. Then Alice's comment about a sick father popped back into my head. I kept the door closed, mind made up.

Since the guys from BBTT still weren't here, I went to the kitchen to search for a plastic baggy to store the poppy in. Unprepared to handle a murder scene, I needed to use what was at hand. The first drawer had a set of keys. I grabbed them hoping they were a spare set, so I could lock up the house when I left. The bags were in the third drawer I tried, and I carefully placed the wilted flower into one. Evidence preserved, I walked through the house. This time I looked for evidence of murder. If any violence occurred here, there would be visible signs, but like Violet's body, the house looked untouched.

The rumble of a vehicle pulling up sent my heart racing. Logic said it was BBTT, but fear and logic were not friends. Looking out the blinds, I saw the BBTT logo emblazoned on the side of the van in the driveway and blew out a breath. The business didn't usually spell out their full name because it would make the vehicle a lot more likely to be vandalized if one forgot to keep the protection charms fresh. My heart rate steadied, and I swallowed. I shook my head hoping the gesture would push the creeping fear back into the deep recesses of my mind.

Opening the door, I greeted the two men getting out of the van. "Hi, guys. I'm Peg. Thanks for coming."

The two introduced themselves as Craig and Dwayne. Craig was the younger of the two, which might explain his earlier references to women's anatomy. Dwayne, on the other hand, lacked any sense of humor whatsoever. It must have made for an interesting work dynamic. Craig gave me a grin, slightly morbid given the circumstances. Dwayne simply grunted, the strong silent type.

"Where's the body?" Craig asked.

"In the last bedroom down the hallway, she's in a metal chest."

Craig and Dwayne accepted that with no comment. When you picked up bodies for a living maybe you had heard more interesting stories than a body placed in a storage container.

"Since this is a murder, I'm guessing Pammy wants the whole shebang?" Craig inquired.

"Uh, first murder here. Not sure what that would entail."

Dwayne looked me up and down and grunted again. The grunt seemed to imply that he found me lacking.

Craig inserted himself before I could respond. "The whole shebang is body process for any evidence and an aura trace on the house for the past forty-eight hours. Plus, we can test anything else you need handled."

"What if the murder happened before two days ago?" Although I believed Violet's death had been well within that time frame, I wondered about the limit.

Craig shrugged, "Part of the business plan. Past forty-eight hours we would need to hire more powerful witches, and they're expensive. They don't grow on trees."

Maybe I should offer my services, but I was no expert, yet. That, and they probably wouldn't hire me. Pammy was a shrewd businesswoman, and I had no doubt that she made sure that her vendors didn't poach the talent.

Craig grinned again "We don't hire Fortunes. Pammy would kill us." He said it as a joke, but what I'd learned in the last three weeks was that the fun woman I had taken tequila shots with at the bar was a façade. The woman was ruthless.

"I came to that conclusion myself," I agreed. "Please do the forty-eight hour aura trace." It would give me one less thing to do, considering I would need to do one on the poppy and perhaps the chest as well. "Also can you test a mug of tea I found? I think it may have been poisoned or drugged."

"Definitely."

"Oh, and you will check her body for curses in the autopsy, right?" I asked as an afterthought.

"Of course."

With that the guys went to the back of their van and pulled out a plastic body bag. I led them into the house and pointed to the bedroom. They disappeared down the hallway. I wasn't sure if they used magic instead of a stretcher when transporting bodies, or if they considered hauling bodies around a cheaper version of the gym. I gave them space, waiting in the living room off the front door.

They walked out ten minutes later, breathing a bit heavy with the effort, each holding on to a strap on either end of the bag. That answered one question. Violet couldn't weigh more than one-ten. Perhaps they didn't want to waste their magic.

I followed them out to the van and remained silent while they loaded Violet in. It didn't seem appropriate to make small talk with the guys until the job was done. Once they closed the back of the van, I had them to follow me back to the bedroom. I pointed to the mug I needed to have tested. The guys produced some plastic containers and plastic bags to transport the teacup and its contents.

I looked over at the chest. "You guys want to take the chest?"

Dwayne grunted, and Craig grimaced. "That sucker's too heavy and too big to fit in the back of the van. Besides, it's empty. We'll leave it here."

I walked them outside, ready to head home myself. I heard the van rumble to life as I pulled out the set of keys I found in the kitchen. The third key on the ring was a winner and slid easily into the front door lock as the van pulled away. With the two other witches being gone, the uneasiness returned, and I glanced over my shoulder. I nearly jumped out of my skin.

A girl stood across the street. Under the halogen street-light, her long dark hair had an orange tint. I couldn't make out any other details, but when she saw me staring, she turned and started to run. *What the hell?*

That wasn't what I'd consider normal behavior. Without thinking I started after her. I wasn't a champion runner, but I had jogged fairly often to counteract my food addiction. The training didn't hurt, but I certainly had never trained at full speed, and the girl easily outpaced me. I called out a few times, but it only made the girl run faster.

I considered zapping her, but she was too far away, and I didn't want to hurt her if she was just some teenager who thought she was being caught out after curfew by a nosy neighbor.

My lungs burned, and I didn't think I could keep this up much longer. The girl was still a half a block ahead of me and turned a corner out of my sight. My pace slowed, but I continued on. When I turned the corner, it was to find a quiet street, no sign of the girl. *Damn.* I bent over resting my hands on my knees, fighting the urge to vomit as my breathing slowed.

Straightening slowly, I looked around the dark street. A little voice whispered in my ear. *What if the girl was bait?* Vampires loved to play that kind of sick game. The thought had me picking up my pace as I headed back to the house, all thoughts of continuing the search gone. I had only run about a half mile, but the walk back lacked adrenaline, and fear pricked at my skin.

To distract myself, I focused my thoughts on the crime scene. The chest seemed to be a statement of some sort, and I needed to figure out what it was saying. Maybe my best friend, Lola, could ask one of her goblin foster brothers if he'd answer some of my questions. I snorted, the sound startling in the stillness of the neighborhood. I looked around again, my paranoia creeping back in. A thought struck. What if the vamps came back to raid the house? Would they take the goblin chest?

Since I needed to perform an aura spell on it, as well as the poppy, it was too risky to leave it at Violet's. I made it back to the house and studied my Jeep. The chest was huge and heavy. I could hypothetically use magic to bring it out to the Jeep, but it wouldn't fit. I needed to call in some muscle. I sighed and pulled out my phone from my pocket.

Bruce was a Pima, or in his native tongue an Akimel O'odham, a bear shifter who owed me after I'd taken his grandma to a doctor's appointment the week before. Normally I wouldn't have cashed in because that's what friends did, but he owned a truck. A blessing and a curse for him—if he needed to move something it was great, but if one of his friends needed to move something, he was on speed dial.

Bruce answered on the first ring, probably thinking I was looking for some fun, given that it was Friday night. "Hey, good looking, what are we doing tonight?"

"I'm glad you asked. We're moving a large metal chest from a murder scene to my house."

There was only a slight pause before he replied, "I don't approve of grave robbing, so you'll have to count me out."

"Nana."

"That's not fair, Peg. It's Friday. Lola and I are going to a poker game. I was going to invite you to come too," he whined into the phone.

"Bruce, you know I wouldn't ask you to move something on Friday night unless I was a little desperate. Think of Cheddar. Who will buy his kibble if I can't solve this murder? Besides, you can still go out. Have Lola meet you at my place."

As a close friend, Bruce knew about my current financial struggle. I milked it even if it was a tad over the top. He was a sucker for children and animals. He sighed into the phone, knowing he was defeated, and asked for directions.

I waited in my Jeep, so I could make a quick getaway if necessary. The rumble of Bruce's F350 diesel engine reached my ears about thirty seconds before he pulled up. Unlike a lot of guys, he wasn't compensating for anything. He used his truck for work as a welder and to haul around his horse trailer.

He climbed out of his truck, and I got out of my Jeep, the nervous tension leaving my muscles at the sight of him. He smiled, his teeth a bright white in contrast to his dark skin, his eyes crinkling at the corners, a result of spending time outdoors in the bright Arizona sunshine. He insisted on being his own barber, which meant every few months he shaved his head and let the thick dark hair grow out haphazardly which was its current state.

"Hey, Bruce, I really appreciate this."

His smile got wider. "You bet your ass you do. It's Friday night."

"So sorry this murder upset your plans," I sniped back.

My comment had no dampening effect whatsoever on his mood. He simply came over and gave me a bear hug, lifting me off the ground. "Ah, small one, life is a circle, until it's a line with a set point."

I wasn't sure if he was being philosophical or if he recently picked up a *Math for Dummies* book. It was hard to tell with him. He was over a hundred and an immortal, in the loosest sense of the term. Immortals would not live forever, but with no violent impediment they could live thousands of years give or take. He was only half-shifter, chances were he probably wouldn't see past six hundred.

The grandma I had driven to the doctor the week before was actually a distant cousin through his mother's side. Didn't matter, he still treated her like an elder, even though he was technically older than she. He once explained that when you had less time to live, you matured faster and had a different viewpoint on the years you experienced. Still, he had a long life ahead of him, longer than mine as long as he never called me grandma.

"Quite the philosophy. Now move heavy things for me."

He smiled again and followed me into the house. Upon seeing the trunk, he let out a whistle. "That there is a work of art. I'm surprised the goblins let it go."

That made two of us. "It really is beautiful, but once you see a dead body in it, you tend to view it as a death trap."

He nodded. "I can see where that might make it lose some appeal. We takin' this death trap to your place?"

"Can you think of a better location for it?"

"Nope, you need a little excitement in your life, girl."

I agreed with him, though my idea of excitement was more like a wild girl's weekend in New Orleans and less murder-filled Friday nights. If I solved this and got some more cases, perhaps I could indulge in the former. "That's settled then. Don't forget to lift with your legs; I don't want to have to take grandpa to the hospital."

"Keep that up because you'll be old someday —Grandma."

"'Grandma' doesn't bother me." I lied.

"It bugs all women. You're a vain breed." With that bit of male wisdom, he bent over and manhandled the chest like it weighed nothing. He also lifted with his back. If he wanted to be ornery that was his business, I wouldn't be around in three hundred years when he wanted to whine about arthritis. He did have a few issues navigating the huge trunk through the narrow hallway without denting the walls. All in all, he had the trunk secured in his beast of a truck in less than five minutes.

"I'll meet you at your house, Peg."

"Sounds good. Can you wait until I lock up?" I looked

out at the seemingly empty street. As if on cue a street light flickered ominously.

"Afraid something's going to get you?" The look he gave me was the equivalent to the one a twelve-year-old boy would give another when calling them a chicken.

Too tired to pretend otherwise, I simply said, "There was a poppy on the body, and I'm not in the mood to donate blood tonight."

The mischievous look he sported disappeared instantly. "Hurry up, girl. Last thing I want tonight is a brawl. Friday's are better suited to poker, dancing, and general debauchery."

Saluting him, I turned back to the house. The keys that I found earlier still dangled from the lock. In my rush to chase the girl, I had left them there. The deadbolt slid into place with little resistance and I pocketed the key. As I walked down the path a strange sensation of someone watching me caused goose bumps to raise on my arms.

I turned again, scanning the yard and the house, and saw no sign of anyone. A shiver ran down my spine. Bruce revved his diesel engine at me and I must have jumped a foot off the ground. I swung my head back to give him a death glare. I couldn't hear him over the engine, but I could see him shaking with laughter inside his truck. I turned all the way then, uneasy about exposing my back to the house and hurried down the path. Relief flooded my body as soon as I was securely locked inside my Jeep with the engine running. *Maybe I was a chicken.*

4

The drive home was slow. Fatigue had me fantasizing about showers and beds. I would have preferred a bath, but I'd probably fall asleep and be the idiot who drowned in the tub. My mother would be so embarrassed.

Unsurprisingly, Bruce beat me to my house. Even when I was alert, my driving compared to a grandma's. Bruce on the other hand thought being in any sort of motorized contraption was a chance to practice the skills he might one day need for NASCAR. At home, I found that Bruce was already let into the house. Lola had decided to wait at my house for him to pick her up. As my best friend, she'd been granted the honor of a key.

She greeted me on the porch, looking like Melody from the original Josie and the Pussycats comic. I was no slouch myself. My curly brown hair, hazel eyes, and even features along with some subtle curves definitely got attention. However, Lola always stole the show, she was simply that stunning. If I hadn't loved her, I'd hate her.

"Hey, Peg, I heard you had some excitement tonight."

Her face warred between a smile and grimace before she dazzled me with a smile in greeting.

I sighed. "Yup, a lot of excitement for one night."

Her smile dimmed, and she looked at me with sympathy but didn't comment. She wasn't a fan of my new career. "Bruce and I are going to an after-hours poker game with some of his shifter friends. Wanna come?"

"Think I'll sit this one out, Lola girl." I considered redirecting her to the living room where we could sit more comfortably and chat, but if I sat down, I wasn't sure if I'd make it to my bed.

She nodded. "Care if I have Bruce drop me off afterwards? I can sleep on your couch, and we can have breakfast."

I gave her a tired smile. "That sounds great. Just use your key, and I'll set out some bedding for you. Oh, and, Lo, don't let the guys take all your money."

Lola grinned again, a bit more toothy than usual. She did love to gamble and was pretty good at making men cry when she wanted to. Tonight, it seemed she wanted to.

"You know that won't happen. I'm lucky."

"That you are. Maybe I can borrow some of that luck. We could go to Vegas. We'll win millions, and then my Friday nights won't consist of finding dead bodies."

Lines formed between Lola's eyebrows, and her voice took on disgusted edge. "I wish you were joking. Still, if someone has to do it, might as well be you," she admitted. "If you were a human, you'd be a policeman, and everyone would respect you, except for adolescent males who are super focused on breakfast foods like donuts and bacon."

I snorted, very ungracefully. "You can be such a weirdo. Where did Bruce put my trunk?"

"What trunk?"

Was she blind? She had to have seen Bruce carrying

that sucker in. "The trunk he hauled over for my investigation."

Bruce chose that moment to appear. "It's in your Arizona Room, Peg. I figured you'd want it where you stored all your crap."

"Thanks, Bruce." I gave him a tired smile. "Lola, how did you not see the giant metal trunk? It was pretty hard to miss."

Lola shrugged. "After I let Bruce in, I went to your bathroom to freshen up."

Bruce took the opportunity to hug Lola from behind, lifting her off the ground, and smell her neck. "And don't you look and smell good enough to eat."

Lola squealed in response, a flirty squeal, as opposed to the dear-lord-I-am-being-attacked squeal. It was my sign to usher them out the door. They were just friends, but their flirting was at a high school level, and I was too tired to watch them without gagging.

House reclaimed, I went and took some aspirin for the headache that began to form. The smell of dead body and poppy was stuck in my nose. The too-sweet flower with a sour undertone scent, made avoiding a shower until the morning impossible. I took a quick one, shampooing the smell away. I threw on a pair of boy shorts along with a camisole. I left out some sheets and blankets for Lola. If she came back really drunk, she would probably just crawl in with me, but I wanted to give her options.

Finally in bed, sleep found me quickly, hauling dreams in its wake. I was back at Violet's house, and someone was watching me. The feeling was so real I woke myself up. Grunting, I stretched trying to get comfortable. My foot hit something warm and solid at the end of the bed.

"God, Cheddar, you need to lay off on the kibble."

"I don't enjoy kibble, but tonight I intend to dine on

the succulent flesh of a thief," a very deep male voice grumbled into the darkness.

My eyes flew open. The moonlight illuminated an attractive goblin sitting on my bed. While eons away from the horrible looking creatures humans wrote about, I didn't want to be anywhere close if he labeled me a thief. My mind flew into flight mode analyzing possible escapes.

The goblin stood on the side of the bed closest to the door. As he lunged for me, I rolled off the opposite side of my bed into the small space next to the wall. I kept a knife on my nightstand, and I reached for it, cursing because I couldn't see very well in the dark, and I doubted he was going to be kind enough to turn on the light. Goblins could see in the dark. A side effect of their time spent in mines.

He hadn't quite made it all the way over the bed on his initial grab for me. I didn't think he'd miss a second time. Goblins were hard to take on, and it was too dark to hit him with a knock-back spell. Even if I could score a single hit in the dark, goblins needed two spells in quick succession due to their thick skin. I couldn't stay still long enough to produce one despite the magic rushing forward, eager to be used. I scampered to the front of the bed, my bed creaking as he reached for me again. His fingers slid through my hair, way too close for comfort.

With him on the bed, I had a chance to get out of my room and ran for my front door. It wasn't far, a short sprint down the hallway away. I didn't bother looking back because it would be a waste of time. Behind me, I heard him bang into the hallway wall when he underestimated the tight turn. The chase was on.

With only three feet to the front door, fingers gripped my hair hauling me back against a hard chest. My scalp burned. Anger boiled through me. What kind of dick pulled a girl's hair? I crouched down quickly, sending an elbow into his groin. I lost some more hair in the process, but his sharp intake of breath made it somewhat worth it. He released my hair, and I went for the front door again only to be clobbered from behind. The last thing I remembered was seeing my solid wood door coming closer to my face.

I woke up with a headache and the feeling of my blankets being too tight. I hated that. I struggled to free myself from the folds when I realized the restriction I felt had nothing to do with blankets. My hands and ankle were bound by what I assumed were zip ties from the sharp sting of hard plastic biting into my flesh. My eyes snapped open in time to see a large hand push my shoulder, re-securing my place on to my couch. I had been teetering perilously close to the edge.

My attacker was kind enough to have turned on the lamp on my side table, which meant, I could now take in the details previously hidden in my moonlit bedroom. The pale yellow light softened his hard features, but just barely. The sharp planes were there, with the pale skin holding a slightly gray undertone. He was handsome with straight black hair tied back and blue eyes that were deep and clear as sapphires.

The goblin remained silent, standing over me while I openly studied him from head to toe. I wasn't sure if he was as tall as I thought he was, or if it was the effect of him towering over my prone form. I bet on the former. His black slacks and V-neck sweater could either be a fashion statement, or his attempt at dressing down for a B&E. He continued to stare down at me. We were playing the silent game.

I never won the silent game. "So, any particular reason you broke into my house to watch me sleep?"

"You should know, thief." His voice was deep and held a hint of an accent, something Old World. That confirmed that flight had been the right choice. His accent indicated he was probably old despite his youthful appearance.

I'd forgotten about the thief accusation, that didn't excite me, but since he hadn't killed me yet, a false sense of bravado had me tipping up my chin. "I haven't stolen anything since a Kit Kat when I was four. It was delicious, by the way. So, you may need to give me a bit more information."

"You have my property here at your house, and you have the audacity to lie to my face? Do you have a death wish, witch?"

"Given my recent career choice as a Fortune, some have assumed so, but no I don't. I don't have anything that belongs to you." Spider webs cluttered my brain making connections difficult but then a little path cleared and I remembered the chest.

While I debated how to acknowledge the goblin chest in my home, he studied me some more. It could be an intimidation tactic, or he could be deciding whether I was telling the truth or not. If I possessed any common sense, I would be scared out of my mind. Apparently I didn't. If he pulled out a knife or his eyes turned gold, a tell that a goblin was using their magic, I'm sure that would change.

"Then why is my safe in the hovel at the back of your home?" He sat on the wood coffee table in front of my couch and leaned forward.

"Hovel?" I instinctively scooted a little further back on the couch.

"The metal safe on your porch."

"Hey now, that is not a hovel. It's an Arizona room that

has been relegated as storage for the time being. When it's cleared out, it's a lovely additional living space." *Why had I just said that?* Maybe I had a concussion. My head hurt, the back from the near scalping, and the forehead from face planting into a door. If my hands had been free I'd have been massaging my scalp. As it was, I shifted uncomfortably on my couch.

"Are you slow? I asked why my safe was in your Arizona room, not its function." His eyes were starting to shimmer, not a good sign. Either he was about to lose it and blast me with some magic, or I really did have a concussion.

"The metal chest? That's witch business," Since he'd confirmed my suspicion there was no use denying it but I still didn't know why he was calling it a safe; there was no lock on it.

"No, the safe is my business, as it is mine."

"It's also the presumed murder weapon in the death of a young witch. Perhaps I should be asking where you were tonight." In for a penny, in for a pound.

"You are in no position to threaten me, witch." He sat up, crossing his arms. A grim smile teased at the corners of his mouth.

"Not at the moment, no, but do you want Pammy coming after you if you harm me?"

"I do not fear Pammy."

"Then you're in the minority. I would have guessed someone as old as you would know better."

His eyebrow quirked. "How would you know my age?"

"I don't, but your hint of an accent means you're fairly old."

He inclined his head slightly and I took that for a confirmation. "I do not wish for issues with Pammy. Some things, however, cannot be swept under the rug. At the end of the day, I doubt Pammy would be stupid enough to try anything against me."

He was either high up in goblin politics or a great liar if he didn't care about starting an incident with the witches. My palms began to sweat. I wanted to think it was because they were bound together, but I knew better. I reached deep inside myself and found my inner snark.

"Yadda, yadda, yadda. Yes, goblins are scary."

"You are impertinent."

"Yep, now can you untie me? I didn't steal your safe. I brought it home from a murder scene to try using a trace spell on it to track down the murderer."

"Why do you insist my safe was involved in a murder? What happened? Was it like a cartoon where the safe was dropped on someone? I smelled no blood, and I assure you, the safe is rather heavy, so there would have been blood."

I rolled my eyes. "A woman was found bound in it. She might have suffocated in it, or possibly been poisoned, and then put in it. Either way, it's obviously a piece of evidence. Now that I know it was stolen from the goblins, it makes it even more intriguing. Once I process it, you can have it back."

He simply stared at me. Okay then, he apparently didn't think it was that simple. "Why would I leave my valuables with you? From its present location, I doubt you understand its worth."

My eye started twitching; the sleep deprivation, a possible concussion, and a self-important goblin made my patience run thin. Bound as I was, there was no way to vent my frustration, hence the eye twitch. "You say that decorative chest is a safe. From what I understand about safes, it's not the safe that's valuable, but what's in it. Yours contained one of my people. Finding her killer is worth a lot more to me than a giant hunk of metal."

His eyes flashed again. If he kept that up, he could get a job as a traffic signal. "Perhaps you do not realize the importance of metals in my world."

This was going nowhere. I silently began to hit my head against the armrest on the sofa.

"That won't help your headache."

How does he know about my headache? Oh right, he slammed my face into a door.

He was probably right, but I wanted to hit something and the only thing I could hit was my head. Since it already pounded, I didn't see the harm. The eye twitch hadn't been nearly as satisfying. I stopped though because I needed to talk my way out of this mess. If nothing else, so I could take two aspirin and return to bed. Even if sleep wasn't advisable with the possible concussion.

"I'm not in the business of securing valuables. I'm in the business of protecting witches. I have no idea how much a safe would cost. I'd guess around five grand. I'm sure the Coven would give you a deposit, since you're worried."

He laughed at me. His deep laugh would have been infectious if it wasn't also bone chilling. "Stupid, stupid witch. That safe is worth closer to a million. The gold on it alone is worth more than five grand," he sneered.

The derision in his voice made me want to say fuck it with the diplomatic approach. It wasn't working anyway, but I needed to get released eventually and didn't want to be carted off to his lair along with the safe. I didn't think that was a possibility, but my mouth had gotten me into some fairly bad places. Finding his lair might make it worth it, if I could bust out.

"Sorry, I guess I'll do my homework the next time I run into a goblin safe."

"You'll never see one again."

"Are you threatening to kill me?"

"Not at the moment, but the safes are treasured, and I doubt a goblin would let you near his."

"Challenge accepted."

"Little girl, you would be wise to forget this. Protect your own people and do not pry into a world you could not survive in."

I snorted. I didn't want to be involved in the goblin world, their hierarchy was downright archaic. They still had a queen for gods' sake. "I'll take that under advisement."

He shifted closer to me, and whereas before his manner had been purely menacing, he now studied me in earnest. He looked me over from my purple-painted toenails to the top of my head. His stare lingered on my hips and breasts and turned heated. A blush burned my cheeks. *Great, apparently sarcasm and stupidity turned him on*. He wasn't bad to look at, but if I were going to be tied up, I wouldn't have chosen zip ties as the instrument. Plus, the entire caveman display of being grabbed by the hair, knocked unconscious, and dragged into a cave, or in this case my living room, wasn't great foreplay.

I hadn't heard the rumble of Bruce's truck, but Lola was suddenly calling through the front door. "Peg, are you up? Why didn't you come to Bruce's to play poker? I thought you were going to bed."

The goblin tensed, obviously readying to attack either physically or magically.

"Lola, do not come in here. Leave right now." My voice was shrill.

She paid me no attention and came in. I heard the not-so-quiet shutting of the front door before she appeared in the entryway. The goblin, who had been ready to pounce, visibly relaxed and sat down again on the coffee table.

Huh?

"Hey, Deval. I didn't know you knew Peg." Her blinding smile made my head throb more as I strained my neck to look at her. Of course she knew this deviant. He was probably her adopted second cousin.

Lola finally clued in to my predicament. "Oh, I'm sorry, Peg. I didn't realize you two were playing sex games. You knew I was coming back here tonight. Why didn't you stay in your bedroom, or put a sock on the door, you kinky minx?"

5

"**R**eally, Lola?" My cheeks flamed.

The goblin, apparently named Deval, gave me a scathing look. "You should be so fortunate."

I wished I wasn't tied up so I could give him the bird. Lola appeared completely oblivious to our exchange. I understood why when she biffed it when the tile of the entry transitioned to the carpet of the living room. Normally she had no issues with the texture change. Drunk Lola, on the other hand, would trip over a grain of rice. She had been about to nail her head on the coffee table when the goblin gallantly stood and caught her. *What a fucking gentleman.*

Lola hiccupped and patted his shoulder in thanks before turning and plopping down on my calves. If they weren't numb from being tied in an awkward position, it probably would have hurt, but because they were numb, it was just aggravating. If I had been in the middle of a sex game, why would Lola decide to crash the party? Then I heard soft snoring.

Craning my neck, I looked and sure enough, she had

passed out. Bruce had given her tequila again. I rolled my eyes, and the goblin laughed. Apparently he had been watching me.

"Now that we're buddies, would you mind untying me?"

"Why would you think we are now 'buddies'?"

"Well, you didn't clobber Lola. That feels like an olive branch to me."

"Lola is a ward of my people; I would not harm her unless she broke our laws, and besides I know she would never be stupid enough to steal from me, even if she is a bit naive."

That was polite because Lola could be a complete ditz. Anytime I mentioned that she held a master's degree in Mining Engineering, the reaction was always "Really?" It tended to be awkward because then I spent five minutes convincing them I wasn't joking. She was actually good at her job, and no, they didn't need to call their second cousin twice removed to advise him to go work at a different company for fear that the walls were going to collapse on them at any minute.

"I know she was raised with you guys. We've been best friends since we were twelve and I always had to host the sleepovers because you wouldn't let me come to goblin land."

"Holding a grudge?"

"Pssh, grudge smudge, my sleepovers are awesome: you guys missed out."

"Is that an invitation?" His dry tone suggested he wouldn't be RSVPing.

"No, it's an invitation to untie me. I've known Lola for fifteen years. Do you think she'd be friends with me if I was a raging klepto with a suicidal streak thrown in?"

"Suicidal?"

"If I were a thief, I wouldn't steal from goblins, or vampires, or fae. If I were a thief, I'd go after humans because they're the easiest prey."

"Thinking about a bank robbery?"

"Right now, bank robbing would beat my current job because at least then I would have feeling in my hands!" I shouted the last part.

Lola mumbled in her sleep and fell further on top of me pushing me further into the cushions. At that point I gave up and turned my face into the cushions. I would smother myself. Thirty seconds later, I realized I must have a will to live because I was lifting my chin slightly so I could breathe.

Something rustled behind me, and I felt Lola lifted off of me. Before I could see where he stashed her, the cool feel of metal slid between my wrist and the hard plastic zip tie. Then he did the same for my ankles.

I sat up slowly and began to massage my shoulders, knowing at any minute the blood rushing to them would bring agony. Deval began to say something, but I lifted my inflamed arm and held up an index finger. I needed a minute, and he should be happy I didn't give him a different finger. I didn't need to be trussed up again, so I practiced good behavior.

It must have been five minutes, but he waited patiently while I rubbed my extremities and bit my lip through the pain. When all that left was a slight tingle in my skin, I looked up and met his eyes. "So, I take it I am no longer on the menu?"

"Figure of speech. Goblins aren't cannibals."

"I knew that, deep in my subconscious, but when I wake up to strange men sitting on my bed threatening to eat me, I tend to get concerned."

"Does that happen to you often?"

"Hmm?"

"Strange men threatening to eat you."

"Nope, most threaten to strangle me. You're the first to suggest making me a snack."

"I take it you aren't a regular at the Poppy Den then?"

"If you're asking if I'm a blood junkie, the answer is no, and you should be able to tell from my lack of clothing that I don't have the telltale scars."

He raised an eyebrow. "You do however have a bite mark on your collar bone."

Damn, he was observant. I shivered, an old fear surfacing briefly. The bite had come after we rescued my aunt. One of her former "friends" came by to check on her. When she was indisposed, he saw me riding my bike and went for a snack. Thank gods he was a low-level vamp, and my parents were strong in their magic. That wasn't something this guy needed to know, however.

"Someone mistakenly thought I was a meal, and you'll notice the tearing along the bite scar. He didn't get the meal he was looking for."

"Must have been painful. Right on the collarbone."

It had been excruciating; the vamp broke my collarbone. Why was he digging? "It did more than tickle, but I survived."

"You consider yourself a survivor?"

"What is this? Twenty questions?" He had gone from my attacker to psychoanalyst. *What was his deal?*

"Just curious." He held up his hands in supplication.

"I do have a strong desire to live; I think all witches do. We all sense that our lives are supposed to be longer than they are because our immortality was stolen from us." I decided to humor him.

Interest shone in his eyes. "Not many witches would

admit that. Still, the curse was long ago, so why yearn for something you should never have expected to have?"

I shrugged, uncomfortable with the turn I had taken the conversation. "Who knows? Now, do you know anything about a witch named Violet Williams?" I needed this conversation to get back on track.

"No, should that name be familiar to me?"

I looked him dead in the eyes. I'd always heard that you could tell when people were lying. I thought of myself as a good reader of people, but he'd probably learned a few tricks over the centuries.

"Well, she was found dead in that fancy chest of yours."

"That is a bit disconcerting, but I don't believe there was any damage to my safe, so I will get over it."

"I can tell you're really sensitive to the human condition."

He shrugged. "Ah, but she was not human; she was a witch. Witches tend to hide behind the fragility their mortal bodies burden them with, but it could be argued as far as magic goes, they were blessed with far more than their share. That being said, I am sure your victim was not innocent." That was a rather bold statement from someone who claimed not to know the victim.

"I thought you didn't know her."

"I didn't, but she must have been involved in something if she was given a coffin worth so much. Symbolically speaking, there was a message here. Perhaps I am over-thinking it, but if you did not steal my safe, then someone with enough connections to my home, my inner sanctum, was involved. My people would not risk so much for a nobody."

"Are you sure someone wasn't trying to piss you off?"

Something passed in his eyes. It looked like doubt but

was quickly gone. He didn't want to believe it was personal. He wanted to blame Violet.

"No, goblins are loyal," he said a little too quickly

"If you say so. Have you pissed off any vampires lately?"

The question appeared to surprise him. "I am sure I have since they are the scourge of the magic users, parasites. Even after the witches' curse, we would not ally ourselves with them."

He wasn't telling me anything new. "There was a poppy found with the body as well."

"Interesting." His voice felt intentionally blank.

"That's all you've got? Interesting?" I leaned back, frustrated.

"Well, did you want me to jump up and yell 'eureka'? There have been no clashes with my people recently. At least none that I have heard of."

"Okay. Would you allow me to keep the chest and run an aura trace spell on it?"

He waited a moment, obviously thinking before he answered. Goblins could control earth, but his magic wasn't fluid like mine. He was right; when it came to magic witches were the superior magical race. Perhaps I was being ethnocentric, but our magic was malleable. With enough intuition, practice, and power, there wasn't much we couldn't do.

"I do see hiring you as a smart choice," he finally grumbled.

I pinched the bridge of my nose, closing my eyes. "Listen, bub, I've already been hired. If you were my client as well, it would be a conflict of interest."

"Very noble of you, but as my interests are also concerned, I would like to know that you will also focus on the thief."

"I'm already interested in the thief. You paying me wouldn't make a difference."

"If you want to keep my property, I need to know you owe me some allegiance."

"I don't want to keep it. I want to perform one spell on it and get it the hell out of my Arizona room."

"You will not be paid unless you find the thief."

"I don't want to be paid at all." That wasn't true, but Pammy wouldn't be happy if I was double dipping.

"Are you sure about that?" He looked around my home with an assessing gaze.

That was insulting, and if I were a shifter, I was pretty sure I would have grown hair and bristled.

"It may not be the Ritz, but I like my home."

"It is…charming. But home ownership can be expensive; it's nice to have insurance should trouble come knocking."

"You're already here, and I don't recall you knocking." It hit me then. *How had he gotten past my wards?* "Speaking of which, how the hell did you get in here?"

He smiled then, his eyes glistening with genuine mirth. "Aw, little witch, your people are not the only ones with secrets." With that he stood up and walked to my front door.

I dogged his heels. "Seriously, how did you get in?"

He simply chuckled and walked outside to a sleek black SUV, the driver illuminated in the vehicle patiently waiting for Deval. He called back over his shoulder, "Have Lola give you my number. I'll expect regular progress reports."

6

I stood on the porch and watched him climb in the passenger seat of a black SUV. My escape would have been thwarted even if I'd made it out the front door. Captain Jackass and his minion pulled away from my house. I walked to the front door and placed my hand on the frame calling my wards. I found them present and intact. For once I wished they'd been stripped or broken.

They had taken weeks to carefully lay. Broken wards would be better than the mystery before me. The goblin found a way in, which meant my defenses were compromised.

I called my power. It came slowly, my body exhausted from the night's activities. I shut the wards down and charged them again. Logic said it wouldn't make a difference, but my sleep-deprived mind wanted to believe my wards behaved like a computer. A restart usually helped. It wouldn't hurt anything.

I wanted to pee and sleep. My rational side told me sleeping with a possible concussion and compromised wards would be foolish. The illogical side decided I would rather be murdered in my bed than spend another moment in the waking world. The deadbolt thrown, I stumbled down the hall to the bathroom.

The mirror was not kind. The goose egg on my forehead resembled a ping-pong ball. My hair looked like I had taken Aqua Net and a blow dryer to it because I wanted to audition for a Def Leppard music video. The piece de résistance being the thinness of the tank top I wore to bed. It bordered on indecent. Not my best look.

My reflection shrugged at me. If you were going to break into my home in the middle of the night, be happy I'd bothered to put on pajamas period. I used the facilities and stumbled into the kitchen. Ibuprofen was needed to stop the throbbing and bring down the bump on my forehead. A moment of genius also had me grabbing a bag of frozen peas from the back of the freezer.

Before heading to my room, I peeked into the living room. Lola cuddled into the pillow I had set out for her. The blanket that accompanied the pillow tucked securely around her prone form. Had she done that herself or had Deval tucked her in? How well did they know each other? Questions for the morning.

Cheddar waited for me in my bed. I crawled in, cautious not to disturb him. He purred loudly from his corner at the foot of the bed, and I petted him with my foot. He must have been exhausted because he didn't attack it. His purr lulled me into a dreamless sleep.

Warm water dripped down my face. The bag of peas had melted in the night. I tried to turn over but a heavy weight lingered on my side. The heavy weight began to purr in a deep rumble.

"Cheddar, you're too fat to sit on my ribs. You're going to fall off any minute, get angry at me for your own gluttony, and take it out on me."

Sure enough he teetered on my rib cage and plopped to the side taking a swipe at my back to tell me how insulted he was. It didn't feel like he'd drawn blood, but my entire body was sore. For all I knew, Cheddar had stolen a kidney. Footsteps from the hallway stopped my musings about damaged internal organs. A moment later, Lola opened the door and popped her head into my bedroom.

"Good morning, sleepyhead. Hope you had fun last night."

I groaned into my pillow and pulled the soggy bag of warm peas off my face. "What exactly is it that you remember from last night?"

"Oh, getting back home and seeing you playing some adult games with Deval in your living room. I didn't realize you were an exhibitionist, Peg. You knew I was coming back. I can't believe he didn't spend the night. I always imagined him as more of a gentleman. Maybe he was embarrassed because I walked in on you guys. Too bad, I wonder if he can make French toast." She said all of that without stopping to breathe.

Lola never suffered hangovers. I hated her for it on a normal day. On a day where I had been assaulted the night before and she mistakenly took my being tied up in the living room for a tryst, I despised it.

Grabbing a pillow, I placed it over my head before mumbling, "Half an hour, Lo. I need a half an hour before I can deal with this."

"Oh, okay. I'll go and make us some cinnamon pancakes. I know they're your favorite." Her voice hesitant. She probably had heard the annoyance in mine. The pancakes were likely meant to be a peace offering. I would take them, along with a little more sleep.

Well, at least I tried to; it was hard to sleep over the noise of the orange juicer. She must have suspected I was really upset if she was making me fresh orange juice as well. The pillow came off my face for good, and I sat up. Cheddar repositioned himself on the corner of the bed. His tail twitched while he glared at me.

"Don't look at me like that. I think Lola is making bacon. Why don't you go pester her?"

At the magic word "bacon," he jumped off the bed and ran out of the room, with surprising agility given his mass, his belly swaying as he ran. Normally I would have gone straight to the kitchen to help Lola. She didn't care what I looked like in the morning, but I needed a shower before I could move with any semblance of normality.

In the shower, I felt my forehead where the goose egg had been last night. It had gone down considerably though my forehead was still tender to the touch. The hot water helped ease the pain, but I should probably take more drugs or a muscle-relaxing tea. I looked down at my wrists. The zip ties had left my wrists with light red marks where they had chaffed. Everybody would think I was into S&M, not just Lola. Further inspection of my body found several bruises on my legs and arms, likely from the fall. All I needed was some dark sunglasses.

Inspection completed, I gingerly massaged mint-scented shampoo into my hair. I hoped it would wake me up. It helped a little as I went through my shower routine. Beauty products were a weakness. My tub was surrounded with various bottles offering to moisturize, volumize, mini-mize, and anything else one could *ize*—a guilty addiction that felt good to indulge in for fifteen minutes before I had to return to reality.

By the time I had gotten out of the shower, wrestled a brush through my hair, and dressed in comfy jeans and a gray V-neck, Lola had arranged a breakfast fit for a queen on the small bistro table I'd jammed into my kitchen. There was a stack of cinnamon pancakes so large I thought for a moment she might have invited Bruce over. Alongside was a plate of bacon and the freshly squeezed orange juice.

Lola was dressed for work in sturdy jeans, a thick khaki button-down, and heavy work boots. Her glorious hair was tamed into a French braid

"I made everything you like, Peg." Lola gestured to the table, biting her lip. "Uh, are you mad at me?"

I sighed and sat down, loading up my plate before answering. She hovered, so I gestured to the other chair. She sank into the chair letting out a sigh. I couldn't be that mad, if I wanted to eat breakfast with her.

"Lo, I am not mad at you. I had the night from hell."

Lola's eyebrows drew together. "Really? I always heard he was good in bed." She paused. "This is going to be awkward the next time I see him."

Hysterical laughter bubbled out. If I had been a meaner person, I would have let Lola think that the worst part of my night consisted of bad sex. I pictured her giving Deval pitying looks every time she saw him and laughed so hard it was difficult to breathe. By the time I managed to get myself together, tears streamed down my cheeks.

Lola looked confused for a moment and then smiled, as if she thought she understood the joke. "Oh, it was so bad it was funny? Now I really won't be able to look at him."

That started me going again, and it was another minute before I took a deep breath, and reached for my orange juice, taking a gulp.

"I mean, I guess because he's the prince, I expected

him to be incredibly hot in bed, you know? Too many fairy tales," she said.

Huh? I choked on my orange juice and turned to the side as I coughed it out, narrowly avoiding ruining my pancakes. Lola came over and pounded on my back before cleaning up the orange juice with some paper towels.

Once I was able to breathe again I asked, "Prince?" My voice sounded strangled.

Lola sat back down and gave me a quizzical look. "Yes, Prince Deval. Didn't you know who you were sleeping with?"

The farce had gone on long enough. "I didn't sleep with him, Lola!" It wasn't necessary to shout, her being whopping two feet away from me, but it felt good.

"What do you mean you didn't sleep with him?" She sat back down and fumbled with her fork.

"What you walked in on was a B&E and a hostage situation! I'm not an exhibitionist. Gods, Lola, don't you know me at all?" My nostrils flared while I stared her down.

She waited a moment before answering, obviously thinking it through, "You're right; that was out of place for you. I was happy you were getting laid, and to be fair I was a bit tipsy."

"A bit?" I raised a brow. My voice lowered to a reasonable volume.

"Okay, I was trashed. You know what it's like to drink with shifters." A light blush colored her face. It would have been endearing if I weren't annoyed with her.

"I do, Lo, and I'm glad you had a fun night. Just next time, if you see me tied up, can you start with the assumption that I'm being attacked? Only go to the conclusion of sex games if I yell out something like 'Ride 'em cowboy'?"

"Oh, so you are into role playing?"

I gave my friend another murderous stare. "Please go

drink a cup of coffee; your wild night has obviously interfered with your ability to think."

Now Lola mirrored my annoyance. That was fine because she stood up and duteously refilled her cup.

"Get me one too, while you're at it."

"Please," she responded in a snippy tone.

"Please."

She brought the pot back to the table and refilled my cup before sitting down. She gazed at me expectantly.

"He thought I stole something from him."

"Oh, that's not good. Goblins are very harsh with thieves." Her hands tightened into a death grip on her coffee mug.

"I got that impression when he threatened to eat me. Before you jump to conclusions, not the fun way."

"Of course not the fun way. Just so you know though, he wouldn't have actually eaten you. Tortured, maimed, and murdered possibly, but definitely not eat."

I pondered that a moment. "Good to know." I shoved a heaping bite of pancakes in my mouth. Instantly my nerves calmed as cinnamon, butter, and syrup hit my tongue. Yep, definitely a stress eater.

"What did he think you stole from him?" She leaned forward, grabbing my upper arm to get my attention.

"A giant metal chest," I said, my mouth full.

"Oh well, there's nothing like that around here." She let out a sigh, releasing my arm and leaning back.

"Yes, there is. Go look in the Arizona Room." I shoveled another bite in my mouth.

She stiffened, rose, and walked around the table to the door leading to my screened in porch. She opened the door and looked out.

"Sweet hell and hades, you are freaking dead! I could ask for a favor. Maybe you'd only be maimed. Remind me, are right or left-handed? We can trick them, and maybe you can keep your good hand."

Turning in my seat, I pointed a pancake-filled fork at her. "Lola, come back and sit down."

She gave me a wild-eyed look and paced back in forth a few times, muttering to herself before she threw herself back into her chair. I could see sweat forming on her forehead and a whiff of tequila permeated the air. She did have a wild night. The safe was obviously as big of a deal as Deval said.

She jabbed her finger at me. "Peg, this is very serious. I don't know the queen, but my foster father does. I can ask him to speak on your behalf."

I grabbed her hand and held it in my own. "Lola, other than that Kit Kat bar when I was a kid, do you know me to have sticky fingers?"

"No, but times have been tough lately. Why didn't you tell me that you needed a loan?"

"I don't need a loan. I didn't steal the chest-safe-thingy. It was used as a casket at the murder scene I went to last night." I released her hand.

Lola wilted into her chair and placed a hand over her heart. "Oh thank gods. He believed you right?"

"Enough to try to hire me. I'm going to share the results from the aura trace I'm doing this afternoon." I paused puzzled for a moment, "How did you not see the safe last night when Bruce brought it in?"

"I was getting ready in the bathroom. You know I need time to prep."

That was an understatement.

She leaned forward and helped herself to a big bite of pancakes, the hand holding her fork shook. She was a stress eater too.

"You actually helped, by showing up. He might not have believed me if I didn't have the connection to you."

She smiled shakily and continued to eat. We ate in silence for a bit. She was recovering from her near heart attack, and I was recovering from my earlier annoyance. Once we ate enough that I was considering unbuttoning my jeans, I asked the question that had been bugging me.

"What exactly is so special about that chest? He called it a safe. Also, how the hell did he get past my wards?"

Lola shook her head. "Nope."

"What do you mean, nope?"

"I can't tell you that if he hasn't already. It would go against my family's code."

"Lola, are you a witch or a goblin?"

She glared at me. "That's not fair. Would you tell your family secrets to another witch just because she was a witch?"

"I would if she was my best friend."

"Well, you've always known the rules, why pout about them now? You were never allowed on goblin territory, and you knew there were secrets I couldn't share. I'll always help you in any way I can, but I cannot, without permission, give you details about safes."

Meeting her stubborn stare, I nodded. She would always have divided loyalties. It just had never affected me directly. "Can you ask if you can tell me?"

"Yes, but you would be better off asking Deval. He's royalty and can get away with more than a ward of the goblins. Also, how the hell did you not know the name of the goblin prince?"

Oy. "I've only ever heard him referred to as Prince Dev. You know I'm not that into the antiquated royal mumblings."

"You are a freaking Fortune, woman. You need to be

better versed on the political comings and goings. This is why I don't like you doing this job."

"What does the goblin royal house have to do with being a Fortune?"

"You're not invested in this. At the very least, you should be able to tell me who the Phoenix movers and shakers are. If you were more interested in learning about the dangers out there and how to avoid them, I wouldn't be worried. You've reluctantly dipped your toe in. If you keep doing it half-assed, you're going to get killed." Lola stood abruptly. "I need to drive to Globe today, and I'm late. I love you, but get your life together."

They were harsh words coming from a woman who couldn't tell the difference between sex games and someone being held captive. They hit home nonetheless. She was right. Lola grabbed her purse and was stomping toward the door when I stood up and followed her. I grabbed her shoulder and turned her around before she could open the front door, pulling her in for a tight hug.

"Thank you. I know I am a pain in the ass, but I needed to hear that. Just to reiterate, in the future if you see me tied up please assume I need help."

Lola, who began the hug with her arms stiff at her sides, laughed and reached up to embrace me. "Deal, and for the record, if you should see me tied up, assume that it's wild sex and leave quietly."

7

D ishes cleared, I turned my attention to the real work. I needed to perform the trace spell on the safe so the goblin prince could come collect it. The trace spell was fairly complicated, so a pre-spell meditation session was in order. Walking through the screened-in porch, I came to my own personal oasis otherwise known as my yard.

It was a large lot with numerous citrus trees, surrounded by a block fence. As long as the neighbors weren't having a backyard karaoke party, I was afforded a peaceful space. Grabbing a cushion off one of the outdoor chairs, I went and sat on it under a large grapefruit tree.

Despite it being November, the ground was dry because it hadn't rained for a few weeks and because I avoided irrigation during the winter months. The weather wouldn't be considered cold by anyone who lived further East, but it was brisk to a native Arizonan, right around sixty. Sitting down cross-legged on the cushion, I leaned back against the tree trunk, resting my wrists palm up on my knees. Meditation wasn't necessary to perform an aura trace, but I found the ritual helpful.

Soon I would be surrounded by wisps of various essences, and I needed to be centered to better interpret what I was seeing. That and the potion to incite the spell would take at least an hour. One wrong stir or incorrect ingredient measurement could lead to disastrous results or just wasted time. This wasn't my first rodeo. I'd done a couple of theft cases in the past couple weeks and on a few secret admirer letters friends had received in high school. Aura traces were always a handy trick to have up one's sleeve.

Sitting outside, I soon reached a meditative level that allowed all thought to clear my mind. Cheddar was kind enough to come sit on my lap a half hour in, breaking me from the trance. I scratched his head before pushing him off my lap, to his disgruntlement. Standing, I stretched. The cold caught up to me a bit, and I rushed back inside where hot coffee waited.

Another mug poured, I set the cup next to the stove and started rooting around my cabinets for my spell pot. In actuality it was a large stockpot as opposed to the cauldron most people thought of. Some witches mastered the art of crock-pot spells. I wasn't brave enough to try that. The idea of walking away from a potion to let it do its own thing for hours on end was too risky for my sensibilities.

Pot found, I began going through my spell cabinet for the various herbs, oils, and odds and ends I would need. Half an hour later, everything was bubbling nicely. I turned down the heat and gave the potion one last stir before putting on the lid allowing it to simmer. The house smelled like lavender and vanilla. It could be argued that aura potions were some of the nicer smelling potions. They contained no insects or small animal parts.

The fact that I had to drink this particular potion made me particularly happy that it lacked creepy crawlies. I went to the cupboard and grabbed my potions mug. I kept one mug for the purpose of potions because I needed to make sure it was thoroughly sanitized every time I used it, like a first-time parent who sanitized every inch for a newborn baby. It directly opposed my usual, 'if it looks clean, it's clean' stance.

The last thing I needed was to have a little leftover aura trace in a cup of coffee and start tripping in public. Even though that wasn't what was happening, it would sure look like it. People often weren't kind to humans who appeared high as kites, and they were extra unkind to witches who did.

I poured the mug about half full and placed the lid back on the pot. The potion would keep for another couple of hours. If the first dose wasn't strong enough, I had extra plus some for round two with the poppy. Mug in hand, I headed to the Arizona room.

I studied the safe for a moment before sighing. There was no better way to do it. Sitting inside it would give me the most accurate aura readings, although I wanted to sit on top where the dead body hadn't been hanging out. But at the end of the day, I knew that would be half-assing it. In I went. It was surprisingly roomy, and I was able to sit cross-legged with my back against one of its walls. Looking at the potion, I took a deep breath. Even though the potion smelled like gourmet lavender and vanilla cupcakes, it would taste awful.

Closing my eyes tightly, I tilted the mug to my lips pretending it was a cheap tequila shot someone bought for me. The trick worked, and despite a slight gag reflex and mild burn, I survived. I set down the mug in front of me, keeping my eyes closed, and draped my arms along the sides of the safe, much like someone would do in a hot tub. The thought of hot tubs made me think of vacations somewhere tropical, and then bam, the potion hit me hard.

My eyes flew open as a tornado of raw emotions and aura signatures raged around me. Colors swirled, and the storm dragged some wisps free of my ponytail. My breathing became labored as the spell tried to pull at me from every direction, I closed my eyes again, shutting out the emotions, and took three shuddering breaths centering myself before reopening my eyes. This time it was not nearly as overwhelming. In fact, compared to other aura pulls, it was relatively peaceful. The safe, being of new construction, had very limited aura signatures on it.

The illusion of chaos was caused by what surrounded the safe. The Arizona room was basically my storage unit, so it contained a lot of memories. The house was also reasonably old and had its own signatures as well. I needed to begin pulling on the threads and reliving the past because as easily as the aura signatures and memories came, they could leave at any time.

What I needed to look at was so transparent and small the rest of the room was trying to butt in. With that focus in mind, I reminded myself to keep breathing slowly and began to search the wisps surrounding me. The most dominant colors that surrounded me were orange and red. Reaching out with my left hand, I touched one. It took the invitation, traveling up my arm and into my open mouth, taking me to a different time and place.

There was fire so hot on my skin I glanced at my arms to see if my skin blistered. Sweat poured off me but the burning sensation was an illusion produced from the spell. Was somebody burned? The sensations cleared a bit and I began to see the trace. An elderly goblin worked at a forge. He was creating the safe, molding it lovingly into the masterpiece it was today.

He was sweating, but he didn't seem bothered by the heat. The goblin's thick skin was allowed him to look fresh as a daisy in the harsh conditions. His head was shaved, which was odd because most goblins were vain about their hair. The slight gray undertones to his skin were much more apparent on his bald head. It was fascinating watching an obvious master of the craftwork. But quickly the vision dissipated. That was for the best. I needed to move on.

The reds and oranges still swirled around me. An educated guess told me they were likely more memories at the forge. It was a bit disconcerting because often red denoted passion or anger. In this case it was a passion for metal work. It was as though the goblin's very soul was linked to the fire he used to lovingly manipulate the precious metals.

Passion could be a reason for murder, but Violet's death felt colder. When a purple wisp passed by, I reached for it. I returned to the forge, but the fires were not burning as brightly. It was rather quiet, compared to the previous crackles from the roaring fires and clanging hammers. This time I saw Deval. He stood with the older metal smith, and they appeared to be performing a ritual of sorts. One that involved Deval sticking his hands into molten metal while remaining silent. I hadn't realized he was a masochist.

Okay, that wasn't fair. Goblins kept their magic pretty secret. I wouldn't want the goblins to mock my cultural history. It hit me then how lucky I was to have received Deval's permission to keep the safe and run the spell. Had he known what I would be able to pull? Or had he thought faces would pop up? *Better not bring it up.*

The scene left me, and I continued going through the wisps methodically, and what felt like hours later, I was ready to give up after having seen various scenes of the making and enchanting of the safe. A new respect formed for Deval's pain tolerance and the metal smith's attention to detail. I also needed a nap, and my ass was asleep.

I kept reaching out for the different colorful strands despite my growing discomfort, the spell hadn't released me, and I still hadn't found what I was looking for. Then I noticed it, or the lack of it. There were holes in the tornado. Normally the wisps weaved together, not leaving much space between one and the next, but there were sections the size of a ruler missing.

Why hadn't I noticed it before? Oh yeah, that's right, because of the level of crap in the surrounding room. The outside auras peeked through to the vortex I was sitting in. How could someone scrub their aura? Now wasn't the time or place to analyze that because, despite my exhaustion, I needed as much information as I could get. I reached for a tiny light-green one.

Finally what I was looking for, or at least part of it. It was Violet that came into view. She was in her room and appeared very tired. She was being set down into the safe, and then there was darkness as she dozed off. The aura left me, and when I snapped my eyes open, the tornado was gone. Damn it. I'd wanted to look at those holes a bit more.

Groaning, I reached my arms above my head and stretched. Twisting side to side, I cracked the kinks out that had developed in my lower back. Back in prime condition, despite my left ass cheek being asleep, I pushed myself up. I let out a soft curse when I pricked my pinkie on some random piece of protruding decorative metal. Looking at the culprit, I saw blood. Dammit. Deval would not appreciate me leaving DNA behind.

That and I would rather not give it to him freely. Sucking on the injured finger, I went to the bathroom. I dumped some precautionary peroxide on the minor cut and placed a Band-Aid over it. Afterward grabbing Clorox wipes to go and take care of the safe. *Did bleach hurt metal?*

I looked at the point where I thought I cut myself and found no sign of blood, odd. I searched the rest of the safe, but there was nothing. Maybe I'd imagined it. The finger was definitely cut, but sometimes it took a moment for blood to rise. I just came off an aura pull. Exhaustion weighed heavily on me, but I still needed to pull from the poppy.

Mug in hand, I went back to where the potion simmered on the stove. The clock confirmed that the potion was still good. What felt like hours with the safe had actually only been forty-five minutes. The poppy would likely have only a few aura traces. I didn't want to be under the influence for as long this time. All I needed was a single gulp. Mug filled to the appropriate amount, I took it and the poppy to the backyard. There was a poured cement slab measuring three feet by three feet.

It had been poured for spell work shortly after I moved in. Not all items that needed trace spells were large enough to engulf one's self in, like the safe. I needed a place that wouldn't get too many interruptions; hence the random square of cement in the middle of my citrus trees. It came in handy for other spells, but I was glad I had it when I became a Fortune.

I plopped down on the square and wished I brought a patio cushion out. But it would have caused some interference. I chugged the small amount of potion at the bottom of the mug and gripped the poppy tight, smooshing the already wilted flower. There was no lull this time around. Having just come off of the spell, I went straight into the vortex.

What I found in the end of my session with the safe

was starkly apparent now. The poppy didn't have as many auras as the safe, but looking around, I saw the tendrils. They were oddly clear, almost as if they were malleable glass. This time I reached for them and found...nothing.

The wisp still crawled up my arm and into my mouth, but what I lived was nothing. I was in a white space, no sound, no breeze, no movement. It should have felt like reaching a high state of meditation, but instead my skin crawled. I reached for the wisps again and again. Every time the stomach sickening sensation returned. There was no color, no hint of Violet or anyone else could be found.

It made sense that I couldn't find her, likely the poppy had been placed after death. But surely there had to be some trace of the person who gave the death token to Violet? I'd never seen anything like it. Coming out of the spell the second time was jarring and uncomfortable. It left me nauseated. Just carrying my mug and the poppy back into the house took a great deal of effort as exhaustion joined the already troubling list of side effects from the spell.

I needed to recharge before I analyzed the pull. A nap was necessary. Nothing brilliant ever came to a witch after an aura pull, no matter what they might have thought in the moment.

Even after trying to analyze everything after my nap, I was just as confused. I wouldn't be able to answer why there were holes in the aura spell, but I knew who could. There was only one place Pammy would be this time of day. I jumped in my Jeep and headed over to a little hole-in-the-wall coffee shop called Bump and Grind. Not the classiest of names, but inside it looked like many other independent coffee houses. There was a checkered floor, a bookshelf with tattered paperbacks, and several well-worn armchairs and sofas.

Pammy was holding court on her couch at the back of the cafe. Not wanting to bother her without an extra dose of caffeine for courage, I sidled up to the counter. The barista had a warm smile that felt at odds with her tattoos and multiple piercings. I ordered the largest iced coffee on the menu and eyed the pastries. A sugar hit on top of the caffeine would be nice. But as I was here to talk, I didn't want to do it with my mouth full. I decided against the lemon bar that wanted me to adopt it.

Coffee in hand and a tip in the jar, I headed back to Pammy. She hadn't acknowledged me when I'd walked in but this was her unofficial headquarters, and she kept her eyes on the comings and goings. It wouldn't go with her badass reputation to wave across the cafe yelling "yoo-hoo." She sat alone on the overstuffed couch while several chairs had been scooted over to form a half circle around her. No one ever seemed to sit on the couch with her, as if it were some great *faux pas*. I didn't want to be the one who broke the trend, so I gave her a nod, set my iced coffee on the table in front of the couch, and began to manhandle another chair into submission.

Her deep voice stopped me. "No need for that, Sug. Ladies, I have business to attend to, scoot along."

"But, Pammy, you said—"

"I know what I said, Aldine. I'll talk to you later. This is business, and you know nothing interferes with my business."

The young woman flushed and rose abruptly, moving to sit on the other side of the cafe. The other two women were already gone, getting up as quickly as Pammy had asked for the space. They were probably her regular groupies and knew the routine. Pammy drew people to her like only a person in power could. Even humans came to her, although not as openly.

She was a mover and a shaker and very dangerous if you let her facade fool you. I knew better. I also didn't anticipate a day that our goals in life would not be aligned. I probably didn't fear her as much as I should.

I sat down on the faded pink armchair that Aldine vacated since it was facing directly in front of Pammy. "How are you, Pammy?"

Pammy liked social niceties. "Good, Sug, better if you tell me who killed her."

"Sorry, I can't tell you that. I need some help with some research."

"Good girl, need help, ask for it. No one needs to be John Fucking Wayne." She took a sip from the mug in her hand. "What's the problem?"

I explained to her the connection with Deval and the holes in the trace.

"Well, shit on toast."

"Yeah, that's what I was thinking."

"The goblins are involved? Hmmm, this is a bit more political than what I wanted to give you. Are you good at diplomacy?"

I thought about lying, but that was never a good route with Pammy. "Uh, normally yes. I may have a hard time with this one."

"Because he knocked you out and tied you up in your underwear?"

"Pajamas, I was reasonably dressed given the time of night," I stuttered, telling myself to remain calm, so I wouldn't flush and give away my embarrassment.

"What ladies call pajamas these days aren't as conservative as the way I was brought up. I assumed, not that it matters, you're not a woman who can get over being in a subordinate position are you?"

"I'm not his subordinate." I wanted to yell but kept my voice even.

"Course not, Sug. Witches are powerful. The others forget, but we won't always be weakened, and we won't forget."

I knew she was talking about the curse being lifted, but if it hadn't happened in three hundred years, it wasn't likely to happen now. If she wanted to believe she would become immortal again and live a thousand years, I didn't feel the need to disillusion her.

"Well, I won't forget. It's one of those embarrassing things I would write as a true confession to one of those trashy women's magazines, if I was allowed to say the G-word in public."

Pammy harrumphed. "Those fools are lucky we haven't outed their asses years ago."

Again I kept mum because I didn't need to tell Pammy the reason we hadn't outed those fools years ago had more to do with the fact we didn't all want to be murdered in our beds in retribution. I had no doubt that would be exactly what happened.

Pammy took a sip of what appeared to be iced tea and visibly calmed down. Her shoulders relaxed, and the hint of a smirk returned to her full lips. "Aw, well, now is not the time to talk about that dreadful business. Now keep working with the boy, try to be respectful. They aren't our enemies, but always remember they are no longer our allies either, and to them their needs will always come above ours. Now, you are saying you believe someone scrubbed their aura?"

I leaned closer, Pammy's voice was strong but at times its deep timber made it difficult to hear. "I can't think of anything that would do that, but I haven't been in the business of hiding my identity."

"Haven't you?"

"Huh?"

"Girl, you are now ass deep in the business of finding people who do need to hide themselves. It's time to take this seriously."

I cringed. "You're not the first person who's said that to me today."

She nodded. "Good, get your head on right. The best Fortunes are the ones who research on the side. By day they're finding the bad guys, by night they're scholars. Course it's your choice, but the more you educate yourself, the less likely someone will be investigating your death."

I started to feel a little snarky. As an adult, there were only so many times you could hear you were being a dumbass before you wanted to do something stupid, like make a request for some rock star Fortune to investigate your death. I brushed over the subject. "What can scrub or hide its aura?"

Pammy sat there thoughtful for a moment before answering, "I haven't heard of an aura scrub, but obviously it can exist. I think, given where the evidence is pointing, you should start with the worst-case scenario, and if that doesn't pan out, you can go ask Alice."

Pammy was oblivious to her literary reference, but I decided to follow her down the rabbit hole anyway. Anything to ignore the dread cramping my stomach, already knowing what the worst-case scenario was.

"Who's Alice?"

"What do you mean 'who's Alice'?"

Damn it. Did every other sentence I uttered have to end in a rebuff? "I'm sorry, Pammy, I don't know who Alice is."

"Humph, baby witches need to learn more about their

community. All up on the Internet with their social media, but don't know the best scholar in their own state. Even if she is batshit." Pammy said everything under her breath, just loud enough for me to hear.

I decided it was meant to be rhetorical and kept quiet. She didn't make me wait long; apparently my punishment for ignorance was being called a "baby witch."

"Sug, we'll talk about Alice if you get nothing at the Opium Den."

I knew it was inevitable, but the cramps were now accompanied by a cold sweat. No witch in her right mind wanted to hang out with vampires.

She ignored my sudden lack of color, raising her hand she called out, "Aldine, go grab my bag from the car."

I peered over my shoulder and spotted Aldine rushing out the front door, as eager as a puppy. Pammy and I sipped our respective drinks while Aldine completed her errand. She returned quickly. Pammy took the leather duffel bag from Aldine's hands and shooed her back to her corner after offering a curt, "Thanks," that made her light up like a joint at a reggae concert.

I didn't know what I was expecting Pammy to pull out of her bag, perhaps a rabbit after all of the veiled Alice references, but a solid silver collar and wristbands was not it. Yep, I was going to the Opium Den. The sight of the collar should have made the cramps worse or brought on another bout of the sweats. Oddly though it brought on a calming force, a sense of resolve. I was doing this. I was a Fortune, not just in name, and damned if I wasn't going to be a kick ass one.

8

_____

I wanted to go straight to The Opium Den, but it was only seven, and I didn't think that my faded jeans and T-shirt were going to meet the dress code. Like most popular nightclubs, The Opium Den wasn't really swinging until later. If I could get away with going early before the crowd I would, but I doubted the higher up vamps would be there until the going got good. Their lackeys would run the joint unless there was a problem. They would just show up for the all-you-could-eat buffet.

I perused my closet trying to find something that would get me entrance but also be good to move in in case I needed to run. My choices were fairly limited. Given my recent financial struggles, I hadn't been on many shopping sprees. When I shopped I usually went for the staples, and thankfully.

I found a pair of black skinny jeans and quickly put them on. Next came a few requisite lunges to make sure they would work if it came down to a fight. They were perfect, form-fitting enough to be sexy but also containing a high enough Lycra percentage to move with the body.

After that, I decided to keep with the simple theme and donned a low-cut black tank top.

The silver cuffs and collar added enough dramatic flair to dress up the outfit. The other customers would think they were statement jewelry, but the vampires would recognize them for what they were: a not-interested notice. Not that they would respect that.

Dressed, I arranged my tools of torture on the bathroom counter to tame my hair when my phone started up with the psychedelic sounds of the Josie and The Pussycats theme song. Lola was calling. She hated the ring tone, but it made me laugh.

"Hey, there."

"What's up, Peg? Wanna get some Mexican food?"

"Always, but I have plans tonight."

There was a pause on the other end. "Really?"

I was a bit of a homebody, but I wasn't that bad, so I hated admitting the next part. "It is work-related."

"Oh, that makes more sense."

"Gods, Lo, I am not that much of a shut in."

Lola coughed delicately into the phone.

"Lola, you're extremely social. No normal person could compete with your social calendar."

Her laugh tinkled through the phone line. "You're probably right. So, what is this work engagement you're going to? Going to interview a suspect or do a stake out?" She sounded excited at the prospect.

"Nope, I'm going to The Opium Den."

"What the fuck!"

My eyes widened. Lola rarely cursed. Admittedly, she was doing it a lot more since I started my new job.

"Uh, you okay, Lola? That was a pretty visceral reaction."

"I know. Darn it, Peg. Not all of us are natural sailors like you."

"Uh, I'll take that as a compliment."

"You would." Her tone was haughty.

"Hey now, don't get nasty, I have to do this for work. You're the one who said to take this seriously. I am. I'm all in. I'm even wearing flat boots I can run in instead of the gorgeous stilettos I bought last year."

Lola snorted. "You can't even walk in heels. You wouldn't wear those heels even if you didn't have the distinct possibility of needing to run."

"You're just being mean."

"The truth hurts. You should sell those shoes on eBay, or give them to me. I like them, and I'll actually wear them."

"I'll think about it." I wouldn't think about it. You never knew, I could be invited to dinner. As long as I was sitting, I was willing to totter from the car to a table. Plus, my ass looked great when I wore them.

"Who's going with you?"

"Hmmm." I was still imagining the perfect scenario to wear my heels.

"The Opium Den, pay attention."

"Sorry, I'm going by myself."

"I thought you said you were taking this seriously."

"I am. I have a silver collar and cuffs."

"God, Peg, haven't you ever watched a crime drama? If you're going into a dangerous situation, you take back up."

"Are you looking for an invite? I wouldn't take my worst enemy to that house of horrors disguised as a night club."

"Well, I wanted to go out tonight anyway." She sounded resigned.

"You do realize that we're not immune to their glamour?"

"Peg, I know I may seem ditzy sometimes, but I'm not five. Every witch knows that." Her tone turned decidedly snippy.

Sheesh. "I know, I know. I just don't want to put you in danger."

"Tough, I'm going. I'll drive. Be at your house in an hour."

Knowing Lola's sense of time, I wasn't surprised when she didn't show up for two hours. She was dressed in a red mini skirt that showed off her tan, toned legs. Her top was a black silk shell that left very little to the imagination. Expecting sky high heels, I was surprised to find a pair of strappy flat sandals on her feet.

"I see you're prepared to run, but Lola, the amount of skin you have exposed is an invitation to take a sample."

"Peg, no man, vampire, witch, goblin, or human will dictate how I dress. Also, I'm a ward of the goblins. The vamps touch me, and they can kiss their butts goodbye."

"You're right. I just want to be cautious."

Lola looked sympathetic. "I know, hon. I'm comfortable in this, but I understand why you want to cover up more, but holy boobs, Batman."

Blushing, I grumbled, "It's a night club."

"Yes, ma'am, and you look great. You should wear the silver more often. Humans won't know what it's actually for, and it looks very dramatic. I like it with the bun and the smoky eye."

"I do know how to clean up. I just prefer comfort."

Lola smiled. "I know, very sassy. Too bad we're going

someplace where the eligible men are either unwitting blood slaves or sadistic bastards. We're wasting great outfits on these assholes."

Damn, that was the second curse word from Lola today. She must be feeling frisky. "We still need to go."

That earned me a pout. "I know but I had to try. Bruce is going to the Casino tonight."

"I'm surprised he didn't insist on coming with us, if you told him where we were going."

"I didn't, for that reason." She lowered her eyes.

"Huh, I thought you were all for backup."

She met my eyes. "You can catch more flies with honey than vinegar. If Bruce showed up, it would turn into a pissing contest. I look a lot less threatening, but if anyone pulls anything, I'm going to name-drop the crap out of the goblins."

"People never realize how diabolical you can be." I grinned.

"I'll take that as a compliment. Now get in the car." She waved to her car.

"Let me grab my purse." After I locked the deadbolt, I opened up my senses to my wards. They were set, and everything appeared to be in order. I still needed to figure out how Deval bypassed them. It made me leery not knowing who or what could enter my home. I climbed into the passenger's seat of Lola's cherry-red Mustang.

Glancing over, I could see Lola's face turn guarded in the glow from the dashboard. "Lo, do goblins have any special talents for bypassing wards?"

"You know that's off limits."

"I understand you can't tell state secrets. I've never asked you too, but that was before my life became endangered." My tone came out hard.

I crossed my arms and looked out the window. There

wasn't much to look at. We were on the freeway, and despite various Southwestern designs on barricades and medians, it was still just cement walls.

Lola let the silence sit for a long time before quietly saying, "I don't want to keep secrets from you. If I thought for a second that Deval would harm you, I would tell you whatever you needed to know to fight him, but he won't."

I knew why she couldn't tell, but it still hurt. "If you hadn't shown up the other night, he would have hurt me. For god's sake, he slammed my head into a door."

"No, Peg, he was subduing you. He would have done that to anyone he thought stole from him. If he was going to hurt you, he would have taken you someplace else."

"Where?"

Another bout of silence. "I can't tell you."

"Fine, but know this, you've been my best friend for as long as I can remember, but if I am in danger, and you don't tell me what I need to know, I don't think I could forgive that."

Her hands tensed on the wheel. "You're being dramatic, but for the record there's no danger to you right now."

My spine stiffened at basically being compared to a teenage girl, but I knew it was time to drop it. I turned back to the window. "Fine."

Tension filled the air for the remainder of our trip. By the time we pulled up to the valet queue, I decided to let it go, for the time being at least. I looked over at Lola. "You ready for this?"

She accepted the unspoken olive branch and nodded.

"Okay, here's the deal, we need to see the main man. I would appreciate if you'd let me do the talking."

She nodded again, already taking my cue.

"Oh, and Lola? If I say run, run. If things get hairy,

even with your name dropping, remember my power levels are a lot higher than yours, and I have been training."

"Yes, yes, Peg, you always were a show-off. I'm sure the three weeks as a Fortune have made you unstoppable." She said the last part with a grin.

A knock sounded at the window, making me jump. Lola, unfazed, smiled at the valet as he opened my door. It was show time.

The Opium Den was on the top floor of a historic building in downtown Phoenix. There were questions during construction as to why the secretive owners didn't build something new and flashy rather then pour all their money into a building that would be better off condemned. I'd never been there before, but it was obvious the building held a certain splendor that couldn't be recreated.

It only increased when we walked into the lobby. The sigh Lola emitted said she was as awestruck as I was. Marble floors flecked with gold were set off by the antique bronze gas lamps. The walls were a deep burgundy. It all felt very classy in an illicit sort of way, and we weren't even in the club yet. Club goers packed into the elevator like sardines. Given where we were headed my mind began to shout, "Tower of Terror." I shook my head.

I should have expected the crowd given that it was Saturday night. But the place would probably be as packed on a Monday. The club was known to be exclusive and nothing drew people more than a chance to tell their friends and enemies that they had made the list. The elevator doors opened into a lobby lined with velvet ropes.

If it had been a human club, I would have been concerned about my chances of getting in. Even in the company of Lola. I didn't need to worry here. To the left there was a smaller nook, the area labeled "VIP," and it was manned by a vampire. Just as my magic began to tingle, telling me I should be running, his head snapped up, and his nose told him his favorite meal was on the menu tonight.

He flicked his wrist and suddenly a large meaty man appeared next to him, and he whispered to the man gesturing in our general direction. Holding up my hand, I waggled my fingers and smiled. Lola elbowed me.

"What? He knows what we are. This will make getting to the boss faster."

"God, you don't have to act like we're takeout."

"I would think the silver cuffs and collar would signify that I'm not on the menu tonight."

"Or that you like to play hard to get." She harrumphed.

"Great, we're the perfect package, you're blonde, I'm brunette, I'm a challenge, and you're an easy meal. We appeal to all tastes. Lola and Peg for the win!" I held my hand up for a high five.

Lola stared me down for a minute before shaking her head, leaving me hanging. Still I saw the twitch at the side of her mouth. She knew I was funny, even if she wouldn't admit it. Before I could say anything further, the giant vampire lackey was before us. "Ladies, would you come this way?"

There were some angry comments along with a few curious stares from the people we had ridden up the elevator with. We were now deemed important to the masses, oh goody. I nodded and followed the man, my hand gripping Lola's elbow. She talked a mean game, but I knew she had to be uncomfortable, to say the least. I was shaking in my boots.

Ninety percent of the time attitude got you through hard times. If you wanted to be a badass, you could be one if you pretended for a bit. So, I put on my best resting bitch face. I had been born with it, so it didn't take too much effort.

We were taken to the vampire at the podium, who grinned, displaying his if extra-sharp second set of canines that looked like a simple dental anomaly if you were observant and knowledgeable about teeth. Vamps were growers, not showers. Evolution was kind enough not to make them easily recognizable to their prey. They were, of course, beautiful as a general rule. Humans might like to laugh at Hollywood glamorizing monsters, but the monsters could only exist if they were able to eat. Beauty was alluring and powerful bait. A power the monsters took full advantage of.

The vamp before me was no exception. He was over six feet, with a powerfully built body expertly contained in an expensive suit. His sculpted face whispered a Nordic heritage. His pale skin and blond hair confirmed it. I assumed his eyes were blue, but I wasn't stupid enough to look into them. Glamour wasn't just a popular women's magazine; it was also a death sentence.

"Ladies, what a pleasant surprise. Welcome to The Opium Den. Can I interest you in the VIP area?" He raised an eyebrow before adding, "Or perhaps a private room?"

Yep, he thought we were easy. "I need to see the boss. If you can make that happen, I'll go wherever. Fair warning though, try to bite either one of us, and I'll use whatever power I have to fry your ass. This isn't a social visit."

The vampire looked crestfallen. I knew better. Vampires were nature's most perfect sociopaths. They were charming, but behind the warm exterior ran ice water.

They enjoyed torturing puppies and playing with their food. "That is indeed disappointing, Miss…?"

"I wanted to remain anonymous."

"If you wish to see Fane, that will not be possible," he said, giving me and Lola a boyish grin. "If you changed your mind about Fane however, I can meet you in a private room. I'll call you whatever you'd like."

"That won't be necessary, Vince. I will see the ladies."

Vince's already pale skin turned a little ashen. Apparently even the deadliest predators were on the food chain.

"Yes, Mr. Dimir," the vamp uttered, obviously wanting his boss to leave as quickly as possible, so he could reclaim his cool.

When I looked at the vampire that scared his counterpart, I could see why. Whereas the VIP clerk was tall, handsome, and lethal looking, this man made him look like a sissy boy who would run to mama. He topped the other vamp by a few inches, putting him at roughly six-and-a-half feet. His body was somehow bigger and yet more graceful than the other vampire's. To top it off, his face was the perfect combination of beauty and ruggedness. His blond hair was a little long and was wispy around his ears and collar, he had facial hair, which was odd for a vampire, but added a rugged appeal. "Do I meet your approval, Ms. Darrow?"

My eyes snapped up before I could stop, and I found myself looking into glaciers. His blue eyes were the lightest I'd ever seen. My magic started tingling with a vengeance, and then I realized what I saw in his eyes was triumph. Oh hell no, I snapped my eyes down quickly before his glamour could take hold.

He laughed softly. "A challenge, I like that."

We found out his type. At least he would leave Lola alone. She remained deathly silent during this interaction.

I glanced to my right to find her staring at the floor in determination not to meet his gaze.

"Ladies, to what does The Opium Den owe the pleasure?"

I kept my eyes averted. "Business." I noticed my voice was gruffer than usual. Perhaps it was trying to counteract the submissiveness that avoiding eye contact insinuated.

"How disappointing." His voice sent shivers down my spine, making me want to hunch my shoulders. It took a lot of effort to make them remain squared. "But I would be remiss to not entertain ladies of your caliber under any excuse. Would you care to follow me to my office?"

Actually, I wouldn't, but it would be careless to discuss our business out in the open. Plus the loud music emanating from the club would not be conducive to a productive conversation. "Sure, lead the way, was it Mr. Dimir?"

His eyebrows knitted together. He was obviously annoyed by my lack of knowledge regarding him. "I'm surprised you didn't know, Ms. Darrow, I'm the clan leader of my kind in Arizona."

Fan-fucking-tastic or fang-fucking-tastic, I sounded completely clueless. As a Fortune, I should have known not only his name, but his face. Hell, as a witch, I should have known. My only excuse was that ignorance was bliss, and up until this point I'd avoided vampires like the plague. Time to play it cool. "Of course you are, I simply wanted to make sure I was speaking to *the* Mr. Dimir. We've never met."

He leaned in to whisper in my ear, "Understandable, I would recognize you anywhere. You have your aunt's eyes."

My magic raced to my palms before I was even aware it was happening. I felt Lola tense, ready to run or back me up. Before I could consciously release the magic, the vampire was five feet in front of us.

Looking back over his shoulder, he tossed out a playful, "Try to keep up, ladies."

His acting didn't work on me. Teeth gritted, I went to follow him when I felt Lola pull on my elbow, in a stage whisper she hissed, "You sure about this, Peg?"

I met her gaze. "Nope, but I still have to do it. If you want to wait in the car, I'll understand."

She shook her head effusively before she started walking, pulling me with her. "No way in hell am I leaving you here alone. If he wants to play, we'll play."

Lola fell into a role. From what I could tell, it was a confident, political mover and shaker. The look of determination creasing her forehead made me glad she was on my side. My stride lengthened to match her pace. *That's right, bitches: we're walking with a purpose.*

We followed the vamp through what appeared to be a catacomb of hallways. The gas lamps lining the walls were the same as those in the lobby and in the waiting area. But instead of the marble flooring, there were wide-planked dark wood floors the echoed every footstep eerily. The romantic ambiance of the public areas transitioned to something more sinister behind the scenes. All the darks shadows had me thinking, "the better to hide your blood, my dear."

The vampire remained five feet ahead of us the entire time, not bothering to turn to see if we were still following. He knew we would; there was no need for the pretense. It felt like we were walking through the halls for a half hour before he stopped in front of large, dark, double doors. He produced what looked like a large antique key from a chain hidden under his shirt.

Even standing a few feet away, I could sense the magic

pulsing off the key. It was witch magic and obviously opened wards as well as the door. How sloppy of him. All it would take was someone pilfering the key for the vamp's office to be free game. Then again, whoever wanted to enter the spider's lair had a death wish. Present company excluded, of course.

He opened the door and extended his arm with a flourish, gesturing me and Lola inside. We entered, my muscles tensed at having him at my back. My magic had a mind of its own tonight and again raced to my palms. I heard the vampire laugh behind me.

It was hard to hide his true nature from his laugh. It lacked any genuine feeling, and I had to force myself not to shiver in response. It was the first time I truly saw the man for what he was, the first time the facade completely dropped. I turned quickly, no longer willing to leave him at my back.

"Tsk, tsk, my dear," he said, waggling my finger at me as if I were an errant child. "There is no need for the magic." His playful mask was back on, but it was as if the metaphorical mask was askew.

Lola decided she'd been quiet long enough. "As long as you know there will be no need for the fangs, buddy." Her voice was authoritative, if lacking the punch that only strong eye contact could make. I elbowed her lightly, making her stiffen.

The vampire seemed to notice Lola for the first time. It was strange, especially when gorgeous Lola was half naked. He looked her up and down, and winked at her, but then his attention returned to me. I knew it was because of my aunt, but I intended to stop that subject from becoming the topic of the evening. I took a seat.

I would have preferred to sit at a desk, but the large intricately carved wood desk only sported a master's chair with no guest seating. The small area before the desk offered two love seats richly upholstered and quite inviting. *The better to eat you with, my dear.* Again, I was making fairy tale references, ugh. Lola quickly took the spot next to me.

The vampire looked disappointed. He considered us, no doubt thinking about trying to squeeze between us. He decided against it and sat directly across from us, leaning back and crossing his legs.

"Mr. Dimir, I am here in official capacity investigating a death in the witch community."

"Another one? Such a waste. Please, call me Fane."

I'd rather have not but didn't want to spend the next five minutes arguing. "Okay, Fane, were you acquainted with Violet Williams?"

"Yes, we were acquainted."

That was easy. "In what capacity?"

"We enjoyed a business arrangement. She provided witch blood, and I provided money and, on occasion, security."

"Great job, on that last one."

He frowned. "I said on occasion. It wasn't necessary in recent years."

"You've had this arrangement for years?" My eyebrows rose.

"Not this arrangement, but we ran in the same circle for years." The look on his face told me that was all I'd get on that subject.

I wanted to push, but he was under no obligation to speak with me, and I didn't know when he was going to stop humoring me. So, I asked what I needed to know. "I've read that vampires have the capability of going invisible, at least the older ones. Have you heard of a vampire being able to hide their aura as well?"

He arched an eyebrow and pursed his lips. Leaning

forward, he grabbed a crystal decanter and unstopped it. He raised his gaze trying to meet mine. "Unless of course you'd care to donate?"

"No," Lola and I said in unison.

"A pity." He filled the rocks glass accompanying the decanter with a dark-red liquid. It was too thin to be just blood. It was probably cut with something else. "You ask a lot of questions, but you don't offer anything in return. That's not how to play the game, Peg."

"It's Ms. Darrow."

His chilling laugh sounded again. "You're going to be such fun."

The conversation was going exactly where I didn't want it to. I tried to rein it back in. "You don't know of any vampires who can hide their aura, effectively scrubbing it from an item?"

"Did you think you would come in here and I would tell you the secrets of my kind? We value witches, but only as a delicacy."

Well, shit.

"I didn't want to start issues with Pammy, but you smell so damn inviting."

"Huh?"

"It's not that you smell better than other witches, your blood just has an extra zing of copper, an extra boost of power. Not everyone would recognize the unique vintage you've brought before me. I'm afraid I can't resist." He struck faster than a cobra. One minute he was sitting at the sofa across from me, the next he had picked me up and was cradling me to him. "I like your accessories, Peg. They're very striking, but they are not a deterrent, simply a nuisance."

Lola jumped up. "I wouldn't do that, asshole."

Fane spared her a glance. "Don't worry, my sweet, I'm sure you'll make a lovely dessert."

"Touch her or me and you jerks won't live out the week. The goblins will kill you and every vampire in the state."

I struggled in his vice-like grip. "Seriously, dude, I'd listen to her."

He smiled down at me. "Ah, my dear, I know your family is not connected with the goblins."

"Well, I am, and she's my best friend. Plus, she's recently become cozy with Deval."

Fane tried to maintain a passive expression, but the name drop worked. His grip on me loosened. "But if she has piqued his interest, it was surely a fling. Deval is not one to commit."

"Even if it's just a fling, he's hired her to look into this murder. Back up before I call him." Lola reached into the tiny clutch and drew out her phone.

Fane released me completely and stood. "What exactly is your connection to the goblins, Miss…?"

"Fahl. I was adopted by them. I'm their ward. Go ahead and harm us. See if I'm lying."

Okay, Lo, let's not bait the hungry vampire. "How about you answer my questions? I eat a very unhealthy diet. I'm sure my blood wouldn't be worth it."

Fane gave me a disbelieving look, maybe I shouldn't have brought up my blood.

"Yeah, you should see how many burritos she can put away in a week."

"Thanks, Lo, it's a skill."

The vampire moved to the space between his desk and the sofas and began pacing, obviously torn. If he let us go, he was acknowledging the goblins were stronger than the vampires. Which they were, but ego was something everyone wrestled with. I leaned back into the sofa, finding it comfortable again now that I was no longer being restrained by my worst nightmare.

Lola remained standing with the phone in her hand, daring Fane to call her bluff. If I became successful at this Fortune thing, I might need to hire her as muscle or the pimp of impending muscle, so to speak.

The vampire quit pacing and turned sharply on the ball of his foot, returning to his previous seat on the second sofa. "At this time, I will refrain from feeding. Why have you brought these questions before me?"

"I found a black-market blood bank in her house."

"I would hesitate to use the words 'black market.' Everyone who donated was aware of what it was for and was compensated appropriately."

"Witches hurt for cash every now and then, but I don't think it's actually legal," I said.

"And fae and shifters, even goblins, still it's a gray area at best," Fane argued.

Lola sat back down quickly, her mouth open in surprise.

My jaw ached to drop as well. "Really, you get fae and goblins too?"

"Of course, every race no matter how affluent, wealthy, and insular will always have its poor drudges, the ostracized. Violet was good at finding them, and I paid her, and them, very well for it."

"Why bother to pay? Those poor drudges would likely show up on your door looking for a little danger." There would never be a shortage of stupid, regardless of species.

"There will always be those, but they often require a courtship process and even the most loyal servants sometimes get away. How is Belinda?"

The back of my jaw tensed and ached at the mention

of my aunt. "That is none of your concern."

"She is missed, so willing with just a hint of defiance. Well, at least initially." His eyes glittered, drawing my gaze before I pointedly focused on his nose.

He was trying to goad me, but I didn't fall for it.

Lola was a bit more susceptible apparently. "Shut it, or I'll tell Deval you attempted to attack us." She was shaking.

I placed my hand on hers to calm her and wordlessly ask for her silence. Her stiff muscles relaxed slightly as she tried to do my bidding.

Fane nodded once, clearly not worried. He knew we wouldn't say anything as long as he cooperated. If anyone got to kill him, I hoped it would be me one day. I wouldn't want Deval to beat me to it, unless absolutely necessary.

"What happens now that your source is gone?"

"Another one will pop up. They always do."

"You didn't have any arguments with Violet?" I prodded.

"No, ours was a strong working relationship. We had a history. I was fond of her."

"You're incapable of that kind of emotion." My nose wrinkled.

His flat grin reinforced my statement. "Even the worst monster can feel affection for a pet."

That was exactly what Violet had been, a pet. "Okay, even if you didn't personally have any problems with her, what about the other vampires in your territory?"

"None would dare."

"The poppy she was clutching would say otherwise."

His eyebrows raised. "What do you mean? A poppy was found?"

"Exactly what I said, a poppy flower was found in her cold dead fingers. Are you saying the poppy flower is no longer your calling card?"

I looked to the painting displayed behind the desk depicting a field of poppies for emphasis.

His mouth thinned before answering, "Yes, it's our calling card, but none would dare, and if they have, they'd have me to answer to. I will need to know about the results of your investigation. It is a great offense to harm one in our possession, let alone to have gone against the sect or to impersonate us."

The most telling word of that statement was "possession." Vampires did not care for anyone. Even their loyalty for one another was only a means to an end. Lola was a member of the goblins, and they referred to her as daughter or ward. Vampires only wanted to own people, and break and discard them at will, just as they had my aunt.

"I would need to clear that with Pammy and Deval. Frankly, why would I give you any information when you're not being forthright with me?"

"Please, child, I have been answering your questions," his tone was snide.

"The bare minimum. Can any vampires scrub their aura as well as their physical form?" Fane inclined his head slightly. It gave him a strange otherworld appearance, like a reptile impersonating a human. He closed his eyes for a moment in thought.

He didn't see me shiver at his strange movements.

Eyes still closed, he answered, "I am the oldest in this territory, and I cannot hide my aura without the assistance of witch magic. We, like every supernatural, evolve, but I have not heard of this talent. I would not say definitively that the talent doesn't exist, because we are secretive, but again I haven't heard of it."

"Do you believe any of your people may have 'evolved' to possess that talent?"

His expression turned thoughtful. "I do not, no. I keep those in the state well in hand. They would not be able to hide this talent long."

"Can you think of anyone else who might want to harm Violet? You mentioned Violet needed security in the past."

He waved his arm, dismissive of the question. "That was child's play a few years ago. An old tryst. I can't even remember his name."

"Are you sure he didn't hold a grudge?"

"No, I am not sure he didn't hold a grudge. I am not all knowing."

"Okay, but do you remember anything about him, if not his name?"

"I remember arrogance. I enjoyed bringing him down a notch. But age doesn't always lead to clear memories. You would need to confer with her friends."

"Is there anything else you can think of that might be helpful?"

He tapped his finger on his jaw for a moment. "No, that is all I know. Will you share your findings with me?"

Damn everyone wants a piece of the action.

"I'll tell Pammy you want information, and she can decide."

"Do tell her that I'd be most interested. Now, ladies, as pleasant as this has been, I grow bored. You may leave."

He didn't bother getting up, but Lola and I did quickly, wanting to leave before he returned to his previous game. He remained on the couch as we hustled out the door. My eyes darted around the labyrinth of hallways and spotted an escort. The human lackey stood slightly away from the door we exited waiting to escort us to the exit. His glazed eyes and smile reminded me of my aunt.

9

W e made it to Lola's car without further incident. She was frazzled and gripped the steering wheel with an intensity one would expect from a teenager in driver's ed. She didn't want to talk about the night, which was fine by me. I had enough to think about without delving into a "we came this close to death" conversation. She pulled up in front of my house.

"Did you want to come in for a drink?" I asked.

She shook her head "no."

I closed my eyes for a moment. "Thanks for being the Hooch to my Turner."

That elicited a small smile.

"I'm going to Violet's in the morning. I'll call you after." I told her.

"Sounds good, I'm exhausted. I'll talk to you tomorrow."

I got out of the car, hyper aware of every shadow. It wasn't until I was in my home with the locks set and my wards double checked that I breathed a sigh of relief. At least until my subconscious gave a little wobble of doubt.

Deval managed to get in despite the wards. *Ugh, there went any chances of a decent night's sleep.*

Sleep didn't elude me, but I woke to an aching jaw and slight headache. Even in sleep I couldn't hide from stress. Nothing some coffee and ibuprofen couldn't fix. It was early, before nine. If I listened to Pammy, my next step would be to take a trip down the rabbit hole. First, I needed to check out Fane's story.

He was adamant that he had nothing to do with Violet's death because she was an asset to him, but vampires couldn't be taken at their word. It was evolution's greatest shocker that they'd organized a government at all. Their natures leaned toward ripping one another apart.

I needed to make sure Violet hadn't backed out of their deal. Just because he considered her an asset, didn't mean she felt the same way about him. If it were a mutually beneficial arrangement, financials would provide a clear view.

In the kitchen, I measured out the grounds and turned on the coffee maker, looking at financial documents would require an extra cup. Math wasn't a foreign language, but it wasn't my best class. Hearing the flop of the cat door, I glanced over my shoulder to see Cheddar trot forward, his hanging belly jiggling adorably as he moved to weave between my legs. He meowed pitifully that I was starving him. We both knew it wasn't true.

Fifteen minutes later, Cheddar was reclined on my bed licking his chops in gluttonous glee while I got dressed, my second cup of coffee on the dresser. Still waiting for the caffeine to kick in, I made the executive decision to take another cup to-go. It was good being the boss. *Lord help me if I said that in front of Pammy.*

Dressed in my uniform of a cotton T-shirt, jeans, and a tattered pair of burgundy Doc Martens, I looked out my bedroom window and saw that it was overcast. Arizona winters were tough. Grabbing a cardigan, I left the house five minutes later, travel mug in tow.

By the time I was at Violet's house, I was fairly awake, thanks to loud classic rock and caffeine. The approach to the house was a lot less ominous in the daylight. The front door was shut and locked like I'd left it. I hoped that meant there wouldn't be any surprise visitors. That was probably wishful thinking The vampires would want their property. I assumed the medical equipment was theirs. I couldn't picture Violet shelling out for the expense.

Reaching in my purse, also known as the black pit from hell, I searched for the spare set I grabbed on Friday. Five minutes of digging produced nothing. It was only after searching my Jeep that I remembered taking them into my house for safekeeping. *What an idiot.*

The lock could be broken, but I didn't want looters to take any of Violet's valuables. Going back for the keys would be a pain in the ass, especially if there was an alternative. I walked around the side yard to the block fence. Despite being five seven, I stretched up on my tippy toes to reach the latch on the other side of the gate.

The backyard was overgrown to degree that suggested Violet hadn't enjoyed yard work and only kept the front yard groomed to keep her neighbors off her back. Chaotic, where the house had been sterile, it was a stark contrast to the impression her home gave. It was attractive with its many citrus trees, if a bit gnarly and wild. The porch had the prerequisite dusty lawn furniture that looked to be rarely used. Its lack of coordination again at war with the uniformity of the home.

I reached for the knob and found it locked as well. *Damn it.* There was no deadbolt in the fifties-styled door. It had a window for the top half, the blinds tightly closed. I considered what would be easier to replace, a door lock or a window. Now I was being silly. I needed to go home and retrieve the keys. Then I noticed the dog door. Childhood shenanigans came to mind, like being dared at a young age to squeeze through a cat door.

Violet didn't have any pets; it was likely a relic from a previous owner. I could no longer fit through a cat door, but this one had been meant for a larger dog breed. I'd only need to get my torso into the door and reach up to undo the lock. This was why I didn't dress up for work.

Down on all fours, I angled my shoulders through the door. I managed to get my torso in easily enough, but trying to push my hips through was futile. Plan B it was, I twisted in the space, my ribs digging uncomfortably into the sharp plastic of the pet door and extended my arm as far as it would go, undoing the door lock.

The soft click barely sounded when I heard a deep voice from the outside. "While I appreciate the view, this seems beneath you."

Fear had me banging my spine against the top portion of the pet door. I scraped my back as I scrambled out as quickly as possible. The sun chose that moment to peek out of the clouds. Blinded by the glare, I threw a jolt of power at the direction of a male figure. A grunt sounded. Just as I readied another jolt a cloud passed overhead, and I could see again. I doused my power. "Deval, what the fuck are you doing here?"

He looked a little pale, which for a goblin meant practically corpse-like. They evolved in the earth after all. "Good gods, woman, I knew you were strong, but you have exceeded my expectations." He placed a hand against the brick wall, taking a deep breath. Goblin magic was slow to work. Their natural immunity allowed them to be impervious to a single jolt of magic.

"Didn't anyone ever tell you not to sneak up on people? I could have killed you!"

His color was quickly returning. "Witch, you would need to do a lot worse to kill me."

Throwing up my hands, I said, "Don't test me," through gritted teeth

He clenched and unclenched his jaw before spitting out, "You are powerful, but do you think I would be the reigning prince if some witch woman, not even a century old, could take me down?"

"I likely won't see a century, jackass." It was bad taste to bring up the consequences of our curse. Just because I grew up knowing I wouldn't live a thousand years, didn't mean that there wasn't a longing encoded in my DNA saying I should be able to.

Something flashed in his eyes. Sympathy? "My apologies, I sometimes forget about your disabilities."

The plastic lawn chair began to look rather inviting. If I hit him over the head with it, it wouldn't hurt him, but it would make me feel better. Nobody could claim I was attempting regicide, or was it princicide? No, that wasn't a word.

"It wouldn't be worth it."

My eyes narrowed. "How do you know what I'm thinking?"

"You're looking at that chair with a longing I have seen in many upset women, and a few men. I will forgive your magic attack, since I startled you, but this would be premeditated. I could not let that go without punishment."

"I'm not your subject."

The corner of his mouth twitched. "Appearances, and all that." He suddenly sniffed the air and looked at me with concern and confusion. "You have injured yourself."

The adrenaline making my injuries painless disappeared. The bruising and scraping along my back began to burn. Twisting from side to side, I felt the pull, but it was just a scrape. "No biggie. I'll need to remember to put some stain remover on the shirt before I wash it." Bloodstains were a bitch.

"I don't know why you're bringing up your domestic skills to me. Turn around."

"No, it's fine, and I was making small talk. Jeez, leave the cave every now and then, would ya?"

His mouth formed a hard line before he closed the three feet separating us to grab my shoulders and forcibly turn me.

"I said I was fine. A scrape never killed anyone." My body was tense, but I didn't see any way to get him to back off without ignoring his warning and actually taking the lawn furniture to him. He released my shoulders, but his close proximity remained, and I didn't think I had been set free. Suddenly, my cardigan and T-shirt rose, and air brushed over my skin. The fabric peeling away from my scrape and the cold air on the cut caused me to suck in a breath.

"Hey, Deval, unless you have a Band-Aid and Neosporin in your pocket, I don't see the purpose of this. If you're trying to see what color my bra is, and in that case, you need to buy me a shot of tequila first."

His low chuckle caused his breath to tickle my ear. It was close, but I managed to not shiver at the caress. He was looking at my injury, not trying to get in my pants.

"You are right. It is a minor scrape." He tugged the

fabric back down gently. "And I don't need tequila to undress women. Your beige color choice seems very functional."

I laughed at that and turned to face him. "Yep, it is that. Not typically men's favorite color choice, but I don't consider myself the femme fatale type."

He chuckled again, the corners of his eyes crinkling giving him a more approachable face. "I suppose you have scientific evidence to back this up?"

"Insomuch as every guy I've ever dated has said as much."

"Has this been an extensive poll?"

My skin heated at his insinuation. "Not that it's any of your business, but no."

Oblivious to my discomfort, he went on, "Ah, so hardly enough for a scientific study. Men may have preferences, but if he's not pleased to see you in your underwear, despite the color, you probably should not give him the pleasure of seeing it. I would not complain at all if you chose to strip down."

I opened my mouth and closed it again, speechless for a moment before I found my thoughts. "Dude, no wonder you have a reputation."

"A reputation?"

"Yeah, you're known as a big ol' man whore."

"If that is to say I enjoy the company of women, I will not apologize for it." The smile accompanying that statement was downright predatory.

"Okay, down, Fido. I'm not interested."

"I know differently, but I will honor delusions. We can continue with our business."

I scowled at him. "You have come back to the witch's house for what purpose?"

And just like that, he turned off the flirt. I wished my

body could shut down as quickly. I wasn't really attracted to him. It was stress, I told myself. Of course I was lying to myself. If anyone claimed they didn't find power and intelligence, wrapped up in an attractive package appealing, they were lying to you. Shaking my head, I forced my thoughts back to business.

"I went to see the vampires last night; they said everything was peachy on the business front. I want to check Violet's finances to verify that. I don't trust them."

He frowned. "Lola said you went out last night. Whereas I understand the need, you two should have brought security."

"I am security," I responded, bristling.

"If you were, Lola would not have needed to name drop."

I shrugged. "Security uses every tool available to them. I could have gone in with a big show of power, but why bother when a little name dropping keeps everything peaceful?"

"Do you really think you could have fought off the ten or so vampires in the building had you not name dropped?"

The answer was no. But why be honest when you could go for mysteriously delusional instead? I gave him a vague smile and turned to open the back door. Behind me he grunted, probably annoyed I wasn't going to admit to my inferiority while smiling and saying, "Yes, sir. Thank you, sir."

If I remembered the layout from the other night correctly, the office was in the hall off the kitchen. Deval followed, his steps light on the ceramic tiles. Going to the desk, I sat in the comfortable chair and turned on the computer desktop. Thankfully, it wasn't password protected, because lord knew, I wasn't very tech savvy. I should probably work on that since there were no master hackers in my social circle who'd let me pay them in Mountain Dew and bacon maple donuts.

I stared a bit blankly at the array of desktop icons to choose from.

"Remind me never to hire you for an administrative position."

"Please, you only hire goblins anyway."

He physically pulled back the office chair, causing me to squeak in surprise. "That is untrue. We are equal opportunity employers at Rouge Mining. Just look at Lola."

Getting out of the chair, I muttered, "Yeah, a ward of the goblins, real diverse."

"Well, is she a goblin?"

"For all intents and purposes."

His shrug said he agreed, but he still said, "Ah, but she is a witch."

This conversation would get me nowhere, and since I wasn't trying to get a job at Rouge Mining, I decided to drop it.

A few seconds later Deval had Violet's financial software up and running and was looking through the spreadsheets like they meant something. Maybe I should get some financial software, instead of winging it. If I found the killer, I'd actually have a little bit of money to keep track of. As it was, I was happy to let him stare at the numbers.

"Hmm."

"What does 'hmm' mean?" I asked.

"This workbook only shows her day job. She's reasonably well paid as an RN, but you said she was in financial straits?"

"Yeah, her Dad is sick, and I think she's been covering his bills."

"He can't provide for himself?" There was a hint of

contempt in his tone only the independently wealthy ever had.

"Not everyone is born to with a gold mine already in his name."

He grunted, unperturbed by my snark. I would have probably lectured him further, but then he pulled up another workbook.

"This seems to be what we're looking for."

I leaned over his shoulder to get a better look. There was a lot of money coming in, but it was going out just as fast. The vampires paid well, but the redemptions showed Violet spared no expense for her father's care. It also looked as if she was paying her donors' premium asking prices. That could easily be explained by the W, F, and S denotations next to the names of the donors. My bet was that these stood for "witch," "fae," and "shifter," respectively. I said as much out loud.

"Yes, that is likely the case. They would not need human blood procured for them, but supernatural blood is a much more difficult commodity to come by. The power it gives the vampires, even temporarily, would be worth a hefty price."

"I don't see any G's for goblin."

"My people aren't that stupid."

I snorted. "Desperate is desperate. Fane implied he had access to goblin blood. Hell, I wouldn't be surprised if a younger goblin did it, just to buy the latest pair of designer shoes. You guys are very materialistic."

He swiveled the chair scowling at me. "What would you know about a goblin's spending habits?"

"Only an observation. Your idea of dressed down is a pair of two-hundred-dollar jeans, mine is a pair that cost a tenth of that."

"You don't know much, Ms. Darrow. There is a reason

for everything. My two-hundred- dollar jeans will last much longer than your twenty-dollar pair."

Someone was getting huffy.

"Perhaps, but if I saw a goblin who wasn't wearing a label, I'd be shocked." Since I wasn't here to debate the pros and cons of bargain shopping, I changed the subject. "She's not in desperate financial straits?"

"She is scraping by. She is paid well, but her bills are high. She would need to continue the blood bank to make ends meet until her father passes."

"Peachy. Well then, shut that down, I need to get going."

"I do not work for you, Ms. Darrow."

"If you want to hang out looking at financials all day, be my guest, just lock the bottom lock when you leave."

Turning to leave, I heard him shutting down the computer behind me. Guess he didn't want to be here any longer than I did. By the time he caught up with me, I was at my Jeep.

"Where do you think you're going?"

"I'm an investigator, Deval. I'm going to go investigate." I crossed my arms.

He gritted his teeth, his entire face going stiff. He still managed to spit out, "Yes, but where are you investigating? You have not given me a report on what you found in the aura trace."

Oh, right. "I found a scrubbed aura. That's one of the reasons Lola and I went to The Opium Den last night."

His forehead wrinkled. "Are you saying you're not powerful enough to see through some aura hiding spell?"

My nostrils flared at the insult. "No, you moron. I've never run into anything like this and neither has Pammy. You should go tell Pammy she's not as powerful as you think. In the meantime, I'll work on finding what can hide its aura."

He crossed his arms, mimicking my pose. "Are you sure you're able to get this job done?"

"As much as anybody," I lied. "You know who did pop up a lot in the aura trace? You and your metal-smith buddy. Yet, I'm intelligent enough to not suspect you, so get off my back." Okay, I might still wonder about him, just a little, but it didn't make sense that he was his own thief. Besides, as far as I could tell, he had no known association with Violet.

"I should be grateful you don't suspect me?"

"Yep. If you want to give me your alibi, or your buddy's, that will take away the need to explore that avenue. Wouldn't want to waste my time."

His face was blank as he stared down at me for a solid minute before bothering to respond. "I was at a goblin function and have any number of witnesses. The metal smith does not even reside on this continent and has not visited the Americas in a century."

"Handy that all of your witnesses are your subjects." I cocked my head.

Before Deval could respond, a black SUV, a twin of the one he parked in front of the house, pulled up. Two large goblins got out, calling greetings to Deval. He glared at me before turning to greet the two men. "Gregar, Vegard. To what do I owe the pleasure?"

"Cousin, we were bored. Are you not happy to see us?" The goblin that approached smiled but his eyes remained hard.

A tick developed in Deval's jaw before he smoothed all emotion from his face. I'd take that as "no."

"Of course, it's always wonderful when you take

interest in my life. What has drawn your attention to me today?"

Both men resembled Deval, although one appeared much younger. He gave Deval a sheepish smile at the question. The older one's smile was anything but sheepish. If he smiled any wider, his face would crack.

"We hear you are hunting, cousin. Quite a pity to have your domain invaded."

Holy passive aggressive, Batman.

Inserting myself by stepping between Deval and the sharper featured version of him, I held out my hand. "Hi, we haven't been introduced. Peg Darrow."

The man sneered down at my hand.

His companion stepped in to take my hand in a quick, but firm, handshake. "I am Vegard. This is Gregar. We are Deval's cousins." His grin turned nervous, probably because his brother was now glaring at him.

Deval reached out and clasped his shoulder in approval. Poor guy, he looked like someone was stuck in the middle of family drama.

"Nice to meet you, Vegard. It's great that you guys decided to stop by. Maybe you could tell me where Deval was on Friday night?"

Vegard turned sharply to look at me, but Gregar just laughed out loud. "He was at a court function with us. He would not want to disappoint Mommy."

I was about to ask where this court function was held, when Deval cut me off. "Ms. Darrow, I need to speak with my cousins. Perhaps you should be going?"

I wanted to stay. Hell, I wanted to pop some popcorn and enjoy the show, but when I looked between the men, I saw that Deval and Gregar weren't smiling anymore, their mouths were firmly shut. They wouldn't say another word in front of me. Vegard shrugged apologetically.

"Fine. I have things to do, anyway."

"What are your plans for the rest of the day?" Deval inquired.

I arched a brow. Seriously? He was dismissing me, and he seemed to think an audience would make me answer his question.

"Peg, answer me."

I considered flipping him the bird, but realized he was playing some sort of power game with his cousin, and it would look bad if I didn't answer him. *Ha, Pammy look, I could be diplomatic.*

"I'm going to go ask Alice some questions."

The stiffness melted from his features and now the crinkles around his eyes seemed to belay actual warmth from a smile. "Alice, such an interesting woman. I would join you, but I have other matters to attend to." He motioned to his cousins, who remained mute despite eavesdropping.

My hackles rose. "Good, because I don't recall inviting you."

He ignored my statement. "If you kept me informed, I would not need to track you down. Whereas, I expedited the process, I am sure you can figure out accounting software. I have other things to attend to."

"So you've said." I managed with a forced smile. I'd wanted to reply with something sarcastic and cutting, but my brain wasn't giving me any material. After congratulating myself on my diplomacy, I doubted calling him an asshat in front of his cousins would be a good idea. I raised my hand to my brow and gave him a mocking salute before turning to get into my Jeep. I heard him laughing behind me as I climbed in. I hadn't meant to amuse him, but then again, I never got the reactions I hoped for from him.

I called Pammy to see where I could find Alice. She muttered under her breath the entire time about ignorant young witches, while I pretended she was talking about her groupies. Five minutes later, I had an address plugged in to my phone's GPS. It said I was going to the First Baptist church in Phoenix. It must be a mistake. I called Pammy back.

"Hey Pammy, I think you gave me the wrong address."

"You calling me senile?" Her voice was not pleasant.

"Uh no, it's just you've given me the address of a condemned church."

"If that's the address I gave you, that's the address you should go to."

My, my, someone is testy today.

"Okay," I tried to sound meek. "Should I call her before I show up?"

"If you needed to call her first, I would've told you."

"Sure, thanks."

There was a grunt before the call disconnected. I wanted to ask more questions, but Pammy obviously wasn't in the mood. I wondered if the Bump and Grind ran out of her favorite pastry.

Traffic was a little rough, but since I was going into Phoenix, as opposed to leaving it, I wasn't sitting on the I-10 for too long. Eight in the morning would have been another story. The First Baptist Church was a stunning building. A fire stole its functionality, but its beauty and historical relevance kept it from being torn down. Someone was probably lobbying to do just that. I hoped they didn't succeed. The building was white stucco and had Italian Gothic architecture overall, suggesting it was a historic landmark, which I had no doubt it claimed. The bell tower soared into the air with a kind of subdued elegance.

I was half tempted to Instagram the sucker, but that would be an Idiot 101 choice for someone who was actively investigating a murder. *Oh, look, vicious killer, here I am, looking into how the hell you've scrubbed your aura. Don't come murder me.* So, I kept my phone in my pocket and looked around.

Perhaps there was a small apartment still functioning somewhere. Finding no trace of one, I approached the chain locked front doors thinking the attempt futile and not looking forward to having to call Pammy back, when a buzzing sensation filled the air. About a foot from the front door, my head shot up. Craning my neck, I saw that what was a beautiful ruin had now become simply beautiful.

What the hell?

Taking a step back, I experienced the same tingle against my skin and the ruin popped back into focus, stepping forward, beautiful structure. I wasn't seeing things. The church was glamoured. Holy hell, the power and knowledge it would take to glamour a building this size had my eyes crossing. The front doors were no longer chained and there was a bell with a pull rope. I grabbed the rope and rang. A rich tone rang, echoing around me.

Did the humans hear the bell? If so, did they think it was a ghost? This was too interesting. How had I never realized this place existed? According to Pammy, it was because I was a baby witch with no respect for the community. She might be right.

I didn't hear any movement inside, and I considered ringing the bell again, when the front door opened with a creak, suggesting the hinges needed oil. The door cracked enough to admit a head. That head was covered in curly grayed hair, dyed with a purple tint, its fine texture, reminding me of the fluff on a baby duck. It stood out every which way, distracting me from looking at the actual woman.

Once I met her eyes, I was taken aback. They were a striking gray that seemed to be far away from the here and now.

"Uh, hi, my name's Peg Darrow. I'm here to see Alice."

The woman continued to stare at me, not really focusing for another five seconds before her eyes suddenly cleared and her thin lips opened up into a wide smile. "Oh goody, a visitor." The woman opened the door, exposing her large frame covered in a lime-green patterned muumuu. It was a bold choice, but somehow perfect, given the purple rinse in her hair.

"Are you Alice?"

"Of course, of course, come in." She grabbed my shoulder and ushered me in.

The church was even more awe-inspiring on the inside. It was not outfitted as a church, but as a massive library. How any single individual could have collected all of these books in a lifetime was beyond me.

"Are all of these yours?"

"Hmm, yes, of course. Did you think I would go around stealing another's books?"

I stuttered a bit, "Of course not, it's just a lot."

"I inherited quite a few, my family always were collectors. Now come in, come in." She clucked and shooed me further into the entry and up a grand staircase leading to a landing. The space held a worn brown leather sofa and two pink velvet wingback chairs that were fraying from use. Alice practically pushed me into one of the latter. "Something to drink?"

I didn't usually turn down refreshments, but despite her size this woman was like a hummingbird flitting here and there, and I didn't want her running off to find me a drink.

If she had a heart attack, I'd never get my questions answered. "No, I'm fine, please don't trouble yourself."

She looked at me with speculation before seating herself. "If you're sure."

"I am."

"In that case, that means more cinnamon bread for me!" she said jubilantly.

I didn't see any cinnamon bread, but then the scent of cinnamon and butter hit making me regret my choice. *Snap out of it, Peg! You're here to get information, not raise your blood sugar.* I smiled. "I spoke too soon."

"Oh, don't worry, I'll give you some to go."

"Kicking me out already?"

"Nope, but you must be in need of some help, if you're willing to turn down refreshments."

"Good point. Pammy sent me."

"How is that pain in the ass?"

I didn't know how to react. Most people worried it would get back to Pammy if they made such a statement to a stranger.

Alice smirked knowingly. "Yes, you can tell that old hag I said that. She calls me batshit all the time. Turnabout is fair play, though to be fair, batshit is a good description for me."

"You seem perfectly sane."

"Honey, you've been here five minutes. I can pretend to be sane for at least twenty. Best if you tell me the information you need, before your time runs out."

Some people you just instantly took a liking to and this zany lady was one of those people for me. "Okay, I need to know what could wipe its aura completely. I ran an aura trace on a piece of evidence, and the auras looked like opaque glass. When I rode them, it was like stepping into nothing, no sound, no noise, and nothing but white."

"Hmm, that's odd. Could be a powerful spell, but there would have to be a lot of intent behind it. Could be another supernatural evolution, though I haven't heard about that one. It'd be a neat trick though, huh?" Alice's eyes took on an excited sheen.

"I don't know, it felt...wrong."

"Course it felt wrong. To erase your aura is to erase yourself. If you're not some angst-ridden teenager, it's not something you should want, but to be able to do it on command could come in handy."

"Sure, if you're a criminal."

Alice tsked. "You're a Fortune. You can't say it wouldn't come in handy to be able to leave no trace on a psychic level when you were investigating. Say you needed to break into another witch's home to do a search and didn't want them to find out. It would be quite a nice thing to have."

"I would never do that."

"Must be new then. Being a Fortune means doing the dirty work for the greater good. As you know, for us it's vigilante justice or nothing at all. Stop watching TV crime dramas. A human's brand of justice cannot work for us in our society."

My face heated slightly. I had been watching too many reruns of *Law and Order*. That mindset was fine for the small-potato cases, but since I was now playing in the big leagues, it was important to remember that breaking the rules could come in handy. "You're right."

"Course I'm right. Now, did you have any suspect you were thinking about? One you want to know if they could pull off not having an aura?"

"Vampires."

Alice gave a delicate shudder, her ample décolletage quivering from the movement. "Those fuckers are capable of anything."

My eyebrows drew together, and I leaned forward. "You mean they're magically capable?"

"Like I said, species magic is ever evolving, but I've never heard of this. Invisible yes, that's frightening enough by itself, completely blank aura, no. Spell work could get you there. They would need a witch, or a specific type of fae, to be able to do it. They aren't spell workers unless they drink it from a witch, and even then, it would be a weak facsimile."

Nodding. I couldn't help my disappointment. She wasn't giving me anything to go on. "What about goblins?" I glanced to the shelves.

"No, they would need a witch's help, too. Vampires are the only ones that can steal from us, even in a small way. Again, if a witch is employed by another race, it can certainly be accomplished. You'd be looking for a powerful one though. I can lend you some books for more research. My time is running out."

Since I'd been admiring the shelves of books, her last comment snapped my head around. I don't know what I expected to see. She looked the same, but now her eyes were starting to glass over slightly. "Yes, thank you. Anything would be helpful."

She rose quickly and marched into the stacks, calling out over her shoulder, "Have you considered the missing aura might be the result of a curse and not self-inflicted?" She muttered the last part of her sentence under her breath, but the echo from the cathedral high ceilings brought the words back to me anyway.

She might have a point. The stark wrongness I sensed earlier during the aura spell came back to me. Curses could be pretty tame, but they could also be the ugliest form of magic. A shiver raced down my spine as I followed Alice. She ran through the stacks, light on her feet as her muumuu fanned out behind her, and grabbed books at what looked random, turning quickly each time to deposit them in my arms.

She piled on a dozen before she was satisfied, turning on me suddenly. "You must go now, dear. They're back."

"Huh, who's back?"

Alice let out a girlish tinkle of a laugh that raised the hairs on the back of my neck. Her eyes were beyond glazed over. They held the opaque sheen of death. I wanted to reach out, touch her arm, to make sure she was okay, but my arms were filled with books. Instead, I turned and fled from her toward the front door. Her giggle echoed through the building, chasing me.

The quick burst of energy left me out of breath by the time I closed the door behind me. The combination of my impromptu sprint and the twenty pounds of books should've left me sweating, instead I was suddenly cold. There were goose bumps on my arms, and after manhandling the stack of books to one arm, I saw that my hands were blue from the cold.

It was a chilly sixty degrees by an Arizonan's standards, but I shouldn't be cold. Shaking my head, I walked off the front porch of the church, feeling more than relieved to leave the glamour behind. The books would need to be returned eventually. Maybe I could get some more answers then. The church felt welcoming when I'd originally entered, but when Alice had said to run, I ran faster than I had the month before when Lola and I went to a carnival haunted house, and a man dressed as a clown chased me with a chainsaw. A mystery for another day, and I was beginning to find that I enjoyed mysteries.

My stomach grumbled as I headed down the street to my parked Jeep. *Damn it, she forgot the cinnamon bread.* Once in the Jeep, I blasted the heater and obtained instant relief from the chill invading my bones. With the books stacked precariously on my passenger seat, I made U-turn and headed back to Mesa.

A drive-thru burrito stand provided dinner. A green chili pork burrito, a churro, and their largest Diet Pepsi added to my bounty. Books and burritos, under normal circumstances I would consider this a pretty kick-ass night.

By the time I got home, it was twilight. The desert sky was painted with reds and oranges. I wished there was time to admire the sunset while I was eating my burrito, but there wasn't. I went to the living room and set the books Alice had given me on the coffee table, only stopping in the kitchen to drop my purse and grab the paper towels necessary when devouring a burrito the size of my head.

Back in front of the books, I noticed they looked old—and valuable. Proper borrowed book etiquette suggested that I didn't return the books covered in grease and green chili sauce, so I ended up taking my dinner to the porch to enjoy my supper after all. I only dived into research after my hands had been thoroughly washed.

A few hours later, my stomach was uncomfortably full, and my brain felt like it was leaking out of my ears. The clock read ten, but I hadn't gotten any closer to the answers I was looking for.

The first book dealt with the evolution of vampires. It was dry, and whereas it made reference to several vampires' evolution, they were all highly individualized with a wide range of powers, one of which Alice mentioned, was the power to go invisible. She was right, that was terrifying on its own. I was happy to read that the particular vampire had been killed. But where there was one, there would likely be others.

The book was scientific in nature and thankfully specific as to what going invisible entailed. Only the vampire's physical form went invisible. Those around him could still feel, touch, smell, and hear him. Mind you, the book was written at the beginning of the twentieth century, and like the book and Alice mentioned, powers tended to evolve. Had the vampire lived, he might now be capable of total invisibility.

After that, I skimmed over a history of goblins. Alice implied they were off the table, but she threw the book on the pile anyway. It must mean something. After reading the first couple of chapters, I realized it was simply a history. Although it was something I definitely wanted to read, I needed to focus on my current case.

The next five books were all on curses and spell work. I started with curses because of Alice's comments, hoping for a "eureka" moment, a specific curse or spell that would explain the scrubbed aura. All I learned was that pretty much anything was possible if you put your mind to it and shoved your morals in the cupboard.

The question became: could the murderer be a cursed victim, who recovered from said curse, only to use another spell to later wipe his or her aura? Or perhaps the scrubbed aura was the result of the curse? It was too much to contemplate tonight. My gut told me the vampires and goblins were a dead end, and I should follow the curse angle. Knowing Violet's history would be essential in moving forward.

10

———————

B right and early the next day, I began my trek to Tucson. Violet's father might know if she had any enemies. At the very least, he would know who to ask. My experience with curses was limited but the curser and the victim usually had a history. Violet was in her twenties, which meant she didn't have much history, and the majority of it should be in her hometown of Tucson.

It was odd. I had been raised in the Phoenix area and had moved to Tucson for college when my family did. Violet had been raised in Tucson but had gone to Tempe for college. We were as two trains passing in the night.

It took most people about an hour and a half to two hours to drive from Mesa to Tucson. For some reason, it never took me fewer than two and a half. But my grandma appreciated my driving, so there was that. It wasn't as if I could afford a speeding ticket.

I had called Pammy on my way to find out the facility where Dusty, Violet's father, was living. She liked that I was driving down to Tucson, rather than calling him. I leveled up from baby witch to respectful young lady. *Goody.*

Around ten thirty I pulled into the Cholla Hospice Center. The hospice center decided to name itself after the cacti I referred to as Satan's plant because it appeared to jump at its victims, and its multiple needles were a nightmare to get out. Gods forbid your pet got near one.

At least the facility had an appropriate desert theme name. There were a number of Arizona establishments that preferred the words bay, lake, river, and ocean in their names. Arizona had rivers and lakes, but trying to give the impression of waterfront property in most of the cities there was pushing it.

Inside the single-story building, I passed the waiting area, noting the collection of vinyl-covered seats in the appropriate southwest shades of teal and pink in a shade somewhere between salmon and Pepto Bismol, as I headed to the receptionist's desk.

The woman who sat behind the desk had a sweet smile that was not unfriendly, but certainly not too happy. Perfect, considering the fact she worked at a place where people went to die. "Hi, how can I help you?"

"Hello, I'm here to see Dusty Williams."

"Family?"

"Friend of the family," I responded.

"I'm glad someone is here to see him. He got news a couple of days ago about the death of his daughter, very tragic." Her voice dropped a few octaves before she added, "Guess she'll be welcoming him at the pearly gates though, which has to be kinda nice."

I nodded, not sure if I agreed with the woman but unwilling to make her feel uncomfortable for trying to find a silver lining in an unexpected death. If she was strong enough to work with loss every day, then she had the right to find whatever it took to get her through the day. "Yes, it was very tragic."

Her voice got even lower as she leaned in. "Do you know what happened to her?"

I gave her a hard stare. There was nothing wrong with trying to find a positive in tragedy, but now she was being gossipy. "I couldn't say." I was unable to keep the frost from my voice.

The woman sat back abruptly, aware that she shouldn't have asked. "I'll go see if Mr. Williams is up for visitors."

While she scurried off, I perused the displayed brochures and found out that cremation was a cost-effective alternative to traditional burial service, lovely. I moved on to reading about high-end coffins for the loved one who enjoyed the finer things when the receptionist returned with an overly bright, "Dusty will see you now."

I followed her down a yellowed laminate hallway. The effect eerily similar to the fluorescent lights in Violet's lab. Dusty's room was located all the way at the end of the hall and appeared dramatically different to the rest of the hospice I had seen. It was painted a deep green color and the floors, while still laminated, were faux wood. The room was surprisingly soothing, despite the hospital bed and a variety of monitoring equipment.

With the help of an adjustable hospital bed, Dusty sat upright. I doubted he would be able to do so without the assistance. His hospital gown hung off his gaunt frame. His forearms gave hints of what used to be ropey muscle, before disease got ahold of him. He must have been a strong capable man. I gently shook his limp hand. "Hello, Mr. Williams. My name is Peg Darrow. I'm sorry for your loss."

He nodded, the movement slightly ruffling the yellowed white hair. To the left was a framed photo of a blond cowboy with a dark-haired woman and a little girl, who matched her mother. Dusty, his wife, and Violet.

"I want to know who would hurt my baby," he rasped out.

"That's what I'm here for. I'll find out who did this." I reached back out and squeezed his hand.

He must have found some reassurance because he gave me an approving nod and his mouth firmed. "Do you have any leads?" His voice weak but clear.

"A few. I hate to ask, Dusty, but are you a witch?"

He shook. "No, ma'am, but my wife was one. She kept no secrets from me. You can speak freely, even if you told me some big dark secret, I'll be dead before I can tell anyone."

I gave him a speculative look. "She told you every-thing?" I didn't doubt him; I just didn't want to give the dying man a heart attack.

"Yes, ma'am. I know about everything and every*one*."

"Okay, well there is a possible curse angle, but there's also a vampire angle."

"That's not good," he replied mildly. He obviously knew about vampires.

"No, nothing they touch is ever good. Did you know about any relationships Violet may have had with vampires?"

"No, ma'am. My little girl should have known better. Her mama certainly drilled it into her head enough. Never talk to vampires: they only want your blood."

Nodding, I asked, "What about curses? Do you know if Violet ever cursed anyone? Maybe an ex-boyfriend or a former friend?"

He shook his head. "No, to me my daughter was a princess and never disappointed me. Then again, she wouldn't share anything that could disappoint me. We weren't close like that. Don't get me wrong, I loved my daughter and would do anything for her, but she never wanted to worry me. She talked to her mom about that stuff before she passed away. I'm not a stupid man, my daughter couldn't have been the angel I believed her to be. Everyone's shit stinks, but I was happy to pretend otherwise."

"Children never want to worry their parents," I agreed. I never wanted my parents to think I was incapable of taking care or myself. Violet wasn't perfect, but she made bad decisions to help her father. I would never tell him that. "If she were going to tell someone about the darker side of her life, who would it be?"

"I'm not sure if they're still close, given that Ivy still lives here in Tucson, but they were best friends growing up. I think they still stayed in touch."

"Do you have Ivy's contact information?"

"Yep, go to the drawer in the nightstand. That's where I keep my address book," he said, his hand shaking as he gestured toward the bedside table. "I told her Violet died. Ivy's a good girl. She came to visit me yesterday and snuck me in some brownies. They don't like to give us sugar here. I don't know why. I'm only hanging on to see justice done for my girl."

I swallowed. *No pressure.*

I rounded the bed to the small nightstand and pulled out the drawer. The photo held my attention for a moment. They seemed like a happy family. Dusty was a shell of the man he used to be, but there was no doubt it wasn't just the disease that did him in. With the way his arm held his wife possessively and his eyes were looking at her, he had certainly suffered that loss.

"What is Ivy's last name?"

"Reyes."

Opening the worn little black book, I leafed to the "R" section and found her name neatly printed. I entered Ivy's number into my phone. "You said she's still here in Tucson?"

"Yep, that girl loves this city. Got a good job, too, at one of the resorts."

"Can you think of anything else that might help?"

Dusty raised his arm to scratch his head. "I really can't, Miss. The surprise of her death should have put me in my coffin, but I'm too stubborn to leave this mortal coil until I have justice for my girl. You're going to give them witch justice, right?"

He was referring to death. There was such a thing as imprisonment for supernatural offenders, but more often they were put down because they were too difficult to contain on limited resources.

"That will be Pammy's decision."

"You tell her I'm for it," his voice was barely above a whisper now.

I nodded. I was undecided on the issue, but I'd share Dusty's wishes with Pammy when the time came.

I reached for my purse and opened my wallet to pull out my card. It was simple, my name, number and email address with no job title. I handed it to him. "If you think of anything else, please let me know."

"That I will, miss. I can't wait to see my wife and daughter, but I need my justice. She should have survived me." A tear leaked out from the corner of his eye, proving just how hard the loss had hit him. A man like Dusty wouldn't cry for much.

I took his hand and squeezed it reassuringly. "I will do everything in my power to make sure her spirit has its justice."

He nodded, closing his eyes. I took that as my sign to go and left the man to grieve in peace.

The receptionist, who was eager and chatty earlier,

studiously kept her eyes on her computer as I left the building. I didn't mind being ignored. The parking lot was nearly empty. I hoped that meant that there weren't a lot of people in hospice, versus no one wanting to visit their sick loved ones.

In my Jeep, I turned the heat up and pulled out my phone. The number for Ivy rang a few times before going to voice mail. It was a generic message, reciting the number in a robotic tone. I left a short message. With nothing left to do, I decided to wait, which translated to visiting my family.

My parents had moved to the area shortly after I'd graduated from high school, and I had followed to attend U of A before eventually moving back to the Phoenix area and taking over the mortgage on my aunt's former home. My parents had chosen a home in in the hills just outside of Tucson in an area called Oro Valley. They lived in a quaint ranch-style home with a pool and a great view of the city lights at night. The only downside was the number of scorpions and rattlesnakes that found their way into my mother's garden. She was constantly looking for new spells to get rid of them, but nature had its own magic and vexed her at every turn.

I didn't need to call my mom before stopping by. Ours was not a family built on societal niceties. We came and went as we pleased, despite last minute changes to plans. So, I took my Jeep past the paved road to the dirt one and rumbled up to my parents' house. There was no doubt that my mother heard me coming from a mile away because when I pulled up in a cloud of dust, she stood on the front porch ready to greet me.

She smiled and waved me forward. "Hi, honey, I'm surprised to see you here today."

I walked through the wards, letting them slip over my skin in a warm invitation. My mother stepped right up to give me a bear hug. Barely over five feet, my mom still managed to give the best all-encompassing hugs.

She pulled back to study my face. "How's my Fortune?" She grinned like a loon.

My mother was the only person who was thrilled at my recent career choice. She had been positively giddy when I'd told her I started working for Pammy. My father had simply said congratulations in a very noncommittal way and had gone off to pray to the spirits for my safety.

Mom was a crime junkie. If there was a special on serial killers, she watched it. If there were a couple of desperadoes robbing banks, she followed every news story. If a trafficking ring was brought down by the police, my mom clapped with wild abandon.

Every Christmas added to her ever-expanding collection of true crime and mystery novels. Her shelves were beginning to buckle slightly.

For some reason, she thought I was invincible, and I did my best to live up to those expectations. "I'm doing well, Mom. I'm on a big case."

"All by yourself?" She squealed reaching up for another hug.

"It's a murder, Mom. You shouldn't be excited."

Instead being admonished, she perked up more. Who did I think I was kidding? Only my mom would be excited about a murder. "That's terrible, honey. Come inside, I'll feed you, and then you can tell me all about your case."

I followed her through the front door and took my favorite seat on the worn leather sofa. Daisy must have suddenly realized I was visiting because the old Catahoula dog burst into the living room with a spring in her step no twelve-year-old dog should have. I had a fairly good suspicion Mom was putting spells on the dog, but if Daisy wasn't feeling her arthritic hip, I had no complaints.

While I petted the ecstatic dog, my mom slipped into the kitchen to grab me food. I made it a point to never turn down food from my mother, nothing would ever taste as good. Plus, my mother always treated me like a goddess for the first two days of my visit. By the third, she realized I was another unwanted houseguest, who happened to be related and the food would dry up.

She came into the room just as I found the good spot on Daisy's belly. Daisy began kicking her back foot appreciatively. Mom set down a glass of ice and a Diet Pepsi and then a big plate of tamales.

"Oh my gods, Mom, did you make these?"

"Ha, I wish; one day I'll learn to. There was a woman selling them by the grocery bag in the Wal-Mart parking lot."

"Score!" I used my fingers to remove the outer cornhusk hiding the delicious masa goodness.

People were surprised when I said the best tamales were sold door-to-door, or out of car trunks. They thought it was unsanitary. I'd never gotten sick, knock on wood, and for these delicious suckers I was willing to take the risk. Daisy got up and placed her head in my lap, looking at me with the love and adoration only a dog could give. "Don't tell Mom, and I'll accidentally drop some in a minute," I whispered into her ear.

"I heard that," Mom yelled from the kitchen.

"Good, now you know I love your dog enough to share tamales with her."

"It is an act of love, dear. I was tempted to tell you to order a pizza when I heard you drive up. But I knew you'd sniff them out, and then you'd be whining about how I love your sister more than you."

"If you gave her tamales and not me, there would be no doubt you loved her more than me."

She brought her own tamales out and came to sit next to me, placing her plate on the coffee table next to mine. "She's been begging me to mail her some to Chicago, but I don't even know how one goes about mailing food. It seems unsanitary."

"Like buying them out of a trunk?" I quipped

"Touché."

We went back to eating in silence. They were red chile beef tamales, and no words were necessary when we were happily stuffing your face. I did, however, take some of the masa and drop it on the floor for Daisy. She gave me an accusingly look for not dropping any meat, but the red chiles weren't good for her. Content after finishing my plate, I leaned back into the couch cushion.

"How's Aunt Belinda?"

My mother gave me a sad look. "She's not having the best day. Why don't you take her a plate of tamales? I'm sure the food and seeing you would cheer her up."

I nodded and stood. I hated seeing my aunt when she was in a state, but I took the good with the bad. It was what family was all about. I grabbed my plate, took it to the country kitchen, and rinsed it before placing it in the dishwasher. Grabbing another heavy stoneware plate, I placed two tamales from the tin-foil container and headed down the hallway to the room at the end.

On my way down, I passed a lot of photos. My mom would never be in *Better Homes and Gardens* for her decorating taste, but she loved family. Every spare surface was covered with one memento or another to prove it. Once at the door, I knocked lightly before entering.

I found my aunt sitting on the edge of her double bed in a well-worn nightgown, her curly hair in a frizzy cloud around her head as she stared out the window. I approached and pulled up the small dressing table stool to sit in front of her. She finally looked at me. It took another five seconds before she recognized me, but she smiled when she did. "Margaret!"

I winced. "Aw, Aunt Belinda, you know I hate that name."

"Like Peg is better? You sound like a pirate's prosthesis. I'll never understand why Peg is a nickname for Margaret, any more than I'll understand why Dick is a nickname for Richard."

Truth be told I didn't either, but I liked my nickname well enough.

"Mom said you're not doing too well today."

"Oh posh, I don't do well most days, but at least my head is clear this afternoon, if a bit melancholy."

Aunt Belinda had run off with a group of vampires when she was in her mid-twenties. My mother tried to free her from their clutches for years, before my aunt showed up on her doorstep, five years later, hysterical and ranting about blood, ropes, and torture. My aunt never went into what happened, at least not to the family, but she saw a witch psychiatrist at least once a week who specialized in trauma.

Mom kept calming spells all around the house, and they helped. Truth was the move south out of Phoenix had helped the most. Not that there weren't any vampires in the Tucson area, but it wasn't as close to the nest that had seduced her and then stolen her innocence and pieces of her sanity.

"I'm really glad. Well, not about the melancholy stuff,

but about the clear head part. Why don't you come to the living room and eat these yummy, yummy tamales."

"No thanks, lovey, but I'll take the tamales. I'm glad you stopped by for a visit, but I need to stay in here today."

I knew better than to push. I handed her the tamales and took her hint, leaving her to her melancholy. My chest tightened. I did understand there was a constant war happening inside of her head. I would respect her boundaries.

I walked back into the living room in time to catch Mom feeding Daisy a bit of tamale. I pointed my finger at her accusingly and an admonishment was on the tip of my tongue when my phone rang. It wasn't a preprogrammed ring tone; I answered it, hoping it was Ivy.

Sure enough when I answered with, "Peg Darrow," I got a response.

"Hi, you left me a message?"

"Ivy?"

"Yes."

"I got your number from Dusty. I wanted to talk to you about Violet, if you have time." I hoped she heard the professionalism I attempted to layer into my voice.

"I have to work tonight, so I don't have long. I need to see you anyway. Where are you?"

That was a little surprising. I gave her directions, and she suggested we meet at a gas station bordering Oro Valley and Tucson. I wanted a coffee shop, someplace we could talk in peace and get caffeinated at the same time. She'd gone silent on the phone for a few moments when I suggested that, but since I didn't want her to ditch me, I agreed to her preference. I said goodbye to my mother, making her promise to give Dad a hug from me when he got home from work.

Ivy said she'd be driving a white Ford Escort, and when I arrived there wasn't one to be found in the parking lot, so I went inside to get a Diet Pepsi. I wasn't desperate enough for my caffeine fix to drink from the burnt coffee pot that was probably brewed hours earlier. Planet-killing-Styrofoam cup in hand, I headed back out to my Jeep and leaned against the door.

Before too long, an older model white Escort pulled into the parking lot. A small woman with dusky skin and straight black hair wrestled with something in her front seat before getting out of the car. Her approach started out strong, but halfway between her car and me, her feet began to drag. I held my hand up in a wave and gave an encouraging smile. It did the trick as her stride got brisk again. When she reached me, she shoved a wooden box at me without a word.

"Uh, hi, I'm Peg. Thanks for meeting me."

"Hi, I don't mean to be abrupt, but whatever is in that sucker had my little sister freaked out." Ivy shoved the box at me again, and I had to turn around to place my cup on the roof of the Jeep so I could grab it. The box was heavy, and I understood why she had wrestled with it in her front seat. "She dropped it off at my house this morning and left to god knows where."

Surprised at the odd introduction, I raised my eyebrows. "Okay, not to be rude but what does this box have to do with me?"

"It was Violet's." She looked at me like I was an idiot.

"Then why does your sister have it?"

"She'd been staying with Violet on and off when she was in Phoenix. I don't know what it is, why she had it, or why it freaked her out. What I do know is that I don't want crazy witch shit in my house bringing death and destruction. I told her I'd keep it for her, but what she doesn't know won't hurt her."

"Wait, she was staying at Violet's house during the murder?" The night of the murder I hadn't gotten a good look at the runner I saw at Violet's, but if memory served, Ivy's build was the same as the woman I'd briefly chased. Plus, the girl had dark hair.

Ivy eyed me warily, her dark eyes flat. Probably thought I was leveling an accusation against her sister. "No, I said she stayed there occasionally."

"I'd still like to talk to her. When did she take this box from Violet? Was she given it, or did she take from the house?"

"Look, I didn't come here to make my little sister a suspect. Violet and I went way back, but to be honest, since she moved to Phoenix, we were more like acquaintances. Imogen was friends with her on Facebook, and that's how they got in touch. Violet was a good girl, but she started hanging with the wrong crowd. I never minded her being a witch, but some of the guys she hung with in college?" She grimaced and ran a hand through her hair. "When I came to visit, it was like she was ashamed I was human. Still, we grew up together. I didn't think twice about Imogen staying with her occasionally, since she's been on her bender."

"What do you mean bender? Is your sister an addict?" Vampires immediately came to mind.

"No, that's not what I meant. She's just needed to blow off some steam, you know?" She blew out a breath.

"Sure." I nodded even though our definitions of bender varied greatly.

"Imogen's boyfriend, the love of her life at the wise age of twenty-two years, died three months ago."

"I'm sorry to hear that."

"Thank you. The idiot liked to ride his crotch rocket without a helmet. I thank god every day that Imogen was not on the back being an idiot with him that day. She normally was. So, she's taken a semester off and has made little trips here and there to blow off steam, mostly to Phoenix. Its close and enough of her high school friends go to ASU that there's always a couch to crash on. Plus, there was Violet. She always loved Imogen. She didn't have any siblings, and she kinda adopted Im as a little sister. I thought it was good for her, and for Violet too."

"Makes sense. But what's up with the box?" I held it up and turned it over. Up close it didn't look like a box as much because there wasn't an opening, just a solid hunk of wood the shape of a large dictionary with intricate carvings.

"Like I said, Imogen stopped by this morning and dropped it off. Asked me to hide it. It's never a good sign if you have to hide something."

"You're right about that. Do you have any way I can get ahold of your sister?"

"Not really, she doesn't have a cell phone."

I stared at her hard. "Do you think I'm an idiot?" My face tightened I hated when people held out on me, especially when their family member could be in danger.

She threw her hands up and shrugged. "I know, a twenty-two-year-old girl without a cell phone. It sounds like an urban legend, but I swear she doesn't, or I should say she does, but she doesn't always take it with her. She calls it an electronic leash. She left it at my house when she left the box."

"That's strange." Still not believing her, I continued, "She still has Facebook, right?"

"She does, our last name is Reyes, in case Mr. Williams didn't tell you."

"He did, but thanks anyway. Now, can you think of anyone who'd want to hurt Violet?" Her sister was a lead, but Ivy obviously didn't know anything about what happened between Imogen and Violet.

"Not really, ever since she moved to go to ASU, Vi was distant. Not at first, but after the first year, she became withdrawn. I think it had to do with her being a witch. People in Phoenix aren't as nice about it as people are here."

Something I was all too aware of. The Tucson population was generally more free spirited, but no matter where you went, you could always run into a bigot.

"She became withdrawn?" I repeated. "Can you think of any instance that might have led that change?"

"Nothing specific, no. I just remember going up to surprise her once. That's when our friendship kinda fell apart." Ivy looked down at her feet and shifted shifting a bit before looking back up.

"What happened?"

"Well, I knocked on her apartment door on a Monday night. She never was the type to party on a school night, so I knew she wouldn't be out. I brought movies and a bottle of wine. I was excited to spend the night catching up with her. When she answered the door, she looked freaked, and told me I needed to go. This guy, or should I say god, walked out of her bedroom wearing a pair of jeans and nothing else. He belonged on billboards. I wanted to give Vi a high five, but I was shocked and couldn't stop staring. He said something along the lines of 'Why not have your friend join us?' It was sleazy, but I considered it; he was that alluring. Violet pinched my arm, hard, and whispered, in this bitchy tone, 'go home.' She looked at me like I was trash."

"That must have been awful for you." I told her

empathizing with the embarrassment all the while knowing that Violet had probably saved her life. There were few men in the world who could be described as gods and make young girls drop all sense of reason. Vampires were some of them. No doubt Ivy met one that night and had been glamoured. Fortunately, it sounded like Violet hadn't been.

Was she immune? There were rumors some witches were, but I never believed it. It would make sense though, since her business dealings with Fane appeared to be a legit partnership, unlike the typical blood-slave relationships that I'd witnessed in the past.

Ivy continued, bringing me out of my train of thought. "Embarrassing really, I felt like an idiot. She apologized later, but it was never the same after that." She checked her watch. "Listen, I'm sorry, but I can't be late for work."

"Okay, is there anything else you can think of?"

"Not off the top of my head. I really do need to go. I manage a hotel, and I'm on graveyard tonight."

I opened my Jeep door, set the box down, and reached for my wallet to pull another card out. "Here, I know my number is in your phone, but a backup never hurts. Please call me with any little detail you can think of; the killer may have had a history with Violet. If you hear from Imogen, please have her contact me. Violet didn't seem to have many friends, and any information Imogen could share would be great."

Ivy grabbed the card from my hand. "I will. Despite losing touch with Vi, I loved that girl like family. I could have gotten over any hurt feelings, if she'd only come to me."

I reached out and hugged Ivy. She stiffened before relaxing into my embrace. Pulling away, she said, "Thanks, I needed that."

"No problem," I murmured, a little surprised at my own behavior. Touchy-feely was not my normal *modus operandi*. Since I'd taken on this case, an unexpected well of compassion had bubbled forth, apparently my new reaction to dealing with upset people was to hug them. My previous response would have been to stealthily leave the room.

She turned back to her car, lifting her hand to wave as she left. I manhandled the box off my seat and over to the passenger side. Stifling a yawn, I fumbled the keys into the ignition. It was going to be a long drive home.

With the help of classic rock, Diet Pepsi, and NPR, I managed to get home without killing anything. Not even the jackrabbit with a death wish, thirty miles outside of Tucson. Back home, I took the box to my kitchen table and examined it. Thank gods Deval was picking up his chest, otherwise I was afraid I would become known as that weird witch who collected boxes. Witch and weird were fairly synonymous, without the addition of any odd collections.

I picked up the hunk of wood, looking it over with more attention to detail. Then I shook it because that was what any professional would do with evidence. On the verge of rolling my eyes at my own behavior, I heard a tell-tale rattle. There was definitely something inside. The wood surrounding the mystery contents was completely solid. It brought to mind a puzzle box. *I sucked at puzzles.*

After another thorough inspection, I shrugged. An idea occurred to me, one I considered before deciding why the hell not? I sent a surge of power through my palms and into the box. At first, nothing happened. Then the carvings erupted in a flash of eye-searing light and a metal thorn shot out of the center like a piston. Great, now I knew what the contraption in front of me was: a blood box.

11

My phone rang at six in the morning, which sucked because I planned on sleeping until nine. On the bright side, it wasn't Pammy's ring tone. Instead the Mesa Public Schools' automated caller offered me a sub position for the day. I didn't want to go in. I had so much to do. On the other hand, if I did sub, I could make an extra hundred bucks.

I didn't know when, or if, I was going to solve the case. I needed to take money where I could get it. Since I planned on spending most of the day investigating via social media, it might work. On the few occasions I had been offered a sub position, the teacher had left me with a video to play for the kids.

Mind made up, I accepted the job before I could change my mind. Not that I didn't want to teach, but sleep deprivation hurt my soul. Job accepted, I got up and headed to the bathroom for a quick shower. I didn't bother washing my hair. Middle school students didn't care if my hair rocked a two-hour blow out or a messy bun. Plus, I was just sane enough not to care if children thought I looked like a hag.

I headed to the school in a simple business casual outfit with my trusty laptop by my side. It should be relatively easy money. Even if the kids were total deviants, come two-thirty, they were no longer my problem. So, when I entered the front office and showed the receptionist my ID, I ignored the look she gave me. It seemed every school receptionist in the state knew my heritage.

Directed to another building, I found out that I would, in fact, be showing a video to the Biology classes, all day. The next few hours passed as expected. The kids came in, and upon seeing me sitting up front with Ms. Darrow printed neatly on the white board behind me, became instantly ecstatic. Students were rarely well behaved for a sub. At best they would be rowdy, at worst downright evil.

The morning group fell into the former, thank gods. So, while the video on organisms and cells droned on during first hour, I busted out my laptop and did what any person with a moderate amount of computer knowledge did, I stalked. Not like scary stalker, just perused around what was there for the taking. Violet, unfortunately, had a private Facebook account.

With limited access, I did the best I could. By the end of first hour, all I knew was that Violet and I had one mutual friend on Facebook, not surprising given the small witch population. Unfortunately, I didn't recognize our mutual friend beyond remembering we bonded over cat memes while drinking at a party, and then decided we would become best friends. That meant we never spoke again. But I didn't un-friend the woman because everyone was a voyeur at heart.

During times like these, I wished for the skills of a master computer hacker. Sadly, my wardrobe didn't contain a Guy Fawkes mask. Next best option was to discreetly text Pammy under the desk, asking for her assistance.

The children's stage whispers raised a notch. An authoritative glare didn't make them pipe down, so I used the only other weapon in my arsenal. "Your teacher implied there would a quiz on this material tomorrow."

A collective groan sounded through the classroom, drowning out the narrator's monotone explanation of single-cell reproduction. For the last ten minutes of class, the students were blessedly quiet, partly because of the threat, and partly because I kept my eyes on them. It would be awhile before I heard back from Pammy. The students were less eager to talk when I actually paid attention.

The bell rang, and they shuffled out as a new group shuffled in, and the process repeated. I spent the second hour looking at more accessible social media. From Twitter I learned Violet was fond of retweeting random scientific facts and inspirational quotations. Ugh, my least favorite kind of twitter feed.

Beyond that, I couldn't find anything of interest. I joined the students and watched the video. For an education film, it was actually fairly well done, dry yes, but still gave a very good overview. This class contained a lot of honor students, so the misbehaving was kept to a minimum. The bell rang, just as my eyes were beginning to glaze over.

The day droned on and after watching the video three times, at the end of the fourth hour I wanted to take a nap or shoot myself. What was dry and boring became unbearable. My phone vibrated before the next class began. I thanked the mysterious beings upstairs that Pammy came through. Violet's login and password were mine. I don't know how she did it, and the little air of mystery suited Pammy's reputation.

Pammy's weren't the only messages I received. Deval texted looking for updates. I let him know I was teaching and would call him after class. His texts got sharper. Apparently the jackass had a problem with me moonlighting. I turned off my phone. With only two more periods left, I wanted to use my time to dig up some dirt on Facebook, not placate a goblin who thought he was my boss.

Despite Violet's login information, I didn't find much. She didn't instant message with anyone, and rarely posted beyond the typical holiday wishes, the occasional vacation pic, and, of course, the sharing of random viral Internet gems. Two years back, I finally found a post where a woman tagged her for Throwback Thursday, otherwise known as, look how thin and drunk we used to be. Better yet, the woman went as far as to mention her new work in the caption.

The woman worked as a realtor and had many listings suitable for her old college buddy. Given Violet's lack of response, I was fairly sure she hadn't encouraged the woman. Which meant she either didn't want a sales pitch on her page, or she didn't want to give the woman her business. The time frame felt right though, maybe the woman would have some information that I wanted.

Violet lacked close confidants, and according to Ivy, that started around college. Until I got a hold of Imogen, Jessica the Realtor became a good option for information. If Violet cursed anyone, it had to be during the time when she was isolated. A move to a different city for school certainly fit that bill. A young woman learning life's ups and downs was likely to place a curse on someone without thinking about the repercussions.

Not that fifty-year-old witches didn't do the same, but

in my limited experience, I typically found that the older, and therefore wiser, a witch was, the less likely they would curse out of spite or anger. It might come back to bite them in the ass. The young and passionate, on the other hand, were more than willing to take the risk.

I would have emailed Jessica to set up a meeting, but the last two hours went decidedly downhill. I had to monitor the crap out of the students, who had gotten bolder as the day went on. I ended up sending two students to the principal for fighting before the day ended. I packed up at the end of the last period. I'd accomplished quite a bit, I thought, as I straightened my shoulders. I'd made a relatively easy hundred bucks, and the next steps for looking into Violet's murder were set.

Outside, the Arizona sunshine heated my skin despite the brisk November air. Between the laptop bag, a tote, various notebooks, and my half-full travel mug, I had a hard time reaching into my purse to grab the keys to my Jeep.

"Need some assistance?" From behind me, a deep voice sounded.

I dropped the coffee mug and tote, barely keeping my laptop bag slung over my shoulder as the lid came off, dowsing the bottom of my dress pants in lukewarm coffee. I swung around, nearly whacking Deval with the purse clenched in my shaking hand. Not sure whether the shakes came from being frightened or furious. I went with fury.

Glaring at him, I reached down to gather the mug and the tote that had let loose all but a few drops of coffee. It appeared my pants were more of a coffee magnet. "What the hell are you doing here?" I hissed in a stage whisper. Teachers and parents were starting to throw curious glances our way.

"You haven't responded to my messages in three hours.

I would think that solving a murder would place higher on your priorities list than babysitting pre-adolescents." The way he said pre-adolescents came across as "sniveling brats."

"Listen here, bub," I pointed my finger into his chest, "not all of us were born with a silver spoon in our mouth, or in your case, an actual silver mine. If I want to pay the bills and feed my cat, I need to take work where I can find it."

"I hardly think your cat is any danger of starving."

My eyes rolled and what started out as curious glares from our unintended audience turned into full-on speculation. I probably shouldn't have pointed at Deval. "I'm not having this conversation here. If you want to talk, meet me at Starbucks."

Deval gave me a look that indicated he would be fine continuing the conversation here. I pointedly fished my keys out of my purse and awkwardly unlocked the door. He didn't attempt to help me or make any comments as I slammed the door. I didn't bother to wait for him to find whatever sleek black vehicle he had brought on his mission to intimidate me.

I left at a reasonable speed for a school zone, so that no one would be able to add reckless driving to any grievance list they came up with. All I needed was for parents and teachers to crow about how I had an inappropriate thug on school property. I didn't know where the nearest Starbucks was, but this was America, I assumed there would be one within a mile. My assumption proved correct.

Since Deval didn't ask where the nearest Starbucks was, I assumed he would figure it out. By the time my soy chai latte was ready, he came through the door. Ignoring him, I walked straight to a table in the corner. The coffee joint was blessedly free of the usual crowds.

Deval followed. I hoped for meekly, but that word wasn't in his vocabulary and certainly not in his posture. He sat down with me without ordering any coffee.

"Aren't you going to get something to drink?" I snapped.

"I'm not in the mood for coffee."

Great, he was a masochist as well as the dick that made me look bad at my place of employment. "Peachy, what was so important you couldn't wait a few hours for me to call you back?"

He folded his arms and gave me what I supposed was his stern look. "The fact you are out working on something besides the murder and theft at hand disturbs me. You indicated in the parking lot you were tight on money. Yet I have offered to pay you. You should be able to see that I find this troubling and unprofessional."

I took a sip of the chai latte as I gathered my thoughts before responding. It was still scalding, but my regular coffee drinking had created a tolerance. The smooth spicy flavor calmed my angry thoughts and when I lifted my eyes to meet the jackass goblin's, I didn't want to maim him, only throttle him. "Deval, taking money from you would be a conflict of interest. We discussed this. I do not work for you."

He made a steeple with his hands. "A technicality, you still need to be focused on the task at hand. What if this man murders again?"

"If I recall correctly, your main concern has nothing to do with a witch's murder but with someone stealing from you. Which is it? Are you mad I'm not out searching for your thief, or are you genuinely concerned that a witch was killed?"

An emotion passed over his face that I couldn't read. "Of course, I am concerned about the witch's death. I am not so old that I am without empathy. However, my priorities will always be to my people. This theft has larger implications than you could possibly understand."

I rubbed my temples. "You're right. I couldn't understand the implications because you won't tell me. For all I know, this murder had nothing to do with Violet being a witch and everything to do with you being a goblin."

"She's not associated with my people, so that is doubtful," he said dryly.

"Yeah, well, the million dollar box might suggest otherwise. Listen, I'm doing the best I can with the information I have. I wasn't just sitting in school all day. I found a college buddy of Violet's, and I'm going to follow up with her as soon as this little chat is over. Get off my back. I don't need a babysitter or a cattle prod."

"Time will tell if that's true or not. I will be by tonight to pick up my property," he said as he rose from his chair.

"Great." I met his eyes. "Do me a favor, and knock this time."

He quirked his eyebrow and gave me a ghost of a smile. I couldn't be sure whether that meant he would knock or wouldn't. If he didn't, I planned to zap him good and risk the consequences.

Comfortably ensconced in my Jeep, I emailed Jessica from my phone, indicating I was interested in buying a new home. Total lie, but bait was bait. Twenty minutes later I arrived home, checked my phone, and was unsurprised by her quick reply. People in sales were cutthroat in their ability to spin bullshit for money. I scheduled a lunch date for noon tomorrow in one of the pricier Scottsdale restaurants because I mistakenly let her pick the location.

Plans set, I got ready for bed, stacking the books Alice lent me in a high pile on the scarred nightstand next to my bed. I flipped through the books, large yawns escaping me every few minutes. Sleep called to me, but with Deval's impending visit to pick up his safe, I wasn't in the mood to give in. Last time he'd visited when I was sleeping hadn't worked out well for me.

I considered grabbing my laptop to see if I'd missed anything online. It would probably be a waste of time since Violet wasn't into advertising her life via social media. Not a bad life choice, but I wished she'd been a little more in tune with her generation. On the other hand, the less crap I needed to dig through, the better. Finding her murderer was already like hunting a needle in a haystack, no sense in piling on extra hay.

Around nine o'clock, I gave up on Deval. For a man eager to reclaim his treasure, he was being lax in his duties. For a minute, worry sneaked in that perhaps some harm had come to him, but remembering who he was made the thought an improbability. Sleep was no longer singing to me, it was screaming in a voice I couldn't ignore.

Sleep came deeply and easily, as did the dreams. Deep in my dreams something called to me. At least I thought they were dreams, until I stubbed my toe on my doorframe. As quickly as the sharp sense of alertness from the pain came, it went. Again the siren song crooned to me from somewhere beyond the room. A reassuring mixture of a deeply toned, warm, stringed instruments played in my head. Warmth invaded my body, giving my mind a fuzzy sense of peace.

I wandered serenely through my house toward the

back door. Opening it, I found what eagerly awaited me, almost as eager as I was to see him. *No, that was wrong.* The chest, or what had Deval called it, a safe? It couldn't be a he, it was an it, or was it?

For a moment confusion muddled my mind before the song pull me back under. I reached out to the glowing metal chest, and my hand passed through soft red light. *Why was it glowing?* Again the song lured me back where there was no need for reason. The lid, much lighter than before, opened easily, and the metal quivered under my hand in anticipation.

That anticipation transferred to me when I looked inside. Stairs, chiseled from rich stone, beckoned me forward. My mind hiccupped again, was it marble? Perhaps quartz? It surely didn't matter. The stairs invited me in, and it would be rude not to visit. Stepping over the chest's edge, I descended into the cold dark unknown. My hand lifted to trace the rock wall that managed to be both jagged and smooth.

My body told me it was too cold in the depths we were exploring, but my mind was unwilling to leave. There was something, some part of the chest that needed me to see where the stairs led. Down I went, strangely not tripping on any of the steps. Time passed, it could have been a minute or an hour for the way time lost importance to me, and then the stairs ended. Before me lay a wasteland of cold rock and purple sky. It should've been ugly, but I never saw anything so beautiful. Unmindful of the tears streaming from my eyes, I wandered around my kingdom. An odd choice of word, but I shrugged the thought away and continued walking until I came upon a large flat stone, light purple in color, with red and copper veining. Sudden exhaustion and cold hit.

Acknowledging the cold in some abstract part of my

mind, translated to my body and every nerve ending rebelling to the frigid temperature. I needed to go back up to the heat. The stone invited me to rest before my journey back. It was a wonderful idea. I lay down, absently aware of the rock's chill seeping into my bones. Unable to hold that realization close, I allowed the chill wind and the rock's lullaby to entice my shivering body to sleep.

Scalding arms encircled my body, hurting my skin, and I cried out. Opening my eyes, I expected to see a fire demon laying claim to me. Only it was Deval, looking down at me with curiosity. "Hang in there, little witch." He pulled me close against his chest.

I wanted to fight, or at least ask him where we were, but exhaustion and cold kept me from doing either. Instead, I buried my face into his chest. The burning warmth from a moment ago was the only thing left to cling to as Deval began an upward climb. I needed to stay awake, but my body continued to betray me, and I fell back into unconsciousness.

My next waking moment was filled with needles stabbing deep, all over my body. Screams, raw and painful, ripped from my throat. I sounded like a tortured animal. Someone smoothed my hair, making shushing noises in my ear. Curling into fetal position, I realized I was in water. The disorientation receded until I recognized a chip in the ceramic of my bathtub. A feeling of security crept in, adding a sense of safety. I was in my own home. As the needles withdrew at an excruciatingly slow pace, I rocked. At some point the petting and sssshing stopped. Their absence made me realize the noises I was making had reduced to the occasional whimper.

The pain finally faded, and I felt a hand in the water by my feet. I would have kicked out, but my frightened mind recognized the brief touch as friend, not foe. A second later I heard the sound of the plug being pulled. Lifting my head, I found Deval kneeling next to my tub. I reached out and wrapped my hand around his wrist, needing to stop him. The cold settled deep in my bones, I needed the warmth of the water.

"I know you think I'm trying to take away the warmth, but this water is cold to the touch." He held my gaze. "I simply mean to drain the tub and fill it again. I hope you have a good hot water heater." His last sentence was muttered, and I managed to release his wrist.

He had a point, the water was cold. Why was I just now realizing that? Had my body been that cold it would chill water in what must have been only minutes?

"If I was that cold, why am I not dead?" Speaking made my teeth chatter, and there was no stopping them now that they had begun.

"That is an interesting question. I have a better one. How did you enter the plane?"

Looking up from my unhealthily blue-tinged toes, I glared at him. I was cold, not stupid. I didn't like him trying to take advantage of my situation by getting his answers without answering any of mine.

He sighed. "Peg, I am not trying to blindside you." He reached into the tub to replace the stopper and turned the water back on. "This may hurt again; the cold has not left your bones and will not for a couple of days. I can answer your questions better, if you answer mine."

My mind warred against itself, the docile half begging me to tell him so we could get our answers. The stubborn half wanted to flip him the bird and gather a witch mob to burn him at the stake for trying to murder me. It wasn't logical. He hadn't tried to murder me, had he?

No, that couldn't be the case because he had revived me. If he wanted me dead, he could have left me down in that death trap. Remembering the beauty, the sense of peace, I balked at the term. As I reminded myself that beauty could be deceptive, the illusion cleared. I didn't know what to think about the experience. My thoughts were all still too jumbled.

Deval sat down on my toilet and studied me. Apparently deciding I would answer his questions, he continued, "Did you find a spell to get into the plane?" His voice deceptively calm.

The hot water level crept back up, bringing both pain and soothing warmth.

"Of course not, like I would experiment on magical items worth seven figures that didn't belong to me. No sub job or bounty for a Fortune would give me the money I'd need to pay that back," I bit out. Pain and vulnerability brought forth my snark.

He gave me a small smile. "Well, Peg, you are going to get what you wish for, answers, but not tonight." He stood up and eyed me. "I will leave you to your bed. I will come back tomorrow."

I opened my mouth to argue, but he cut me off. "Take as many hot baths as your water heater will allow. If your magic is able heat the water, continue even after that. The warmer you get tonight, the sooner this will pass. When you are finished, dress as warmly as you can. Take a shot of whiskey and sleep with an electric blanket, if you have one." After his instructions, he turned to leave.

"You're taking your death trap though, right?" I shivered pitifully in the tub.

He glanced back and gave me an odd smile. "No,

witchy woman, it looks like the safe has chosen its mistress. While that might vex me, I know better to than to fight against these things."

I made a noise half way between a sputter and a squeak. I didn't need a magical box that wanted to kill me via hypothermia. Still, the idea of Deval taking the safe away both appealed to and frightened me. The sound of the front door closing made his decision final.

Instead of dwelling on my recent inheritance, I focused on heating my body. Two hours later, after filling my bath twice more, the water came out cold. My aunt had put in a large water heater when it had been her home, praise the gods. My magic was oddly abundant, despite my near-death experience. I warmed the water twice more before I got out of the tub in search of some heavy-duty flannel pajamas.

Once in my room, I caught my reflection in the full-length mirror hanging from the back of the closet door. Oh dear gods, the bulky white shirt bordering on matronly that I had worn to bed, now clung to my body like a second skin, showing every nook and cranny. Thank gods I put on yoga pants rather than my original inclination to sleep in my underwear.

Oy, every time I saw that man after hours, he caught me in an unintended state of undress. I'd probably light up like Rudolph's nose when I saw him next, since he could now describe my nipples in detail.

The violent shivers returned, removing Deval from my mind. I stripped out of the wet clothes and dried aggres-sively with a threadbare towel that I hadn't gotten around to throwing away yet. The friction felt good, warming my skin slightly. Every time I began to feel warm, the chill flooded my body. Flannel pajamas my grandmother had bought me a couple of Christmases ago were found at the back of a drawer. These were liberally layered over a pair of yoga pants and a long-sleeved shirt. Three pairs of socks finished my look. I wished I owned a ski mask; even my nose was cold.

A plastic container under my bed held the electric blanket I knew I owned but didn't remember buying. Once it was plugged in to warm up, I went to the thermostat in the hall. I cranked the heat up to levels I would normally avoid in deference to my electric bill.

Procuring a bottle of tequila from my kitchen, I didn't bother with a glass. Instead I took the whole bottle to my bed. I might need a warming nip later. Last stop of the night was at the front door to lock it and reassure myself the wards were in place.

Burrowed in bed, I took a swig from the bottle. Never in my life had I enjoyed the burn as much as I did now. That said something, since I was one of the rare breed who truly loved tequila. Between the burning-dust scent of the rarely used electric blanket and the taste of tequila in my mouth, I worried I would have a hard time sleeping. I didn't.

12

————

I awakened to the chattering of my own teeth. It was, if not the worst waking of my life, definitely in the top three. I considered closing my eyes and sleeping another hour, but I wanted answers and that Fortune check, so I could afford to go somewhere warm. Okay, that was an exaggeration. I would not be cashing in my check to go to the Bahamas. After tonight, I wanted the option to turn down dangerous assignments. I was starting to get an inkling that I might not be cut out for my new job. Squashing my doubt, I sat up to an irritated meow from Cheddar, who kindly slept on my legs and acted as a portable space heater. He gave me an irritated look before scooting to another part of the bed and returning to sleep.

Standing up sucked because it meant I had to give up the warmth of the electric blanket. Grabbing the tequila bottle, I headed for the kitchen. If I managed to be murdered today, I didn't want my mother to come pack up my house only to find a bottle of booze on my nightstand. She'd lament that I had been a closeted alcoholic, and she should've gotten me help. Bottle safely tucked back in the cabinet, I went about preparing coffee.

While it brewed, I found the largest ceramic mug I owned. Normally, I would add cream and sugar to the heavenly mixture, but today I would be drinking the coffee for warmth rather than pleasure, so black it was. Cream would take away some of the heat, and I couldn't have that. Even black, it was still coffee and not wheat grass juice. It could be worse.

While the coffee maker rumbled and hissed, I took the hottest shower of my life. My skin turned a lovely lobster red, bordering on scalded, but I still wasn't warm. Wrapped in a thick robe, I went about finding appropriate clothing. In Arizona, the nights could get pretty low, but not low enough to warrant serious winter gear. I had to make do. The warmest clothes I had were what I called my camping gear.

Sturdy man-jeans that were the wrong wash and cut to be considered as anything close to fashionable. A bulky hoodie that was my takeaway from some long-ago failed relationship. Appropriately layered with more yoga pants, various tank tops and T-shirts, and doubling up on the socks, I still had a definite chill going on, but it was bearable.

The clock on the nightstand read eleven, and my lunch date with Jessica was scheduled for noon. Throwing my hair up, I added a touch of makeup in an effort to not look like the frozen corpse I felt like. Having to forgo the giant ceramic mug, I left my house with a to-go cup of blessedly hot coffee.

Scottsdale made me feel self-conscious on the best of days. The area catered to the wealthy, more so than the surrounding cities. The women leaned toward Stepford, and the men were tan and wealthy, or at least faking it with credit cards and labels. My attire was entirely inappropriate for Jessica's restaurant choice, and the expression on her flawlessly executed face when the hostess escorted me to her table indicated she was not thrilled to be seen with me in public.

Things went downhill from there. It didn't help when she found out I already owned a house and wasn't interested in a vacation home in the White Mountains. Who was I kidding? I was very interested, just very unqualified to buy.

"If you don't want a house, what have you dragged me out here for?" Jessica flicked a strand of her immaculate blonde hair over her shoulder. She was rockin' the business Barbie look: blonde, body toned and tanned with curves that may or may not have been purchased, and tight designer clothing.

"Sorry to mislead you. I'm a Fortune and your friend Violet has been murdered. I was hoping you'd have some insight into her history."

She didn't seem perturbed by news as she flagged down a waiter. In a tone that managed to be condescending and flirty all at once, she ordered a white wine spritzer. Looking to me she added, "Just so you know, if you want to talk, you're paying the bill."

Looking down at the menu, I stopped myself from visibly swallowing. Pammy told me the Benefactor would cover expenses, but I wasn't sure that included twenty-dollar side salads. "No problem," I bit out.

She studied me briefly with a hard look, before a mask slipped over her face softening her features and adding a million-dollar smile. The realtor persona came out. "So, what is it that you think I can tell you about Violet? Haven't seen her since college. She didn't even buy her house from me." She pouted.

"If you haven't seen her since college, how do you know she owns a house?"

"Oh, one of my old sorority sisters lives on her block. She was quite shocked when a witch moved into the neighborhood." She leaned forward, framing her impressive cleavage. "Don't worry though, I told her she was harmless."

The derision in her tone made me say something I shouldn't, "It would be a mistake to think any witch harmless."

She stiffened slightly, the wariness in her face moving me from trash to a possibly useful subhuman. "I suppose you're right. Violet did come in handy a few times. I wouldn't have minded keeping our acquaintance intact, but she wasn't always very agreeable. She had quite the reputation."

"Oh?" I quirked an eyebrow, wondering what this woman would consider a bad reputation.

She leaned closer and said in a conspiratorial tone, "Let's just say that she liked the boys."

Who didn't? "Is that really that unusual for college?"

She leaned back, frowning when I wasn't willing to slut-shame a woman who could no longer defend herself, even if defending herself wasn't necessary. "She was quite popular. Not many witches at ASU and she thought she was hot stuff. Got a lot of attention before the boys realized she was just a slut."

At least she was no longer playing coy, and her prejudices were out on the table. "Did you stop being friends because you thought she was a slut, or because she was a witch?"

Jessica's gave a small shrug. "I'm not old fashioned. I like witches fine enough. I didn't like the reputation she was getting. When I told her, she wouldn't talk to me anymore."

I doubted it was that simple. This woman was the type to call someone out in the most humiliating way possible.

At that point the waiter returned. Jessica ordered a fifty-dollar plate of salmon, and I ordered a cup of soup and a hot tea. My teeth wanted to chatter, but since that would show something I wasn't willing to show, I clenched my jaw. Not that Jessica could harm me, it was still better to avoid the impression of weakness.

"Do you know if Violet used her magic on any other students?" I tried for a casual tone, but Jessica's gaze sharpened even as I detected a hint of quickly covered fear.

"Why do you ask?" she asked, fiddling with her napkin.

"Her death may have been curse-related. Know any old boyfriends who might have wanted revenge?"

Jessica waved her hand in the air as if to dismiss the notion. "Of course not. The boys always left her. It became a game of who could bag the witch." When she caught my look, she hastily added, "Violet was a willing participant. She had plenty of fun."

"But there's something you're not telling me." I sipped on the hot tea the waiter brought me. It was delicious and warmed me, if only briefly. Poor guy was going to be refilling my hot water often since I was planning on getting as much bang for my buck as possible with these prices.

We sat there, me sipping my tea and Jessica examining her perfect pink manicure for several minutes. I was in no rush, but she would tell me the big secret by the end of the meal, or so help me gods, I would follow her out to whatever ever luxury vehicle she currently leased and curse her myself, damn the consequences. I was about to tell her as much, when the waiter returned with our food. It bought Jessica a couple more minutes.

She seemed thrilled at the distraction and concentrated on eating her salmon. My soup wasn't bad, some sort of wild mushroom, though the portion was rather small. Thankfully it came with a slice of thick, crusty bread, so I didn't feel too deprived after having eaten the whole thing in the time it took Jessica to make it halfway through her meal. Not wanting to stick around and give her the opportunity to order dessert, I flagged down the waiter and asked for the check. Jessica eyed me peevishly at being dessert-blocked. Yep, her plan to charge it to me, take one bite, and declare it too rich was all too easy to read.

"Jessica, what is that you don't want to tell me?"

"What do you mean?" She shoved another bite of salmon in her mouth.

"I mentioned curses, and you tensed up. Why? I'm not here to punish you for some petty issue you had with a dead woman." Though truth be told, I wanted to.

Putting down her fork, she stared at the table and mumbled something.

"What was that?"

"She cursed someone for me."

Oh, that was rich. "Who did she curse and why?" I kept my tone deceptively even.

"My college boyfriend, Ronnie. He cheated on me."

"So, she wasn't good enough to be friends with, but you'd let her take care of your dirty work for you?"

She didn't even have the grace to look chagrined. "Hey now, I was her friend," she said in an affronted tone.

"The worst kind," I agreed.

The waiter came with the bill, and I was grateful I had

my credit card with me. How one white wine spritzer, salmon, hot tea, and a cup of soup could come out to ninety bucks was beyond me. I handed over my credit card with a wince. "What was his full name?"

"Ronnie Merola."

"Any other magic you can think of?"

"Candle tricks at parties. She helped a freshman clear up her acne for a dance."

"Great." The waiter brought back the check, and I left him his twenty percent, since he would have to to deal with Jessica after I left. After carefully replacing the card and the receipt in my wallet, I stood. Jessica still had a decent amount of food left, but there was no point in pretending we were enjoying our lunch. "I'd say it was a pleasure to meet you, but honestly, it wasn't. Thank you for the information."

Her mouth drew into a prissy line, but she nodded. I strode out the door, looking forward to letting my teeth chatter freely and blasting the heat.

In the Jeep, I inhaled deeply and let it out. The restaurant had felt like a fish bowl, and I had been the minnow surrounded by exotic tropical fish. Normally the tropical fish would be the ones watched, but being the odd fish out meant the opposite. It wasn't as though I couldn't fit in, if I'd been prepared. My mood wasn't improved by the fact that I felt as though I had trekked the arctic in a bikini. My layers weren't doing jack squat.

I turned the key in the ignition and my engine turned over with a grumbled purr particular to older vehicles. I wanted to blast the heat, but it would need a minute to warm up. In the meantime, I pulled out my phone, my teeth chattering at will, and did a simple search for Ronnie Merola. Gods, I needed a hot bath.

He was all over social media. Given his current occupation as a mixologist—his description, not mine—that wasn't surprising. Ronnie was kind enough to leave his Facebook public, and announced he was working the outdoor bar at a local roadhouse in Chandler tonight.

Gila Monster's was fairly well known. I'd been there a couple of times with Bruce. I could go alone but decided to be social and give him an invite. Bruce's chipper voicemail informed me he was either working, sleeping, or two-stepping with some fine young thing. I would have left a message, but in my current state, didn't feel up to competing with some fine young thing.

Enough time passed, and I turned the heater on full blast, carefully pulling out of my parking space, hyper aware of the expensive machines surrounding me. My insurance policy was decent, but I doubted it would cover damage to a vehicle that could be safely labeled as a midlife crisis. I considered the hot bath again, but if I went home, I wouldn't be able to force myself back out of the house. Coffee would have to cut it. I briefly debated going to Bump and Grind, its Tempe location halfway between here and Chandler, but some little voice in my head told me not to. Maybe because I had no desire to tell Pammy about mystical goblin safes that doubled as stairways to freezers.

I also didn't think Deval would appreciate me telling her about my little adventure. Why I didn't want to betray his trust, or lack thereof, was beyond me, but I needed to hear him out before I gave away state secrets. So, I went to another of the many independent coffee shops. This one was called Piestewa Perk, a pun regarding a popular hiking peak.

The barista eyed me speculatively when I came in but offered a small smile when I came to the counter. "Come on now, it's not that cold," she offered, her smile widening.

Lord, she had no idea. "What can I say? I'm a native; my blood's pretty thin."

"I hear ya. My dad's from Boston. Maybe I built up a tolerance from all those Christmases visiting grandma."

"Must have," I agreed, and ordered an extra-large coffee, requesting it as hot as possible. Coffee in hand, I headed over to an armchair sitting in front of an electric fireplace. The building was in a strip mall and too modern to have the genuine article, but the fake logs, with their synthetic orange glow, mimicked the coziness of a real fire. Blessedly, it gave off heat.

I meant to do a little more research on the cursed boyfriend angle, but I fell asleep. The barista woke me by clearing her throat and asking if I wanted anything else before she cleaned the machines. Fishing out my phone from my purse, I checked the time. It was almost eight. Good lord, I had slept for hours.

Deval never called. If I had to make Bruce deliver the safe to the bottom of the Superstition Mountain to get the goblin to take it back, I would. I ordered an extra-large mocha latte to go. The chill was still hanging around, and according to my impromptu nap, apparently I needed caffeine. Taking a few minutes to stretch out the crick in my neck due to sleeping in the chair, I walked to the counter where my latte waited. I paid the woman and after leaving a five in the tip jar, I headed back out. Time to visit a monster.

Gila Monster's was packed for a weeknight, unsurprising given its location in a suburban area. All the locals would stop by on their way home from work. It was one of those bars where the action could be as wild or as subdued as you wanted it to be. If it turned into a wild night, you could walk a couple of miles home or pay for a ten-dollar cab ride. Arizona, as a whole, enforced strict DUI laws. Many nights spent visiting other such bars, I heard waitresses warn their drunk patrons that a twenty-dollar cab ride was cheaper than a ten thousand dollar DUI and summer camp. Summer camp being the nickname for those idiots stupid enough to ignore the waitresses' kind advice and end up spending a few weeks in Tent City.

I didn't bother going inside because Ronnie's post said he would be at the outdoor bar. Given the chill in the air, I wasn't looking forward sitting on the patio until I noticed all of the propane heaters lining it. There were even a few electric ones hanging overhead, making the chill bearable. So, I edged up to the cement bar decorated with some haphazard southwest inlay. I didn't study the decor too much. Like most roadhouses, it had kitsch down to a science. I sat on the sturdy cushioned stool and waited patiently for a bartender, hopefully Ronnie, to appear.

Two young women had decided to put on a show at the other end of the bar, performing body shots off one another. I'd probably be waiting a while. One lay prone on the bar, with her shirt lifted to expose a lacy bra barely containing pert breasts, while her friend drank tequila from her belly button. Turning away, I studied the beer selection from a menu left on the bar. I wasn't a prude, but my days of body shots were definitely in the past. I perked up when I found they carried one of my favorite beers from a brewery out of New Orleans. A Hot Toddy would be a better option but the price point was significantly higher, and I wanted to be in and out. The crowd roared. Glancing up, I caught the finale of the body shot. The friend took the lime out of her friend's mouth in a move I would call a little drunk and sloppy, but based on the average leer, the surrounding men would label sexy. With a shrug I went back to reviewing the beer menu.

"Hey there, hope you haven't been waiting long. What can I get you?"

I looked up to a lopsided grin displaying a dimple on a very attractive man. Swallowing, I found my voice, "Uh, an Abita Purple Haze."

"Aw, that's one of my favorites. Ever been to New Orleans?"

I nodded mutely and waited for my brain to re-engage. Which took longer than usual. I blamed the cold. The bartender didn't bat an eye at my sudden loss of voice and turned around to the horse trough doubling as a beer cooler and returned with my drink.

Thankfully, my brain caught up with my mouth. "Yep, New Orleans is a lot of fun. I didn't catch your name."

The dimple was back. "Ronnie, and you are?" He extended his hand, quite the gentleman, or a trained bartender who knew how to rake in the cash. I extended my hand and he shook it, his grip strong, not trying to prove anything by maiming me. His warm hand felt nice on my cold one.

"Whooee girl, cold hands, warm heart?" he said with a grin. He pulled out two shot glasses and poured from a bottle of Fireball that appeared out of nowhere. He handed over one of the shots and lifted one himself. "I gotta try and warm you up somehow, don't I?" He gave me a devilish wink before raising his glass.

I raised mine, and we clinked glasses before taking our shots. He took my empty shot glass and showed me another hint of his dimple before turning back to other customers. Damned if I wasn't smitten. No wonder he never stopped bar tending, he was perfect for it. Handsome, friendly, with the right hint of sexual innuendo for the ladies, and enough manliness to be able to talk shop with the boys. Scanning at the bar, I didn't doubt that he would make a killing tonight.

Unfortunately his luck was my problem. He was the only bartender on at the moment, which made it difficult for me to talk to him long. I had his attention for a minute, and I wasted it by falling for his sexy bartender schtick. Oh well, because of the shot, I needed at least an hour to burn the alcohol off before getting behind the wheel. I watched Ronnie work his magic.

He was a chameleon, being whatever the patron needed him to be: Italian heart breaker, good old boy, music expert, therapist. What did that say about me? Probably that I looked down on my luck and needed a little pick-me-up from a handsome stranger. That was fine; I did need the pick-me-up. I sipped lazily at the Purple Haze; it would be my only one tonight. I waited patiently for the bar crowd to die out. Over the next hour, Ronnie only had time to give me the perfunctory "need another?"

Around nine-thirty, the patio started to clear out. If it had been the weekend, I would have been screwed, but people had jobs and the steadily dropping temperature made everyone's cozy beds that much more appealing.

I needed to leave soon. Deval warned me to stay warm, and I was anything but; however, when Ronnie made eye contact on his latest round, I called him over. "Hey, Ronnie, you got a minute?"

"For you? Sure thing. Need another one?"

"No thanks, I have to drive. I actually came here to speak with you tonight."

He gave me a once over, which should have been offensive, but the boyish grin he gave made it hard to get mad. "Well now, I won't be off 'til two."

I rolled my eyes. "I didn't come to have sex with you. I'd have dressed up if I was trying to take someone home tonight," I answered peevishly, wanting to hit myself for feeling a little flattered.

"Oh, my bad, but you look cute, like you're out camping."

"At least someone gets my fashion choices," I answered dryly.

"Sorry, I get hit on a lot. I'm single, so I take the bait." He winked.

"Okay, but as we've established that this is not sexual in nature, stop winking at me."

That only made his smile wider.

"I'm here because I'm looking into something for a friend. Did you know Violet Williams?"

The color drained from his face, and he took a step back. "Hey now, Violet and I are on good terms now. I haven't done anything to piss her off. Hell, I haven't even seen her in over a year."

"I'm not saying that you've pissed her off. You said you were on good terms? Jessica Wright mentioned Violet might have performed some magic on you." Not that Jessica struck me as reliable.

He lowered his hands, but his face still lacked the healthy warm tone of someone of Italian descent. "Yeah, last year she came in here. Met some tall, Nordic-looking fucker. He was a scary looking guy. We get some guys in here that are a little rough around the edges, but this guy had a look in his eyes like he would gladly murder puppies. I saw her out with him and a few of his friends when we were in college. I even told her I thought she should stay away from them, but she laughed it off. Told me she knew exactly what he was, whatever that meant."

Hmm, sounded like Violet was running with the vampires for quite some time, and the likelihood of her having a resistance to glamour increased. It didn't sound like she was listlessly following orders. It'd be odd for a vampire plaything to last that long, and that was exactly what I thought she'd been, a plaything, only later turning into a convenient business partner. "I think I know the guy you're talking about. You're right; he's no one to mess with. So, what exactly did Violet do to you?"

He blushed, color returning to his skin. "She cursed my ass."

"Uh huh, but more specifically?"

"No literally, she cursed my ass. I had boils the size of quarters covering it. I would have reported her to the dean, but witches scare me. At least they do now, and besides she came over the next week to reverse it."

"You apologized to her?"

"I apologized for hurting her friend."

I sipped on my bottle of Abita wondering what could have been so awful. "What exactly did you do to Jessica Wright?" I didn't want to take anything Jessica said at face value.

A man called Ronnie's name from the other end of the bar and held up his empty glass. Ronnie went about refilling it and checked on his other patrons before returning to me. "Jessica and I had a thing in college. We both worked at Stacks. I was a bartender and she was a waitress. It wasn't anything serious. I thought she knew that."

Stacks was a library-themed bar on Mill Avenue where the waitresses dressed in Catholic-school-girl skirts with white button-ups tied to display their "stacks" and midriff.

Fake glasses added the final piece to the costume. The guys were shirtless with ties and the same empty frames. The bar was still legendary to students and alumni trying to recapture their glory days.

"What, she found out she wasn't the only girl?"

"That was common knowledge she chose to ignore, until she walked in on me with a new waitress bent over the bar. It was a quickie, only my ass was out. Jessica thought it was poetic justice to have her witch lackey perform a curse on it." He grimaced, then grabbed a rag and wiped at the bar aggressively, not making eye contact. "Sorry, I shouldn't call her lackey, but freshman and sophomore year Violet followed Jessica around like a puppy, until she wised up and realized what a bitch she was. Violet's pretty cool, even if she did maim me." He met my eyes again.

Maim seemed a little strong since his ass looked just fine to me. "You don't have any lingering resentments toward her?"

He gave the question some actual thought. "Fact is, she scarred me. I wish she hadn't done it, but a lot of people make stupid choices in college."

"Do you know if she continued to make stupid choices in college?"

"If she did, she was much quieter about them. That's part of the reason I forgave her. Right after that, she stopped talking to Jessica. Maybe she realized that all the people surrounding her were looking at her like the token spooky friend. She may be a witch, but she's a good person."

I wondered what he would think about her latest career choice. "Is there anything else you could tell me?"

"Uh, I didn't know her all that well. She drank a few

times at a couple of bars I've worked at, but we didn't keep in touch."

Opening my purse, I took out my wallet and handed him my credit card. He took it and went to settle up my tab. When he brought back the check for me to sign, I handed him my business card. "If you remember anything else about Violet in college or after, boyfriends, friends, enemies, can you please call or email me? It would be very helpful."

He looked at my card and his eyebrows rose in surprise. "A Fortune? Holy shit, I didn't think you guys were real."

The corner of my mouth twitched trying to go into a smile. For some reason humans often thought that Fortunes were urban legends. "Yep, we're real all right."

"What did Violet do to have the witch police chase her down? This can't be about my ass. I don't want to press charges."

"Nope, this has nothing to do with your ass. Violet is dead."

His mouth opened like a guppy before snapping shut. He gave me a quick nod and turned back to his patrons. Standing up, I regarded my half full beer bottle wistfully. I wanted to down it. It cost me five bucks, but I was driving and didn't want to risk it, safety first. Slinging my purse over my shoulder, I headed for the Jeep. The cold hounded me as soon as I left the comfort of the various heaters.

Exhaustion made a comeback, much like it had every waking hour of the past few days. Screw a tropical vacation. When I solved this murder, I would indulge in a stay-cation, only leaving my bed to brush my teeth twice a day and to answer the door for Barro's, Venezia's, and Burrito Express. Variety was the spice of life.

Almost to my car, I didn't hear the footsteps behind me until a figure suddenly appeared in front of me, standing in a median filled with gravel and a bush directly under a halogen light. My magic roared through my chest and instantly flew to my palms. Well, hot damn, I hadn't been this charged in I didn't know how long, and for a blessed moment warmth actually returned to my body.

Ronnie nearly fell over when my glowing palms extended toward him. "Whoa, whoa, whoa, lady. I'm not stupid enough to try to hurt you. I wanted to know if you might be able to help me."

I kept my hand up but put the metaphorical safety on my power, and the glow dimmed. Unfortunately, the chill returned.

Before I could consider what that meant, Ronnie turned around and dropped trou, thrusting his butt in my general direction. What I saw conflicted with what I imagined of the Italian Stallion. Under the yellow glow of the halogen lights, his ass looked like the moon, no pun intended. There were craters of scar tissue the size of quarters all over it. Poor guy, his butt was firm, but I doubted he kept the lights on during more intimate moments these past few years.

"Okay, Ronnie, I see the problem. Care to put your pants back on?"

He pulled his pants up quickly, which was none too soon as a police cruiser pulled into the parking lot. Typical, they tended to cruise bar parking lots later in the evening. He waved at the police officer, whom he obviously knew, before turning to me.

His face was red. "I'm sorry I did that; it was impulsive. I've been living with those scars for years. Violet said she wasn't powerful enough to fix them. I realized, as a Fortune, you must be. Can you please help me?"

Oy, I didn't have time for this. Violet should have asked someone if she couldn't fix her own problem. I shook my head. It became fairly obvious that Violet didn't have a strong support system of either humans or witches to turn to for these problems.

Maybe Ronnie could make it worth my while. "Yes, I can help, but I need something in return." Granted black-mailing the guy wasn't nice, but he was in a better position to get the information I needed. Creating a potion to clear up the scarring would take the better part of a morning, time I could be spending on the investigation.

He looked at me warily. "What do you want?"

I poked him in the chest, which was, of course, also firm. "Quit looking at me like that. I'm not going to ask you to sacrifice kittens to Hecate. I need information. I need to know who Violet dated in college, or if there were any other cases of her using magic on someone. I'll even take rumors at this point. I'm assuming you've maintained your college connections?"

He nodded, looking relieved. "I can do that."

"Good, this is time sensitive. Get me all the information you can by tomorrow afternoon. I'll make your cure, and you can come around for it."

He looked like he wanted to hug me but settled on a quick nod and a whispered "thank you" in my ear before turning to head back to the bar.

13

─────────

While I was making the magic cream for Ronnie, I began to wonder if Violet lacked power or education when it came to her magic. Her father was human, but her mom was a witch. She should have been able to handle this with no problem. Maybe she didn't care to fix the problem beyond the basics? Plenty of witches only partly embraced their magical sides. They were in the magical closet, so to speak.

I could have done that. Witches were fairly rare these days, and my family lived in Tucson. I probably could have lied and gotten a job as a teacher. I shook my head; they'd have found out.

It was the cold making me second-guess myself right now. It made everything bleaker. Thank gods Deval said it would only be a couple of days. When he came over later, I needed to grill him. A couple of days sounded like no big deal, but I needed specifics, like when this would go away, why it happened, and how to avoid it in the future. Well, the last bit was easily solved. Deval needed to take his damn box of doom back.

A knock sounded at the front door. I hoped Deval had arrived. I stirred the mixture in my spell pot once more before lowering the flame to a simmer and placing the lid on it. The visitor knocked again.

"I'm coming," I shouted, walking toward the front door. A peek out the peephole told me why the person was impatient. "Seriously, Lola, why can you never just give me a minute to answer the door like a normal person?"

She wrinkled her nose. "Duh, Peg, you know our generation likes instant gratification. It's why credit card debt is so high among our peers."

I quirked an eyebrow at my friend before ushering her inside. "Did Deval send you?"

"Huh, no. Why do you ask?"

"He's supposed to be by today to pick up his killer freezer."

She frowned. "What do you mean killer freezer?"

"That safe he left here. It enchanted me in the middle of the night and forced me into its cold depths."

"Seriously?" Her eyes widened.

"Seriously, there was a stairway and everything. It was so cold down there, if it snowed, I'd believe it was Narnia. At least before Aslan killed what's-her-nuts."

Her mouth drew into a hard line, not even smirking at my joke. "That shouldn't be possible."

This dance was getting old, but the steps were familiar, so I would waltz along and not bother with any illegal moves. "What shouldn't be possible?"

She walked past me into the kitchen and went to the pot Ronnie's ass cream was simmering in. "Are you making beauty products?"

She obviously smelled the lavender and chamomile I threw in on a whim. The potion could be a little harsh, and I didn't want Ronnie's ass to suffer more than it had already. "Sort of, I'm trading a potioned-ass lotion, say that ten times fast, for some info. You should hang around. I've got two eligible bachelors coming by today."

"Now hardly seems the time to start a wild love life, Peg, but better late than never." She paused, turning all doom and gloom. "I hate this you know."

"Hate what? That murder brings all the boys to the yard? I'm not serious anyway. Deval probably has an arranged marriage set up with goblin royalty. Ronnie's a hottie, but I'm not into guys who regularly enjoy a quickie in a bar parking lot."

"A quickie never hurt anyone." She gave me a strained smile.

"Oh, it would hurt him. I doubt I'd be happy when I caught him with his windows all steamed up with some lady other than myself. Ronnie seems like a nice guy, but I don't think anyone will get him to settle down before he turns into the silver fox he's destined to be. Even then, she'll be five years younger than I am now with boobs the size of cantaloupes."

Lola did laugh then, deep from her belly. "Oh, one of those, huh? Bright side is if you don't sleep with him, you can be friends, and you'll always get interesting stories."

"I'm not sure I want those kinds of stories. If I'm hankering for stories like that, I could always get a subscription to *Penthouse Letters*." I walked over to the stove and playfully hit Lola with my hip to get her out of the way. Lifting the lid, I stirred the potion a few more times and turned off the burner. I left the lid off so that the mixture would thicken as it cooled, and then I could put it in a Mason jar for Ronnie.

Lola placed her hand on my back tentatively. "I meant that I hate that I can't tell you everything. I'm afraid if I tell their secrets, that my family would disown me."

Turning around, I pulled her into a hug. Her parents' death had left her with abandonment issues, and even though they hadn't left her on purpose, she felt guilty for being angry with them. Lola's adoptive family loved her, and I didn't think they would really disown her, but it would put them in a bad position. Despite my griping, I didn't want her to have to deal with that. She always had my back, even if she couldn't share state secrets.

"It's okay, Lo," I said, pulling away. "Deval is stopping by later, and he can tell me. Even if I have to find some zip ties in the closet and beat him at his own game. If you see him hogtied on my couch, walk away quietly."

"Pssh, sure thing. If he comes back later and blames me for leaving him to be tortured and maimed, I can play innocent and claim I thought it was a tryst, it is after all my M.O."

"Want some coffee?" I grinned at her.

"Got some Bailey's or Kahlua to spike it with?"

I opened up the cabinet above my microwave and stood on my tippy toes to peer around. "Nope, but it looks like I have half a bottle of peppermint schnapps from last Christmas." I grabbed it and turned around to display the dusty bottle to her, my eyebrow quirked in question.

"Oh god, Peg, I was joking. I so would though, if I didn't have paperwork I needed to do later this afternoon."

"You're playing hooky this morning?"

"Nope, I'm not scheduled until this afternoon. Sadly my entire shift will be spent in the office. Bleh." She made a face that I hadn't seen since second grade when a little boy from down the street threw a gecko at the prissiest girl on the block.

"When you told me you would be a mining engineer, I thought it would be all digging and no bureaucracy."

"You should know better." Lola waved her hand

dismissively. "Every job has paperwork. If you want to use explosives and heavy machinery to dig holes without compromising the foundation and nature, there is going to be so much paperwork your eyes will cross," she replied morosely.

Grabbing a mug out of the drying rack, I filled it, added the flavored creamer she liked, and handed over the mug. After topping off my own, we clinked glasses. "May your paperwork be quick and painless," I said solemnly.

"May your ass cream work like a charm," she responded, and we drank in solidarity. "By the way, what is potioned-ass-lotion?"

"Aw, it is really just a scar removal cream, but as it's going on Ronnie's derriere, I can't help myself."

Her eyebrows drew together, and she took a seat at one of the two stools at my tiny bar. "Huh, that's an odd place to have scars. His ass was in the fire?" She grinned at her unexpected joke.

"You can say that, he was caught screwing around with his pants down. Unfortunately for him, the girl who caught him had a witch friend, or lackey as the case may be."

"Your murder victim?"

I leaned against the counter opposite the bar. "Yep, she cursed his ass." I responded, not able to stop my escaping giggle. "I'm sorry I'm being juvenile, but it's the gift that keeps on giving,"

"Poor guy."

"I should call him, see if he has some info ready to trade." I grabbed my phone and went to the contact listing I added to my phone the previous night. While it rang, I gripped the mug a little tighter, letting the warmth absorb into my hand. My teeth were on the verge of chattering again. I was mid-gulp when Ronnie answered.

"Hey, witchy woman, I've got some info for you."

I nearly sputtered coffee, but managed to swallow before answering, "Already? You work fast."

"Yeah, well, I was worried you wouldn't give me the cream if I didn't have the info. Plus, I was pretty popular in college. I have a large social circle to get the information from."

"So modest, no wonder you were popular," I sniped. "What's the rush? You've had the scars for five years. What's another week?"

He didn't miss a beat. "I want the option to wear a thong."

I cringed. "Ugh, too much info."

"Hey now, I didn't say I was going to. I said I wanted the option."

"Uh huh, I'm sure. Well, it's ready if you want to stop on by."

"What's the address? I'll be right over."

I rambled off the address, he advised he'd be at my house in twenty minutes, and I hung up the phone. Setting the phone down, I looked at Lola. "Looks like you get to meet bachelor-number-one after all. Fair warning, apparently he likes thong underwear."

"Ugh, on dudes that's weird," she responded, wrinkling her nose.

I nodded. "To be fair, a piece of fabric up your ass is weird on any gender. It's just not as socially acceptable on guys." I didn't know why I was spouting off about gender stereotypes and underwear choices, especially considering the fact my underwear drawer had its fair share of skimpy fabric pieces.

Lola waved off my argument. "Peg, how do you know this dude's not the killer?"

"My instincts say he's innocent."

"When did you become clairvoyant?"

"I'm not, but my mama always told me to trust my gut," I said giving her taste of southern twang.

"Your mama, my ass. Your mother would research the crap out of any question of guilt."

"Hmmm, maybe. Lord knows that woman loves a research project."

"You should make her your research assistant," Lola said thoughtfully.

"Not a bad idea, if I could afford to pay her. I can barely afford my own upkeep without adding another person to the payroll. Plus, she'd probably demand a dental plan."

"She's no spring chicken, and she's bound to need a bridge at some point." Lola laughed.

I joined in, letting the laughter roll through my belly. It was the best I'd felt in days. The laughter kept the chill at bay. It also erased my underlying tension with Lola. She'd been my best friend for so long, I considered her family. I hated it when we were on the outs.

Our laughs subsided, and I picked my mug off the counter for another sip before gesturing toward the living room. Lola hopped off her perch and followed. Downtime never felt so good. We sat on the couch and shot the shit for another twenty minutes before a car pulled up outside.

Peeking through the window, I saw Ronnie squinting at my house then down to his phone, probably double checking the address. He stood next to a vintage Chevy truck. I didn't know enough about cars to know much beyond the fact that it was a vintage Chevy, and the glossy paint and chrome screamed "expensive." Yep, Ronnie excelled at his job.

Lola let out a low whistle. "Well, damn if he isn't a cutie. Check out his wheels. I didn't think bartenders made that much."

Looking at her, I added, "But I bet he doesn't have dental," then winked.

That sent her off into another peal of laughter while I went to get the door. My wards hummed through the house, letting me know I had a human visitor. Ronnie made it down the walkway and knocked assertively.

I looked up to the ceiling. "Oh, now, you work just fine," I muttered while I opened the door.

"What?" Ronnie asked, obviously thinking that I was talking to him.

"Oh, nothing, come on in," I said, letting him pass through the wards. A minute shiver ran through his body. Interesting, most humans couldn't feel them. Maybe he had some magical blood somewhere in his family. He walked into the entryway and paused, waiting for direction. He scanned every inch of the house and ran a hand through his hair; perhaps he thought I'd lured him here for nefarious reasons. In five minutes, Lola would make him feel right at home. I walked past him to the living room, gesturing for him to follow.

"Lola, this is Ronnie. Ronnie, Lola." I introduced them and then excused myself from the room to go and ladle the now cooled butt cream into a jar. From the kitchen, I couldn't make out their conversation, but Lola's usually sultry voice went up in pitch. A sure-fire indication she was flirting. Ronnie's answering deep laugh made me chuckle. No man was immune to Lola. Shrugging, I screwed the lid onto the mason jar and joined them.

I handed him the jar. He looked at it with both trepidation and hope.

"Ronnie, I wouldn't give you something that was going to hurt you. It's just scar cream."

"Ass cream, really," Lola piped in and started to laugh.

He pinked a bit but let out a nervous, good-natured chuckle. "She told you, huh?"

"Peg tells me everything. Don't worry; it could have happened to the best of us." She placed a reassuring hand on his arm and gave it a squeeze before jumping up. "Well, you two, it's been fun, but a girl's gotta eat. I'm off to the salt mines, or copper mines, as the case may be."

Ronnie rose as she grabbed her purse and made her exit. After the front door closed, he sat back down, and I took Lola's place on the couch next to him.

Leaning into the arm, I put space between us. "So, what did you find out?"

"Lots of stuff." He gave me a flirtatious grin.

"Would you care to elaborate? I will repossess that jar," I teased.

His grip on the jar tightened reflexively, as if it were a lifeline.

I sighed. "It was a joke. I don't need a jar of scar cream. Spill."

His shoulders relaxed, and he set the jar on the coffee table. "Violet was quite popular in her freshman and sophomore years. She started hanging out with Jessica, who was practically the social queen of the campus. Jessica encouraged Violet to be a little, uh, promiscuous.

I rolled my eyes. "Jessica said as much."

"Jessica knew how it was done, since she liked her men, but not to the level she encouraged Violet. Hey, we were all young, no big deal, do what you want."

"Is that still your excuse?" I asked, deadpan.

He clasped his hands over his heart. "That hurts. These looks will eventually fade. Gotta have some fun while I still got it."

"Bull, but please, continue."

"Yes, ma'am. I think about halfway through sophomore year, Jessica got bored with their friendship and jealous of the attention Violet got. She started telling everyone how easy Violet was, though she used stronger adjectives than 'easy.' Then she spread rumors about Violet casting curses on people. I only ever knew about the one she cast on me, but I didn't say anything because I didn't want to bring her attention back to me."

"You think she might have placed another curse on you?" That would paint a different picture than what he previously told me.

"No, not now. She wasn't the vicious type. That was all Jessica. When Violet started getting bullied, she removed herself from the scene completely."

"You didn't say anything about her being hazed when we talked before." The cold that laughter had kept at bay returned. I stood and walked over to the tiny fireplace in my living room to stop the shivers. The logs were already set up in the hearth. With a quiet incantation, the fire came to blazing life.

I turned back to Ronnie as he gulped audibly. Starting the fire with my magic wasn't meant to intimidate him, but sweat dotted his forehead nonetheless. "I didn't know before. I talked to some of the sorority girls that used to run with Jessica. One of the girls felt kinda guilty about it."

Turning back to the fire, I willed the heat to seep into my bones. I'd always loved fire. Right now I wanted to bathe in it. I looked back over my shoulder. "And?"

"Apparently some of the girls and guys printed out pictures of witch burnings and put them on her dorm room door. The sickest thing they did was set up some fire wood and a wooden pole right outside her room. That's about the time she moved out of the dorms."

I turned, putting the fire at my back. "Did she retaliate?" I had a hard time getting the words past my clenched teeth. I grasped my hands in front of me, unsure of whether they were shaking from the cold or the anger. This could be the big break I was looking for, and I needed to push past my own feelings of outrage.

He dropped his eyes, not meeting my glare. "Nope, like I said, after she cursed me, Violet wasn't as vicious as I thought."

Or she no longer had the back up to get away with it. It made me think about her relationship with the vampires.

"She dropped out of the social scene, minded her own business, and went to class."

"Not sure this info is worth the scar cream," I commented dryly.

He looked to the cream sitting on the coffee table and reached out as if to grab it before catching himself and pulling his hand back. He looked at me sheepishly. "But there's more. A teacher disappeared."

"Why didn't you start with that?" Exasperation coated my voice.

"I thought you wanted all the info I found out."

He had a point. "Okay, go on." I gestured with my hand.

"Senior year, Violet had an upper level biology class with one of the girls I knew. Violet kept to herself, like she'd done for the past two years, but my friend noticed she went to the T.A. a lot after class. She even saw Violet coming out of his office one day, too."

I shrugged. "She needed extra help and asked the T.A."

"But Violet never needed help. She was smart. Before she was ousted from the group, she'd help all of the sorority girls with their homework."

"A lot of people have subjects that are harder for them than everything else. I was fine at algebra, but my mother hired a tutor for geometry."

"But biology wasn't that subject for Violet. She loved it, and my friend saw her walking to the parking lot with the T.A. one night, way after office hours."

"How late?"

"About ten. She thought it was weird."

"Why would she remember this five years later?"

"Because the next week, the T.A. stopped showing up."

"As in quit?"

"No, as in, he didn't lecture anymore. He'd still grade things, but he never showed for class."

I bit my lip. "That's odd, but hardly a case of a missing teacher. Someone, his faculty member, would've reported him missing. Maybe he turned out to be agoraphobic?"

"No, I'm telling you there was something not right about it. I wasn't even a science major, and I knew who this guy was. He was good looking, came from money, and way too narcissistic to stop showing off his knowledge to all of the adoring coeds."

"Why didn't you mention this when we talked before?"

"I didn't know it before. I knew *of* him, but I wasn't a biology major. I didn't think anything about it."

Now that the fear my teeth would start chattering diminished, I walked back to the couch and sat down. "Okay, do you have a name for this guy?"

"Yep, Grant Vonn. He's actually a professor now, but he teaches online. Most teachers do recordings where the students can see them, but his lectures are always Power Points with his voice recorded."

"If he really is the narcissist you think he is, that's out of character."

"My thoughts exactly."

"How did you find this out? You've been out of school a while now."

"I'm a bartender. I know plenty of people. I called

around, but one of my regular's little sister is getting a biology degree and took a class from him last semester. If this guy is unwilling to show his face, I can't help but wonder if she did to him what she did to me. Maybe in a much more visible area."

"I take it back, Ronnie. You've definitely earned that cream."

His tense body went boneless, and he leaned back into the cushions of my couch.

"Anything else?"

"Shit, woman, I only had twelve hours."

My hands went up. "You're right; you're right. Thanks, Ronnie, if you could keep your ear to the ground and let me know about anything else you hear, I'd owe you one."

He smiled and sat forward grabbing his cream, finally clear to take his bounty.

Another vehicle pulled up to my house, and when I looked out the window, my eye began to twitch. There was only one person who could afford to drive a car like that, and the trunk space left a lot to be desired for someone who was supposed to be hauling off a large object.

I stood up, and Ronnie hastily followed suit. "Uh, I guess I better get going then."

"Hmm?" I turned to him, suddenly remembering my manners and pasted on a smile that felt brittle.

He winced. "I don't know what he did, but that is definitely my cue to exit."

"Smart man," I muttered.

"You're not a good bartender if you can't tell when the shit's about to hit the fan." With that astute observation, he hastily made his way to my front door, clutching his bounty. I trailed behind ready to greet my next visitor. Ronnie opened the door. Deval's hand was raised to knock.

Ronnie gave Deval a brisk nod and squeezed past him to safety.

Deval watched him go before turning back to me. "The look he gave me was meant for a man being carted to the gallows."

"Hmmph," I uttered, crossing my arms.

"Ah, I've managed to anger you yet again. Let me in, you can tell me all about it."

"You've had no trouble bypassing my wards before. What's different now?"

"Let me in, and I might tell you."

It was a tempting offer, though I wasn't sure if he actually needed to be let in, or if he was faking it. I reached out with my magic and sure enough, the wards were holding against him. Huh, now my curiosity was piqued. That and one of my nosier neighbors was on the sidewalk going for her morning constitutional.

Waving my hand, I opened the wards. He knew exactly when they released and walked into my house with an authority he shouldn't feel though his shudder as the wards passed over him was satisfying. We stood in the entry, and I looked over at his vehicle. "Why are you driving that midlife-crisis-on-wheels and not something that would accommodate a magical goblin safe, or as I like to think of it, a maniacal death freezer?"

"I have decided to gift it to you."

My jaw dropped before I had the sense to close it. He looked at me with expectation.

It took a moment for me to realize he expected gratitude. "Oh, hell no. That thing tried to kill me."

"No, it simply wanted to meet you."

"Now you're saying it's sentient? That's just great. That information would've been important before it tried to kill me!" My voice got progressively louder the longer I spoke.

Since I was standing in my entryway with an open door, my neighbor heard my shout. She gave me a look. Normally I'd be self-conscious about my neighbors' negative attention, but I was too pissed to care. So, I gave her the stink eye right back and slammed my front door closed. It was so quiet in my home that I was able to hear the woman utter a shrill "How rude!" through the closed door.

I turned back to Deval. "Now my neighbors think I'm insane," I said, my voice as calm and reasonable as I could manage at the moment.

He shrugged, turned back toward my living room, and sat on my sofa.

"Go ahead and make yourself at home," I muttered, hands propped on my hips.

"I did, thank you. The fire adds a nice homey touch. I'm starting to find your home quite charming."

Throwing my hands up in defeat, I went to sit with him on the couch. A few days before he implied my home was a total dump. What was with the personality change? I stared at him waiting for him to speak, before letting out an exasperated sigh. "Fine, you win. Why are you suddenly willing to part with a magical object you recently told me was worth seven figures?"

His mouth twitched. "What did I win?"

"As if you don't know. Answer my question."

"No, I truly am puzzled. What did I win?"

I rolled my eyes. "The silent game."

"I did not realize silence was a game."

"You know what? I found the game frustrating a moment ago, but I've changed my mind, just shut up for a minute." I sat back on the couch, closed my eyes, and rubbed the bridge of my nose. The ebb and flow of chilling waves returned, and my teeth chattered away. With Ronnie, I didn't want to appear fragile, but with Deval, I didn't care. He knew what was going on better than I did, and I no longer had the energy to pretend to be anything other than tired and cold. A hand gave my knee a squeeze, and I opened my eyes. Deval gave me a look that was either empathetic or pitying. In a rare moment of benevolence, I decided to assume it was empathetic.

"I really do not know this game you speak of, but since you seem a bit out of sorts, I will ask Lola about it later."

I snorted. "Must be tough to be old enough to be everyone's great-grandfather but look like you are still in graduate school."

"Only among the witches and the humans."

"Mmmmhmm. So, your highness, please tell me why you don't plan on taking the safe."

"It's worthless now."

"Excuse me? You said it was worth close to a million dollars. How can it depreciate that much in one week?"

"What I am about to tell you is not something we advertise. You will have to promise not to tell anyone, at least no one who doesn't already know. I will give you permission to gossip with Lola, since she is already privy to our secrets, but no vampires, shifters, fae, or humans. Some may already know, but do not make that assumption because those who know have been bound by magic and honor to secrecy."

"If you wanted me to join your secret club, why didn't you say so? We can build a club fort in my backyard."

"I don't think you're taking this as seriously as you should be."

I rubbed my temples. "You're right. I'm probably not. What happens if I don't promise? Will you take your safe then?"

"No, you will be helpless to its powers."

"Peachy, fine, I promise, as long as by keeping the

secret, no harm will come to me, my family, or my friends." I bargained.

"You can set your terms, but that in no way means you will not have repercussions. Just possibly a little leeway."

"Whatever, Deval, tell me what I need to know."

"What exactly do you understand about goblin magic?"

"It's earth-based, and you have stronger protections, but that's more biological. You guys are built like tanks."

"Yes, evolution was kind enough to allow us to survive in a mine collapse, which I have on a couple of occasions."

"Really? That's pretty awesome." I doubted a witch would be able to.

"I didn't mean to get off topic. Our magic is earth-based, but we are born with different capacities to wield the magic."

"Like every other magical being, duh." I rolled my eyes.

Deval ignored me and continued, "The strong prevail among us. Being born strong does not guarantee that one will remain the strongest."

"Of course, practice and study will give you an edge," I sniped.

"All fine and good, but still the most powerful are the wealthiest."

"Yes, I know. Money equals power."

"Of course, but I'm speaking in a literal sense."

I sat forward intrigued. "What do you mean, literal?"

"Why do you think so many goblins are miners or work with precious metals and stones?"

"A natural proclivity, having evolved underground, your apparent ability to survive mine collapses?" I rattled off.

"Yes, but like you said, we gain our power from the earth. I will always feel the stones around me, but certain mined metals and gems are more powerful than an entire semi of dirt. The more wealth I have, the more power I can call upon. This means even the weakest magic users among us have the potential for great magical strength, especially if they acquire enough gold, silver, copper, diamonds, rubies, et cetera."

"You're saying if I were a goblin, and I owned a ton of gold, even if I only had the capacity to move a grain of sand before, I could potentially create a crater in the earth because of the power I could get from the precious metal?" Mind officially blown.

"Exactly, which is why we gather wealth from a young age. We value wealth because it keeps us in power."

"That explains why you guys are such hard asses about stealing. That and your general reputation for being greedy."

His mouth twitched. I wasn't sure if it was in annoyance or amusement. "Is it greedy to eat a meal that would give you strength? To get a vaccine that would keep you healthy? Those with a low capacity will be frail unless they acquire wealth. My children will never want for gold and gems because that is what they will need to keep them strong."

"No wonder goblins usually have small families. Good lord, and I thought having elementary school kids compete over who wears the best labels was bad."

"Exactly, you will note Lola's family has two sons, but wanted to try again for a girl. They didn't, knowing a third child could not be provided for, without taking away wealth that needed to go to their sons."

My face scrunched. "Boys are more important?"

He laughed. "Don't let my mother hear you say that. No, if they had two daughters and wanted a son, the same would apply. There is still some misogyny among our kind. Being old means adjusting your world views. My uncle, for example, looks to European monarchies of the past and thinks that he, as the younger brother, should have been king instead of my mother, his older sister, even if the goblins' way was never such. It's funny how individuals will bend their beliefs and heritage to fit their own desires but will never rule."

Isn't that curious. I didn't think he would elaborate further, so I changed the subject. "Having Lola suddenly parentless was something of a morbid blessing?"

He nodded.

"Then where does the safe fit into this?"

"I cannot access the power from my wealth if it is sitting in a bank. It is not a safe option to put that much power into a place someone else has access to. No matter the current political climate, there will always be upheavals in governments and wars. I do not trust humans to watch my power, and goblins cannot do it."

"Why can't goblins own banks?"

"They can, and they do, but if another goblin has physical possession to my wealth, then he could steal access to my power. It would be quite foolish to give another goblin my power."

"If you're not carrying around a backpack of gold bars, how do you access that power?"

"What you have in your cluttered Arizona Room is a safe that leads to a space in the goblin plane. It is sentient and had begun to bond with me. If I had retained possession of it, the bonding would be completed already. As it is, the safe decided to be ornery and chose you to be its mistress, something that should not have been possible."

"Why shouldn't it be possible?"

"Are you aware of any witches that are able to access a goblin plane?"

"I never even knew it existed."

"Exactly, because it should not exist to you. After I found you sleeping in your newly claimed plane, I spoke with my mother. She's never heard of a witch accessing our territories and claiming a plane. The only explanation is that you have some dormant goblin blood that is coming forward."

"I never claimed anything. Second, I don't have any goblin blood." I was having a bit of an identity crisis

"There is no other explanation. Besides people are never as pure blooded as they want to believe."

"Meaning you might be part witch?" I asked caustically.

He didn't hesitate. "I may be, but it would be in small amounts since I have shown no signs of possessing any witch power."

"Well, it's not like our two groups intermingle that much."

"That is a recent occurrence. When witches still held their long life spans, it was not uncommon to see a witch and goblin couple. It's not as though it is impossible now, just inconvenient."

"Wouldn't want to slum it?"

"Inconvenient was probably the wrong word. I wouldn't want to love someone and have to watch them die."

"Isn't love supposed to be worth the sacrifice?" The whole "inconvenient" thing had really raised my hackles.

"Yes, but I do not know if I am willing to have so little time with someone, or to worry that my children will only get half the lifespan they should have. There has not been a discernible pattern for how long the children live. Some live a human life span, others are still living, but no one knows if that will be for five hundred years or a thousand, as should be their birthright."

"I guess that would be hard, not knowing how long to expect to see your children live, but it seems a bit cowardly. A thousand years is promised to no one. Not even you. You just have the possibility." I thought about Bruce. He estimated that he had a good five hundred years and didn't seem concerned with his 'shortened' lifespan.

His posture stiffened at the word cowardly, and he leaned away from me. "I don't expect you to understand. I may not be promised everything I desire, but I can still make choices that will give me the best possibility of the outcome I want." He changed the subject. "So, you're unaware of any goblins in your family line?"

"I already said that."

"It is curious, that there would be no family rumors. How many direct relatives do you know?"

"Well," I listed off relatives in my mind. "I knew two great-grandparents on my father's side before they passed within six months of each other when I was seven. My mom's grandparents were already dead when I was born, but I knew her parents. Three of my grandparents have passed, though I know them all. Only my mom's mother is still alive. I can ask my family, if you'd like."

"I would. The safe has bonded with you, and you now have your own piece of the goblin plane. You should bond with it regularly, so no one can invade your territory, but it seems bonding with it may hurt you, due to your mortality. If you find out how far back the blood came from, I may be able to assist you."

"How?"

"Just find out, Peg. Surely your family will be able to assist you with that. Also, spend some time with the safe, perhaps it will recognize how fragile you are and not accidentally kill you." He got up quickly and walked to the front door without even saying goodbye.

"Nice to see you, too," I called out, not bothering to get up.

He looked over his shoulder. "Keep me updated. I don't like having to track you down." With that, he turned the corner in my small foyer, and I heard the door open and shut firmly when he left. Well, at least he closed the door.

After Deval left, I walked to the front door and locked it. Safety first, even if the only thing bent on harming me sat in the Arizona room. As long as it kept its siren song to a minimum, I was sure we would get along just fine. Deval told me to spend time with it, as silly as it seemed, so when I decided to cyber stalk Grant Vonn, I took my laptop to the safe. The lid was closed, I hopped up on it and sat cross-legged.

While I searched, I stroked the safe and baby-talked it. "Who's a good safe? Who's the prettiest safe in the world?" When I talked to Cheddar like that, he was way less interested in murdering me in my sleep. Here was hoping the safe would feel the same way. Besides, it really was pretty. If it decided to not try to murder me in my sleep, I knew of a corner in my living room by the fireplace where it would look pretty spectacular.

It was a fairly productive afternoon. I found pictures of Grant, and it was no wonder Violet had become infatuated with him. He was all sandy tousled hair, lean tanned limbs, with khakis and button ups. He reminded me of a young Kennedy. The pictures I found were from around the time Violet had been in school. Nothing later though, which leant weight to the theory of some sort of maiming being a real possibility.

I found a faculty email for him at ASU and sent a quick message, asking to meet. I didn't say what I wanted, hoping the ambiguous email would make him assume I was a student. I could fake wanting to buy a house, but faking enough knowledge about science to fool an academic was beyond my acting skills. When I met with him, I would be honest.

That done, I went to my room and grabbed the blood box Ivy gave me. I should have worked on unlocking it two days ago, but between the unexpected sub call, a night trip to the goblin plane, and making butt cream, I had been a little distracted. The sucker needed to be opened yesterday. I grabbed the box and headed out to BBTT morgue and lab.

BBTT Morgue and Lab didn't have any of Violet's blood available. However, they did have her toxicology screen back and the results from the aura sweep they'd done on the house. As I'd suspected, her blood came back positive for ingested opiates, not a surprise that the tea left in the cup also came back positive. The house was a wash. One of their employees, a woman named Susan, had run a sweep trace and found only Violet, and a young girl, who I assumed was the missing Imogen.

She'd also made note that there were traces of other supernaturals coming and going but nothing within the forty-eight-hour time frame. I suspected that had she performed a concentrated trace instead of a sweep, she would have found the scrubbed traces as well but performing an aura trace of an entire house would have been tedious and not what we had agreed to. After BBTT confirmed the death as homicide, they followed through with Dusty's wishes and cremated her body. My visit had been a long shot anyway.

I had some ideas for my next steps. Up first, breaking into the blood box. With the time that passed since the murder, I didn't want to waste any more. That meant going to see Pammy. I was prone to avoid her, even when I wasn't under the effects of strange goblin magic and bundled up like someone on an expedition in Alaska. The cold had faded to more tolerable levels, I reminded myself that I would be miserable all summer in the Arizona heat, gritted my teeth, and carried on. I entered Bump and Grind in my new uniform of thick jeans, tall hiking boots, thick sweater, a scarf, and beanie for good measure.

Pammy was in her usual spot and raised an eyebrow at my appearance. You had to look pretty odd for Pammy to judge you. I sighed and headed over to get a mocha with the blood box held tightly under my arm. This time when I approached, her flock had flown. The same girl from the other day gave me the stink eye again. Huh, I wasn't trying to be Pammy's new lap dog; the girl needed to chill. I took a seat in one of the temporarily abandoned armchairs and set the blood box on the coffee table.

Pammy leaned forward to get a better look. "A gift for me, Peg? You shouldn't have."

"Ha ha. This was Violet's, and since I don't have any of her blood, I'm not sure how to open it. Do you know if her father's would work? I already tried getting some from BBTT, but the body has been cremated, and they didn't have any samples left."

"Dead blood wouldn't work anyway." She picked up the box and slowly turned it over.

I'd suspected as much. Nice to get a confirmation for once. A slight tingle went across the back of my neck, a telltale sign she was forcing some of her power into the box. The thorn snapped up and she promptly placed her index finger on it, pushing down, allowing her blood to cover it before pulling her finger back. She didn't even flinch. The thorn pulsed twice, before the blood sizzled off the thorn, magical steam rising.

"These boxes can have multiple people keyed to them, but it wouldn't have rejected me so quickly, if it had more than one master. I'd say the drive out to Tucson wouldn't be worth your time."

I nodded in agreement. Usually I enjoyed road trips, but there were currently too many balls in the air. I'd rather skip the trip, even if it meant forgoing asking my mom about possible goblin relatives face to face.

"Where'd you get the box? Did you search Violet's house again?"

"Nope, I got it when I went to see Dusty a couple of days ago."

She gave me a little glare. "And you're just now trying to bust it open?"

"I've been following other leads." I explained Jessica, Ronnie, and the apparently agoraphobic T.A. I left out the part about the safe and possible goblin heritage because I wasn't supposed to talk about it. Besides, Pammy would find some way to use my newly found heritage.

Her glare faded, my discoveries so far must have met the minimum requirements. "Hmmm, you're doing pretty good, baby girl. Though this is taking longer than I had hoped."

"Me too, but you can't rush progress," I replied, knowing Pammy wouldn't agree.

"You can, and you will. What you need to do with this box is hack it."

"Is that an ancient witch term?" I barely kept the sarcasm out of my voice.

She acted as if I hadn't bothered to try. "No, smart ass, it's a word your young ass will understand. Every day you need to force your magic into it and prick your finger on it. Depending about how much magic she used when creating the lock, it will eventually rewrite its magic to switch over to you. You've got plenty of power to force into it."

Well, that sounded unpleasant, and not just the part about stabbing myself on a thorn every day. Power was not endless, and with my luck lately, I wanted to hoard as much as possible. There wasn't a question of what else could go wrong, it was when would the shit really hit the fan. "Okay Pammy, thanks for the info."

Standing, I grabbed the box, deciding to dismiss myself before she had the chance. Checking to make sure the thorn was retracted, I tucked it under my arm again. Throwing my purse over my shoulder, I was halfway to the door before she called after me.

"I know you're hiding something, sugar, better not let it interfere in your duties." Her voice boomed through the room and the displaced lackey smirked at me.

I bared my teeth at her, and she swallowed. I turned back to Pammy. "It won't." I continued toward the door. It was a half lie. I might have acknowledged I was hiding something, but hell if I knew whether it would interfere. It wasn't her business. I respected her, but not enough to put my trust in her keeping my secrets. She would always look out for number one, and trading in secrets was part of her job. I didn't feel even a twinge of guilt as I climbed into my Jeep.

The first thing I did when I got home was check my email. No response from the T.A. I hadn't expected one because the notification would've pinged through on my phone. Still, I checked my spam folder to be sure. No dice. Well, since there was nothing better to do, I decided to force some of my power into Violet's blood box. I hadn't performed any aggressive magic today, so the power I channeled into the box came easily. After five minutes, I stopped and looked at the thorn with apprehension. Pammy had no issue placing her finger on the sharp point.

I placed my finger on it, swallowing, my mouth dry. The anticipation of pain was always worse than the actuality. Biting my lip, I took the plunge and shoved my finger down. I pulled my hand back almost immediately. My blood pulsed on the thorn twice, before sizzling off. If my power levels stayed high, I would try again later.

Pammy was right, I should have asked about it two days ago when I first retrieved the stupid thing, then it might already be open. Oh well, couldn't change the past. I placed the box securely in the back of my closet before impatiently checking my email again. Still nothing. I considered babying the goblin safe again, when my cell started ringing. It was Bruce. "Hey, good looking."

"Well, honey, I'm glad you're not here to see me blush." He responded in his flirty tone.

"Mmhmm. What are you up to today, or do you need me to take your grandma to another appointment?"

"That wounds me, Peg. I don't just call you to ask favors. That's your M.O. If I didn't have a truck, I don't think you'd ever call me."

"Not true, if you didn't have shifter strength to go along with that truck, I'd never call you. I can always rent a truck, but I'd need four regular guys to lift what you can with one hand."

"Right to the heart, and here I was going to ask you out dancing."

"Let me guess, I should invite Lola along?"

"She also enjoys dancing, so I thought we could make a night of it."

The three of us did have fun together, but he often used me as the go between. "Why don't you ask her out already?"

"We've agreed to be friends. I like her company, yours, too. Are you available tonight, or are you gonna be sleuthing?"

"I'm not Trixie Belden. I investigate," I responded primly.

"Who's Trixie Belden?"

I sighed. "Nancy Drew's less appreciated counterpart."

"Uh huh, you wanna go dancing or what?"

I looked at my laptop again. Still no response. I was kind of at an impasse until I heard from Grant. If he didn't get back to me by the morning, I could always go hunt him down. In the meantime, the only things to do at home was feed the two boxes. The goblin safe needed attention, the blood box needed power and blood. I was the crazy box lady. Yep, I needed to go out. "What time were you thinking?"

14

————————

Lola came over to my house to get ready, so Bruce could pick us up in one go. I hadn't bothered asking where he was taking us. He was a country boy, so it would be some sort of country bar which was fine by me because country bars didn't judge you if you didn't wear heels. Lola and I dudded ourselves out in jeans, fitted plaid shirts, and boots. Then we both did pageant hair. Lola's process consisted of hot rollers, teasing, and hair spray. My already curly-do only needed me to flip my head over and spray heavy-duty hair spray before letting it dry. By the time our hair was done, our new motto could be "the higher the hair, the closer to the Lord." I didn't know about the Lord part.

By the time that we arrived at Denim and Diamonds, we were ready to drink beer and two-step the night away. It was one of the nicer country bars. Even knowing it would be a country bar night, the question was whether it would be a dive, a honky tonk, or something a bit more fancy. We danced, drank beer from mason jars, and since I wasn't driving, I accepted the tequila shots Bruce presented to me.

By ten, Lola and I were bundled up in the back seat of Bruce's truck singing some Dolly along to the radio with terrible pitch while Bruce laughed in the front, playing our chauffer. I was dropped off first. I walked up to my door and unlocked it. I turned to the idling truck in my driveway and gave Bruce the thumbs up to leave. He reversed and headed out. Still humming Dolly I let myself in.

Unexpected dread took a moment to penetrate my intoxicated mind. Barely in the foyer, I froze, inching backwards until I could place my hand on my front door to touch my wards. According to them nothing was wrong, no one had tampered with them. I shook my head, wondering if I was being silly and continued back to my bedroom. Once there, I stopped, turned and studied the darkened spaces of my home. My skin was crawling, I couldn't get over the feeling of being watched.

Pushing out my magic, I tried to pinpoint what was out of place. Everything seemed normal, nothing was there. It took a moment for that to filter through. *Nothing* was there, just like the "nothing" when I searched for the aura on the poppy and inside the safe. That nothing stood to the left of my doorway. My heart raced, fear sobering me. I needed to get out of the room before whatever was watching attacked.

I dropped my gaze not wanting to let whatever it was catch on that I knew it was there. I forced my shoulders into a casual shrug, as if to say "Well, I guess that was nothing" and started walking toward my door. To keep up the ruse, I called out, "Cheddar, it's dinner time."

Whatever was there let me pass. That ruled out a vampire or a shifter. They would hear the staccato of my heart. I walked calmly down the hall finding it difficult not to turn back and check behind me. My gut screamed it was there, but my need to get to the door kept me moving. This was the second time in a week I needed to flee my home. The first time had been a race and exhilarating. This slow exit was excruciating, every part of my being wanted to turn and attack, but with no idea what was lurking, I didn't know what I was fighting. *This may be the only chance you get to catch this thing,* doubt whispered to me. On my shoulder, logic told me not to fight something I had no knowledge of.

When I got to the end of the hall, my choice was taken away. Cheddar trotted up, obviously responding to my earlier declaration that it was dinnertime. He stopped dead in his tracks, his focus behind me. His fur bristled as he went to his toes, hissing and spitting at whatever was behind me. I ran, but a hard shove from behind sent me to the floor. The ceramic tiles bruised my knees. Before I could react, a hand in my hair yanked me backwards. My hands flew to my scalp, trying to pry the fingers lose, but they didn't budge.

Whatever attacked me didn't have supernatural strength. It still hurt, but I didn't think I'd be scalped. I dropped my hands, let myself be pulled back, so I could get in range. I rammed my elbow back. It hit what felt like a thigh, and I heard a masculine grunt. On the second try, I aimed a bit more center. The hold on my hair disappeared, and I heard a terse "Fuck" behind me.

Scrambling to my feet, I started toward the front door. A hand grabbed wrapped around my elbow digging in and using my forward momentum to change my direction to the kitchen. My hip hit the corner of the entryway. Sharp pains shot down my leg. I gasped and tried to right myself, but that damn hand was back in my hair again. This time he wasn't trying to hold me back. He pushed, causing my injured leg to shriek in protest, before I hit the floor. I rolled to my side, trying to get up and figure out where the attack was coming from. A swift kick landed in my stomach.

Power raced to my hands, and in desperation, I blindly threw my power out. I heard glass break but didn't hear any telltale grunts. I tried to sit up when another kick whipped across my lower back. Crying out, I curled into fetal position, helplessness rising. *How do I target a faceless enemy?* Suddenly an angry feline yowl filled the air, and fur brushed against my arm. I uncovered my face in time to see Cheddar flying over me, claws extended. He clawed into my faceless attacker as the man cursed. The raging ball of fur appeared to be doing some shredding. Blood hit the floor.

With a possible target, I thrust my power out again, careful to avoid my magnificent attack cat. The large surge had no effect. How could a cat's claws hurt someone, but not my magic? I stared dumbfounded. Cheddar suddenly flew across the room, hitting the counter. He let out a small pained yowl and retreated to the living room. I wanted to go and protect my baby, but I couldn't even protect myself at the moment. The invisible attacker was between me and my front door. With limited choices, I turned and ran through the Arizona Room, aiming for the back door, sending up a prayer that my kitty was in one of his hiding spots until I could get to him.

I made it onto the enclosed porch before being knocked forward again. This time, I landed on top of my safe. Its power rushed out, trying to connect. Belly down on top of the safe gave me an idea. It was the perfect position. I mule kicked as hard as I could, ignoring the protest of my aching hip. My foot made solid contact, and a pained inhale sounded. With no idea if he fell or was catching his breath, I pushed into a crouch and opened the lid before scrambling inside the safe.

Behind me, a man laughed manically. "Eager to die the same way as Violet, bitch?"

The joke was on him. The arrogant ass made no effort to stop me. Probably believing I'd suffocate like Violet. Two days ago, he'd have been right. Not tonight though. As soon as I was in the safe, the bottom turned into stairs. I tumbled down a few feet, my body protesting at its continued assault before I was able to stop and gingerly stand up. Everything hurt. I carefully took another step down into the darkness, not sure if the tumble would hurt worse than the pain shooting through my hip with every step down. For a moment, the darkness lifted. Hand against the stone wall, I looked back up over my shoulder. The ceiling of my enclosed porch stretched above the open safe.

"What the fuck? Listen you fucking witch trash, I don't know where you went, but I will find you."

Okay, my invisible attacker couldn't see me either. I held my breath and waited, afraid to move and change that fact.

"I'm going to kill you and your fucking familiar too. You bitches will rue the day you thought you could break me with your curses!" With that, the lid slammed shut, and the stairway became dark again.

Did he really say "rue the day?" I shook my head. I bit my lip when I thought about Cheddar, hating hat I couldn't help him. I sent up another prayer he would go to one of his hiding spots, trying to remind myself how even I couldn't find Cheddar without magic sometimes. With nothing left to do, I started the long descent to my newly acquired plane. Hopefully I made the right choice. I didn't know what would be worse, being murdered in my home where it was warm, or dying in a frigid barren plane that wanted to claim me as its own. If I did die down here, it would be a very permanent claiming.

I debated staying close to the door in case I needed to exit the plane quickly but decided against it and continued down. I hated to admit it was out of fear of the man or thing that attacked me. The feeling of helplessness was a new sensation. Even when a vampire attacked me as a child, I hadn't been so helpless. Of course, I could see the vampire, and my parents had immediately come to fight for me. It warmed my heart that Cheddar tried to protect me, but it also made me feel more worthless.

The trek down the stone steps was considerably more difficult when you were lucid and injured. Deval mentioned the plane would bond with me. As I continued my hobbled descent, I hoped it meant the plane might calm down on the arctic weather in an effort not to kill its mistress. The cold didn't seem as horrible as before, but it wasn't a balmy summer day either.

I stepped off the final stair. The rocky dirt crunched under my boots. The bluish-purple mountain and rocks surrounding me were less stark this visit and somehow more alive. More pink than last time. My mind might be playing tricks, considering the last time I was borderline unconscious. Finding the long flat rock, I vaguely remembered lying on before. I chose not to lie down this time. Too much of a risk. I wasn't cold yet and hoped it wasn't the adrenaline giving me a false sense of reality.

I sat cross-legged on the stone and experienced a small epiphany on how I could get help. Deval had been tied to the plane before it chose me. Maybe he still had some sort of bond with it. He said it was useless to him because it bonded to me, but that didn't mean it wasn't still bonded to him as well. It explained how he'd bypassed my wards. If I sent the magical equivalent of the bat signal through the plane, hopefully he would come running. Even a leisurely stroll, at this point would work. I needed help.

The cool rock went through my jeans raising goose bumps on my skin. I closed my eyes and focused on my power. It should be depleted, but for some reason it was at full capacity. The plane appeared to be a supernatural battery. If I had known that, I wouldn't have been upset when Deval gifted it to me. Pushing my power out with all my might, I chanted Deval's name over and over again, praying I wasn't wasting my time and energy on nothing, and he could still access my secret club house.

Roughly twenty minutes later, I opened my eyes as gravel crunched. Craning my neck, I saw an irritated Deval in jeans and a t-shirt coming up behind me. He looked good, and it wasn't because I was desperately happy to see him. Not wanting him to get a big head, I reined in my reaction. "Thank gods, you're here."

"What are you playing at? Any goblin in a plane within fifty miles would have heard your call. Did I forget to mention that a goblin plane being in possession of a witch is not something we were going to advertise?"

I stood quickly but winced and teetered a little on my bad leg.

His eyebrows drew together. "You're injured. Did you fall down the stairs?"

I hobbled forward to meet him. "No, I had a visit from the murderer and your thief. I came here to escape, but I don't know how safe it is to go back upstairs on my own." It wasn't something I wanted to admit.

"I thought you were powerful. Why are you cowering down here?"

"Way to rub salt in my wounds, asshole."

He crossed his arms and gave me a glare, his eyes flashing copper. "Explain."

So I did. Fifteen minutes later, his arms were still crossed, but his eyes were no longer flashing, and I didn't think he wanted to murder me. "Fine, you had good reason to call me. I will explain to my mother."

"Mama's boy," I muttered under my breath.

He obviously heard me, and his lip twitched in what I didn't think was meant to be a smile. "Be that as it may, we need to get you out of here. You are obviously adjusting well to the plane, but you are still unused to it. Even when you are, it would be unwise to spend excessive amounts of time here."

"Will you always be able to come here?" I tilted my head to the side.

"Is that your new plan? To use this as a safe room and call me to come save you?"

I bristled. "No, I wanted to know. It's not like I could call Pammy," I bit back.

"No, you could not, if she even knew about it." He searched my face as he said it. Probably concerned I had spilled the beans.

"No, Deval, I didn't tell her."

He nodded and walked over to me, lifting me into his arms with little effort.

"What are you doing?" I squawked, trying to push away from him.

"You're injured, and we need to get you out of here."

"I'm not a damsel in distress. I can walk on my own two feet."

"Didn't you tell me that you were injured? I need you functioning; do not aggravate your injuries before you see a healer. Besides, it seems it will be tradition for me to carry you out of your plane." He ended his sentence with a sigh.

I harrumphed but said nothing. At the moment I was the stereotypical needy woman, and I didn't want to dwell on it too hard. He carried me up the stairs as if I weighed nothing at all. When we got to the top, I tensed in his arms, worried we would be attacked as soon as we opened the door to my earthly home.

Deval obviously had the same thought because he set me on the step behind him before opening the lid to the safe. "Reach out with your magic and tell me where he is."

If he's still here. I complied with his order. My magic felt endless, like it was in the plane. Was that because I was still technically in it? I searched through my house looking for nothing instead of something. This time that wall of noth-ingness wasn't there, but I found Cheddar, though he felt both agitated and lethargic. Not good.

"Nothing," I said to Deval, pushing his lower back to get him moving.

"Are you certain?"

Losing patience and wanting to get to my injured kitty, I gave him a sharp slap on the ass. "I said that."

He turned quickly, glaring down at me. "You will never do that again."

"Move it. What's the big deal? A little spanking never hurt anyone." Did I say that? Kill. Me. Now.

He looked at me with a different kind of interest. "While that may be true in one context, we are not currently enjoying foreplay. If you don't want me to assume that's what your love tap meant, I would advise you to desist from doing it in the future."

I groaned because the twelve-year-old in me viewed that as a challenge. I wanted to do just that, but the adult side won out. I was in no way prepared to deal with those consequences. I waved my hand impatiently toward my house.

He smirked. "That's what I thought, but do let me know if you change your mind." With that, he turned forward and went up the final step. I hobbled behind him, willing myself not to blush. When I reached the top step, the staircase vanished, and I was standing on the metal bottom of the safe. I was still studying it when Deval reached in and swooped me out. I almost protested but then realized climbing out when the side came up to mid-thigh, would be very uncomfortable. He put me down gently.

"Thanks."

"My pleasure." He then turned toward my back door and let himself in. I was right about how he'd been able to bypass my wards. The question now was how the other guy got in. I sighed. Questions for tomorrow. Right then I needed to find Cheddar and use the small balance left on a credit card to check into a motel. I'd have to sneak the cat in, because lord knew, I couldn't really afford a room and a pet deposit.

I gnawed at my lip doing mental calculations for the cash I had available when Deval called back to me from inside the kitchen. "Get in here. You need to pack a bag."

"I'm going to," I called back in irritation, hobbling into the kitchen.

He turned around at my approach and smiled. "Good, I thought you'd be difficult about coming with me tonight."

"Uh, coming with you where?" I scrunched my nose.

"To my house, obviously."

"I'm not coming with you; I'm going to a motel." I clarified.

He scoffed. "Don't be ridiculous. We don't know what or who attacked you. A roadside motel is hardly a safe place to stay."

I had planned on going to a mom and pop motel on Main Street, because I liked their neon diving girl sign, but that was a silly thing to admit. Plus, he was probably right, now wasn't the time to look a gift horse in the mouth. I nodded and went to the hall closet where an emergency duffel was packed. Pammy suggested it when I started because I never knew when or where a job might come up. Up until now, I'd never needed it. If I managed to solve this, that might change. A perk, or downside, of more advanced Fortune jobs. The cat carrier was also conveniently located in the closet, thanks to a recent trip to Tucson that I'd graciously taken Cheddar on. He hadn't appreciated it, but it was easier than leaving him home alone.

Items ready to go, I started searching for my brave kitty, calling out endearments and offering treats.

Suddenly Deval appeared with Cheddar loosely held in his arms. "You should talk to everyone like you talk to your feline. You might get better results."

"Sure, I bet that offering you treats and calling you 'my handsome boy' would have worked wonders when we met. Sorry if being threatened and assaulted didn't lead to that."

"You're forgiven."

I rolled my eyes and walked up to him, taking a look at Cheddar. I reached out with my magic and found a hairline fracture on his hip and rib. He was in pain, though it wasn't life threatening. Still I poured my magic into him, healing his injuries. My normally ornery boy purred in response. It had to hurt a little, but despite our human versus cat squabbles, Cheddar trusted me and thought of me as his mother. It gave me a little positive boost to know that I could actually help him, especially after he had helped me. All healed, Cheddar relaxed, remaining boneless in Deval's arms. Under normal circumstances, I would have called him a traitor, but I was too happy at him being okay to care.

I held up the cat carrier, and Deval put Cheddar in, butt first like a pro. *Must not be his first cat wrangling.* Cheddar yowled a little bit in irritation, but it seemed to be a reaction to Deval putting him down, rather than his being in the carrier. Regardless of his feelings, I wasn't leaving Cheddar behind to fall victim to the invisible madman I strongly suspected to be the missing T.A. Pretty hard to lecture, if your students couldn't see you.

Wordlessly, Deval took the cat carrier and the duffel bag. I grabbed my purse, which still held my phone, and followed him out, locking the door even though it felt pointless. I hobbled behind him to my Jeep. Since he came via the goblin plane, he didn't have his car. He opened the passenger door and threw the duffel in the backseat, before placing Cheddar on the middle consul. I started to walk around to the driver door, when he gave me a look that indicated there was no way in hell he was letting me drive.

I swallowed back the words I wanted to say because I wasn't really in any shape to drive. I tended to be a bit of a control freak. It was hard to let someone else drive my Jeep. "Fine," I muttered, as I held out the keys.

He took them and then graciously picked me up and deposited me in the passenger seat. How he had known I'd been dreading pulling myself into the seat was beyond me. He got in and buckled his seat belt before starting the rumbling engine. I meant to stay awake so I could see where we went, not knowing where the goblin lived, but the exhaustion the followed too much adrenaline overtook me, and I slept, lulled by the soothing vibration of the Jeep.

I woke up when Deval lifted me out of the vehicle. My eyes wouldn't stay open, almost as if someone injected me with Benadryl. "Cheddar," I managed to mumble.

"I will not leave your feline hero in your car overnight. I may even give him a can of tuna to celebrate his victory."

I thought I heard Cheddar meow in agreement, but I passed out before Deval closed the Jeep door.

I woke disoriented. The large bed with a fluffy down comforter that I currently occupied didn't belong to me. The only thing I recognized was the fat orange cat sitting on the second pillow, eyeing me with concern.

The night before returned to me. "Good morning, handsome boy." I reached over and scratched his head. He purred happily. To his chagrin, I sat up and looked around the room. It was beautiful, done in beiges, pinks, and whites. Every item was chosen for comfort, and it showed. Looking down at myself, I was surprised to find fresh silk pajamas and not the dirty flannel and jeans covered in blood and dirt from the night before. I wanted to be mad, but looking at the white bedspread, I just appreciated that I didn't have to offer to pay to get it cleaned.

Standing, I waited for the sharp pain to ring through my hip. Sleeping on an injury like that never made the best wakeup call, but surprisingly I was completely fine. Huh, had a healer seen me? Or were my injuries less serious than I thought? As disturbing as I found the idea of sleeping through a healing, I was more worried that I had overly exaggerated my injuries. It was bad enough to call in the cavalry for a rescue, but if I was a wimp, too, I didn't know what that said about my future as a Fortune.

Only one way to find out. I headed to the door and opened it. I half expected Cheddar to follow me, but it was obvious that the bed was too comfortable to leave. I half wished I could stay there as well, but avoiding my problems wouldn't solve them. Ready to face Deval, even though he had seen me in my drawers...again.

To my disappointment, he was nowhere to be found. He had, however, left a note telling me to eat and wait until he came back before leaving. Considering the fact that he had my keys, leaving wasn't a likely prospect. I considered my options. It was noon; Lola would be at work. I didn't want to explain to Bruce why he was picking me up smelling like goblin and lord knew what else his sensitive shifter nose would pick up. The only other option would be Pammy, but that would lead to too many questions. Wait I would, while I devoured a sandwich I made out of the gourmet cheeses and cold cuts that I found in the fridge, along with some freshly baked artisan bread. If turn-down service and delicious food were the result, I needed to be rescued more often. When I found a pumpkin cheesecake in the fridge, I then seriously contemplated being a damsel in distress as a career.

By the time Deval came in an hour later, I was show-ered and dressed in the outfit from my overnight bag. My freshly laundered and mended clothes from the previous night were left on the bathroom counter, so I had shoved them into my duffel. The food-driven euphoria was gone, and the independent lady was back. Deval walked up to where I sat at the kitchen bar, drinking a Diet Pepsi.

He looked at me for a moment before reaching into his pocket and withdrawing my key chain from his pocket and setting it before me. "I'm glad to see that you're feeling better. Your injuries were worse than I thought."

Oh, thank gods. "Yeah, about that. I'm assuming a healer came by?"

He nodded.

"Was it witch or goblin?" I'd never been healed by a goblin before, so I was hoping it was the latter. Perhaps goblin healings were gentler than their witch counterparts.

"Of course it was a witch. Goblins don't have the power to heal witches. At least, not so extensively. We just discussed how goblin power comes from the minerals."

"Who is this healer? I didn't feel anything." I tried to keep the worry out of my voice.

"Oh, that's what you're concerned about."

"I'm not necessarily concerned about it," I lied, none too convincingly.

"Please, your entire body is tense with anxiety. Your jaw looks so hard, you're in danger of cracking a tooth. Our healer is on the payroll. She won't tell anyone, not even Pammy."

I only then noticed that my jaw was aching and made an effort to relax. "What do you mean, she won't tell Pammy?"

"I mean just that. She is paid well enough, and Pammy has enough self-preservation not to meddle in goblin affairs, at least normally."

"Huh, good luck with that, but that wasn't what I was worried about." Though in retrospect, maybe I should have been.

"You know how you always lose the 'silence game'?" Deval rubbed his chin.

"Yeah, so?"

"Well, I don't like to play the 'guess what' game, so please tell me what you're worried about."

"Since you've asked nicely, I will. I'm sure you've been healed by a witch healer or maybe you haven't. Regardless, it is excruciating. If you're telling me I was in bad shape, I don't know how I slept through it. With all of the symptoms I've been experiencing from the plane, that worries me."

He shrugged. "Oh, that. I kept you under."

I stood up from the bar stool and turned my back to Deval. Walking the length of the bar, I turned around. "If a goblin healer couldn't heal me, how could you, a goblin, keep me unconscious without using drugs or knocking my lights out?"

"Goblins are fairly hardy; we rarely need healers, but when we are injured, it tends to be catastrophic injuries, like those of a mine collapse. Our bodies will mend themselves, but we need to be in a restful state to do so. It's hard to rest when the pain of having your bones ground to dust is keeping you awake. Goblins have a magic that allows them to help keep another goblin under."

I strode back toward him, not sure if his explanation was a relief or more frightening. I hopped back up on my stool and took a gulp of my Diet Pepsi before talking. "I'm not a goblin, so how did you keep me under?"

"I told you, you obviously have some goblin blood."

"Yeah, but having some great-great-relative shouldn't leave me vulnerable to goblin magic."

"Ah."

"You know it's really annoying how you always say 'Ah', as if you understand my worries, but that they're small and beneath you." My eyes narrowed.

"My using 'ah' as an affirmative is in no way a reflection of my opinion of your senseless brooding. In this case, it simply meant that I understand what has upset you."

"Feel free to share with the class," I responded snarkily.

"You're worried I will be able to knock you out on a whim."

"Isn't that exactly what you did?"

"Do you understand the concept of benevolent magic?"

"Meaning it's not malevolent?" Sarcasm coated my voice.

Deval ignored my tone. "Exactly, the goblin physiology is a lot more accepting of spells aimed at them to their benefit. Goblins' subconscious will allow for spells aimed at them for healing when they are severely injured and have shut down. Had I been trying to knock you under with malicious intent, such as trying to smother you with a pillow, your body would have fought the compulsion."

"But what if you hid your intent?"

"You cannot hide the intent for this magic. It is a true blessing."

"How do I know you're not lying?" I asked skeptically.

"Ask Lola. Your friend would not lie to you."

I hadn't realized my hands were clenched until I released them. "Sorry, I know that very few people know about my surprise heritage, but the idea of an entire super-natural race being able to will me to sleep on a whim is terrifying."

"Even if they could, they wouldn't. It is beyond taboo. It would mean death or banishment."

"You said it was impossible, so why are there sentences for impossible crimes?"

"Magic evolves. If a man cannot trust his people to protect his health, even if they disagree on other points of politics, what can he trust?"

I met his eyes, my stare hard. "Fine, we'll agree that you weren't attempting to murder me. It's still a lot to take in."

He shrugged out of his suit jacket. "What's hard to take in? You used to feel pain during a healing, now you don't have to."

"If you suddenly found out that part of your history was different then what you had been told, and that it would have a direct influence on your life that you hadn't expected, you would be put off, too."

Deval ignored my complaint and walked over to the fridge, opening it and taking out a Perrier. "You're being melancholy, Peg. All of the changes have been to your benefit. You have your own goblin plane. You can use it as a magical escape hatch, put whatever you like down there, though it pains me to think of you using it as storage, when you could have rented a space at a storage facility for quite a bit less." He shook his head seeming to want to rid himself of the thought of his million-dollar safe being turned into some sort of secondary storage.

"I should be grateful that I no longer have to worry about where to store the Christmas tree next year?" I asked, deadpan.

"And that the next time you are seriously injured, you can have a goblin put you under," he added helpfully.

"Great, so call you? Was being my personal magical anesthesiologist part of your plan?"

"I said any goblin."

"You're the only one I know."

"What about Lola's parents?"

"They dropped her off at my house. I barely know them."

He threw hands up in the air. "Fine, if you are seriously injured, feel free to call me, and I will come, if I'm available."

"Wonderful," sarcasm dripped from my words. It didn't really matter that I survived being healed by a witch while unconscious. He was trying to sell me on a lifestyle change I had no control over. I wasn't buying. "I need to head home and get working. Any chance Cheddar could spend the night again?"

His eyebrow quirked. "Personal anesthesiologist and pet sitter?"

"He's a cat. Which means no work other than pouring food into a bowl twice a day. I'm worried if I take him home, my mysterious attacker will go after him."

"Take him to Lola's."

"This is going to sound paranoid, but I can't see my attacker. I'm worried he'll follow me to Lola's."

"He didn't follow us here."

"How can you be sure? He was invisible, and I wasn't conscious to make sure no missing auras were following us."

"Fine, I will have my assistant procure a litter box."

"I didn't realize you had an assistant," Of course the prince had an assistant. He probably employed a whole team of them because I seriously doubted that he had done my laundry.

"Who do you think stocked the fridge for you?"

"I assumed you would have food in your home."

"This is not my home."

Huh? "Whose is it then?" I gave the living room and kitchen a more studious appraisal than before.

"It is a safe house for the royal family. We do not bring witches into our homes lightly."

"I don't get access to your super-secret club house? Here you said I'd get all the perks."

He looked at me speculatively. "Perhaps one day you will."

15

———

My home no longer felt like my sanctuary. Oddly enough, what did feel like a sanctuary was my goblin plane. Two days ago, I'd thought it would be the death of me. Today, it felt like a safe, no pun intended, albeit cold, inviting place. I debated the need to come home, but knew it was like the old saying about getting back on the horse. I needed to reclaim my home. Oh, and I left the blood box there. I needed to put more power into it because even though my gut and the evidence led me to believe that the murderer was the missing T.A., I had no idea how to find an invisible man. The blood box was my next best lead.

As I walked to my front door, my skin went clammy and the warning signs of nervous sweat broke out. I needed to calm down because nervous sweat smelled awful, and I didn't have time for a shower plus the scene from *Psycho* came to mind. If I was this apprehensive about walking to my front door, the thought of being caught unaware, naked and vulnerable in a shower, was way too much to contemplate. Taking a deep breath, I reached for my power, and my stomach clenched. My reserves were gone. I shouldn't have been surprised, I'd undergone a massive healing according to Deval. Great. The energy I got from the goblin plane had become a little too comfortable and made me sloppy, until I started to count on it.

Well, who wouldn't? I used a lot of what little power I currently had at my disposal and scanned my house, looking for nothing. What I found was a whole lot of something. My fear from the night before left an aura on the house. Only one way to fix that. I marched up to my front door with more confidence. Seeing a piece of white paper in between the door and frame, my confidence faltered. *Please be a passive aggressive note from a neighbor.* No such luck.

Nice disappearing act, witch bitch,
But that's really more my style.
I'll be seeing you,
But you won't be seeing me.

Good thing he hadn't gone into English Literature academia. His poetry left a lot to be desired. On the other hand, one of the first things I learned in English class was to identify the purpose of writing. His purpose was to scare me, and it worked. I looked around before sniffing myself. Sure enough, I reeked of nervous sweat.

Taking the note, I checked my wards and walked inside. My first instinct was to burn it, but I didn't think Pammy would be pleased if I decided to destroy evidence. I set it down on the coffee table and went to retrieve what I'd come for. I went to my closet and was pleased to find the box still there. Pulling it out of the back of the closet, I examined it, reaching out with my small store of magic. While Violet's essence was still dominant, I could feel mine rising underneath. I was making headway with the box. I didn't have the magic available to push into the box, which was my original plan.

A thought nudged. Duh, I needed to take the box into the goblin plane. My heart gave a little patter of agreement. Damn, I did feel unsafe in my own home. Well, I'd feel better with my batteries charged even if the plane was becoming a crutch. The jeans, thin T-shirt and flip-flops from my duffel bag weren't going to cut it. The plane no longer seemed to be inadvertently trying to kill me, but some hardy work boots with pairs of socks and a thick sweatshirt were better choices.

After changing, I used the last of my magical reserve to scan my house one more time. Still nothing as in no "nothing," and I hoped it would be the same when I exited later. Opening the safe, I stepped in and the stairs formed at my will. With less trepidation than before, I went down, closing the lid behind me. I didn't think the safe would let in any Larry, Moe, or Curly, but I didn't want to leave the lid open in invitation.

I descended into the plane, every step bringing a little more relief from the fear. I needed to name the plane because I was already sick of calling it "my plane." I sounded like I owned a private jet or read too many science fiction novels. If I had a blog, I could put up a Name My Plane Contest! Deval probably wouldn't like it, and I didn't have time to devote to a blog. Besides, only my mother would read it.

My feet hit the sandy gravel, and I couldn't help but think the air felt, dare I say, warm? I remembered that Deval mentioned the plane was sentient and would try and adjust for me. Perhaps he could create a lecture series for me: So You're Part Goblin? Life Tips and Lessons from Prince Dev. Lecture series made me suddenly think of my attacker, an involuntary shiver ran through my body. Pushing that thought from my mind, I walked over to the flat rock I'd begun to think of as my throne, again taking a cross-legged position on it.

I shifted, settling the box on my lap and reached for my magic. It roared through me with the plane boosting what I already had. I poured my magic into the box, hoping to spend five minutes inundating it before getting back to hunting down Grant. At two minutes, my eyes widened when the thorn turned green and made a little click as if giving me the go ahead. Without thinking too much, I pricked my finger on the thorn. This time, a glowing pattern emerged on the box and a second distinct click sounded as the wood folded back on itself leaving the box open before me.

Inside lay a simple journal. I was not sure what I'd expected, but a journal felt a little anti-climactic. Nevertheless, I snatched it out, paranoid the blood box might realize its mistake and snap shut. Setting it to the side, I held up the now empty box. I pondered the relative ease with which the task had been accomplished. Did the planes act like magical amplifiers for everyone? I didn't think Lola would volunteer to be my guinea pig, even if her family invested in a separate safe for her.

Placing the empty box aside, I lifted the journal and opened it. I flipped though the pages noting that Violet had started writing it in her college years. I flipped to the final page and saw the date was two days prior to her death. I inhaled sharply. Temptation gnawed to read the final entry straight away, but my elementary school librarian taught me no good came from reading the end without getting the whole story, so I started at the beginning.

The first bit of the journal carried no surprises; in fact much of the journal reaffirmed what I already suspected. Maybe I wasn't as bad at this Fortune thing as I feared. Violet was a sporadic journal writer at best.

> *Mom was so worried when I moved three hours away.*
> *"Don't trust humans," she warned me over and over*
> *again. My best friend Ivy is human, so I don't under-*
> *stand what Mom's deal is. Jessica is introducing me to*
> *everyone, and we're having the best time. We even*
> *manage to study a bit. Sometimes I worry that people*
> *like me because I'm a novelty. They've never hung out*
> *with a witch before, but I think I REALLY fit in!*

She continued in that vein for a few entries even proclaiming that Jessica was her new best friend. I rolled my eyes at that one. Just like Jessica and Ronnie had said there were quite a few boys mentioned, Violet being a typical college girl, letting loose. After the revolving boy period, there was a lull in the journal. When it picked back up, Violet went from a happy carefree girl, to one who felt completely ostracized.

> *I don't think I can handle this. Everything my mom said was*
> *right. I have no friends. I can't go anywhere without*
> *being tormented. They've put things, horrible things*
> *outside my door. I started crying when I saw the pile of*
> *wood and pictures of burning witches.*

> *Everyone on my floor stood outside their doors and watched me crying. They laughed at me. I know it's weak, but I can't take this. I would be better off if I wasn't here. I should drop out...if this is what the world is really like I'm not sure I even want to keep trying.*

My chest tightened. I had never had it that bad, but I knew discrimination happened all the time. Tears pricked at my eyes just thinking about the pain and humiliation.

Even worse, she thought she had found a brief haven in her T.A., who told her everyone else was being ridiculous, and that it was a wonderful thing to be a witch. Once again, she fell for the "you're different and therefore interesting" crap. It was painful to read because it was an exact repetition of her previous experience. Right after he got her into bed, he callously told her he had always wanted to fuck a witch but couldn't date students, let alone freaks.

> *He called me a "witch bitch."*

He still really loved that phrase. Violet's pain was evident in the tearstains dotting the journal, with the heartbreak and fury etched in the words. The whole shitty situation set Violet up to view meeting a vampire as a good thing. I could almost understand.

> *I met Fane last night. Yes, the Fane, world famous vampire king! Every warning I ever heard was a lie. I can look*

*him straight in the eye and feel nothing. I mean other
than lust. He is the most handsome man I have ever met.
Even better, he loves that I'm a witch. He loves that he
can't turn me into a love-sick puppy. Why did I even try
with humans?*

He found her when she was at her most vulnerable. If
her classmates found her being a witch novel, I could
only imagine Fane thought of his new glamour-resistant
pet. His attention meant Violet's suicidal entries stopped.
This was the only positive side effect of their
"friendship."

He encouraged her to bring some of her old tormentors for *dinner* and even to curse her old TA. Thankfully no
one was killed, but she enjoyed watching her tormentors
become the tormented, even if they didn't remember it the
next day. It was a private pleasure for her when she saw
them at school. She mentioned how she always wore a
secret smile on her face. Picturing that smile, I shivered.
The tears that previously stung at my eyes dried up.

The more sinister entries continued until Violet's
mother became ill. Her mother didn't approve of her new
associations. To keep the peace, Violet managed to make a
clean break. Apparently Fane was okay with it because he
had a new witch to play with. I had no doubt if Violet
hadn't returned with a business proposition, Fane would
have eventually tracked her down. Vampires didn't let their
toys go without breaking them first.

I went from reading every detail to skimming. I wanted
to know which curse Violet had used. It wasn't until an
entry near the end that my heart tightened. What was it
that Deval had said earlier today and Alice before him?

Magic evolved? And that was exactly what happened to Violet's curse.

> *I don't know what to do. How can I protect myself from someone I can't see? The curse shouldn't have made him invisible to me, and it didn't initially. When Fane told me to curse him so he was invisible to women, I thought it was inspired. Since Fane is a narcissist, I thought he'd know the best way to punish another narcissist.*

> *What I hadn't planned on was the ass not being willing to apologize. There's no doubt he treated me horribly, so if he wanted to be free from the curse, why not apologize? How was I to know his father raised him to believe that all witches were, to quote the ass, "Satan's whores"? Regardless, I cannot see him anymore.*

> *I think he's been in my house. I can't protect myself. My magic can't even sense him. I only know he's there because of his notes. Even worse, I think he's been talking to Imogen. She thinks he's the ghost of her dead fiancé. I need to go see Pammy. I can't live like this. I should send Imogen away, but what if he follows and hurts her?*

The journal ended there. Maybe I should have skipped to the end after all. I shivered and stared down at my fingers grasping the journal. They were white, bloodless. Much like Violet, I wondered how to stop someone I couldn't see. Thoughts tumbled and twirled, until it hit me. The curse's focus was on women. The million dollar question now was:

could men see him? I amended my to-do list. First, find Imogen, second, talk to Pammy, and gods help me third, I needed another conversation with Fane.

I emerged from my plane feeling like I had gotten twelve hours of sleep and drank a Big Gulp-sized coffee—which was good because I wasn't sure if I'd be sleeping until I found Grant and put him in the early grave he deserved. Where some might think Violet deserved her grisly end, having cursed Grant first, I saw it differently. She'd offered to lift the curse. He was the stubborn ass who'd refused.

What humans didn't realize was the initial curse placed by Bridget Bishop on witches centuries ago, was two-fold. She meant to punish the humans as well but left a loophole. In order to lift a curse, the human needed to apologize to the witch who set the curse in place. Sometimes it was fair, but too many times it was like having rape victims apologize to their attacker for brutalizing them. If humans didn't still fear us, we would see a resurgence of The Trials. So far our luck was holding; although if you watched the news, you might expect the inevitable.

At the top of the stairs, I used my newly recharged magical batteries to scan my house, happy to find no sign of "nothing." I wasn't comfortable showering in my house just yet, but a new shirt was necessary. I changed quickly, not enjoying the momentary blindness caused by taking the shirt off and putting a new one on over my head. New shirt in place, I grabbed my purse and left.

I plugged my phone into my car charger, the battery dangerously low after not being charged since yesterday. With the journal tucked safely in my purse, I was on my way to see Pammy. I called Ivy, who didn't answer. I left a message hoping she was screening her calls and not outright avoiding me.

Pulling into Bump and Grind, I saw that Pammy's old white Ford Taurus was not sitting in its usual spot. *Please don't be off courting another fortune over tequila.* Maybe one of her groupies was chauffeuring her around. I went in, and Pammy and her court were nowhere to be seen. It was kind of surreal because I had never come here in the afternoon without finding her here. A childish part of me was tempted to go claim her seat on the couch, but I didn't really have time to give into stupid impulses. I did however have time to get coffee. I ordered an extra-large iced mocha to go and went back out to my Jeep, drink in hand.

In the parking lot, I called Pammy. She answered on the first ring. "What's going on, sugar?"

"I'm at Bump and Grind. Where are you?"

"Oh good lord, can't a woman take one day to have a nice afternoon at home without every witch and wannabe in the state calling her asking where the hell she is?"

"Sure," I agreed. "You've just sort of set a precedent."

Pammy grunted in the phone.

"I know who the killer is. Catching him, however, may be a problem."

"It's always hard to get the bastards, but you're half way there. Come to my house."

Pulling the phone away, I stared at it for a moment. I had never been to Pammy's house. Putting the phone back to my ear, I scrambled to find a pen and an old receipt to write down the address she as she rambled it off.

It was only a few miles away, and I made good time. Parking on the street in front of the newer stuccoed home with desert landscaping, I could see Pammy standing out front in a voluminous black caftan, her braids artfully secured in a head scarf, waiting. She didn't invite me inside, but rather led me around back to a patio. Thank gods the chill that had invaded my body for days had all but dissipated because it was a little chilly.

Pammy didn't explain not inviting me into her house. She didn't need to. Some old school witches guarded their homes fervently. They didn't want other witches to take personal items to be used against them later or let anyone read the house's energy to see what kind of magic was performed there. The temptation to get a read on the house flirted with me. I could probably pull it off, even from the backyard, but I wasn't sure if Pammy's talent felt when magic was being worked. It would be rude, being invited to the house was an honor, even if I wasn't going to be let in.

"So, kid, who done it?"

I took a sip of my mocha before answering. "An old boyfriend, Grant Vonn. He was a T.A. who threw Violet to the curb after she slept with him. He seems to have pretty strong prejudice against witches."

"I would, too, if I was human and cursed."

Taking Violet's journal out of my purse, I handed it to her. "Definitely, but what from what I read, Grant had strong feelings prior to sleeping with Violet. I believe 'Satan's whore' is what Violet said he called her. He wanted to experience the novelty of sleeping with a witch."

Pammy winced as she took the journal from me. She studied the innocent looking blue book, running her hand along the spine. "Sounds like the fucker had it coming then."

I nodded. "Yeah, but the bad news is, the curse evolved."

Her brow creased, and her already husky voice lowered a notch. "What do you mean evolved?"

"She cursed him to be invisible to women, but initially she could still see him."

"Makes sense, given she should be able to see through her own magic."

"Yeah, well, he wouldn't apologize."

"Idiot." She snorted.

"Mmhmm, the magic evolved to the point where she couldn't see him, magically or otherwise. Neither can I."

She leaned forward in her chair. "What do you mean, you can't?"

I told her about the attack the night before, leaving out the part where I retreated to a goblin plane. Substituting that I managed to run out my door and met with Deval and a healer.

"Who's their healer, these days?" Her question was too casual.

Not liking her tone didn't change the fact I couldn't answer her if I wanted to, given the fact that I was knocked out. She obviously wanted the inside scoop on the goblin's witch. I embellished my answer with a simple solution for not knowing. "I was blindfolded. I couldn't see who the witch was."

"Well, those fuckers sure do like their secrets," she replied, buying it. "What did her magic feel like?"

"Painful," I lied without blinking an eye.

"Too bad," she muttered, obviously bothered by the fact she wasn't privy to every witch-related secret in her state. Since she had more than her fair share, she'd survive not getting the goblins' as well.

"The question now is, can men see him?" I steered us back on the right trail.

She studied me. "They could originally?"

"Yes."

"Then they should, but with the way it evolved, we can't be sure."

The word evolution brought my thoughts back to Fane. He liked games, and my gut told me that he may have left out a few key pieces of information. "I think the vampires would know."

She nodded. "You're probably right. Looks like you need another meeting, but I'm coming along this time."

My stomach turned. It was not what I wanted to here. "Huh?"

"I know your aunt's history. You're tempting to them. I want to make sure they know you're not without allies."

Color me surprised. "I didn't know you cared."

"Of course I care, even more so now so that those fuckers know I'm still in charge here."

Ah, that made more sense.

Before I could comment, she wedged her phone to her ear. "Fane, it's Pammy. We need a meet." A mean little smile bloomed. "Ah now, sugar, I'm not coming to your territory. Gives you fellas the wrong idea. Bump and Grind in an hour. See you then." She hung up and nodded to me.

"Why are they willing to come to your territory if you're not willing to go to their's?" I wondered out loud before I could stop myself.

Pammy didn't miss a beat. "The fuckers think their dicks are too big to get caught in a witch trap."

"Well, all right then." I nodded.

"Still got that collar?"

"Not on me," I admitted.

"No time to go get it. In the future, you should have a gear bag ready in your car."

I nodded. "Do you have one?"

"Nope, I usually have one available if a Fortune needs

223

it, but I haven't replaced the one I gave you. I don't wear one anyway. They'd view it as a weakness."

My fingers trembled as the sudden desire to slap Pammy overtook me. I clenched my fist instead. "But you sent me into their den wearing one."

"Now, Sug, I didn't send you anywhere. You went as part of your job. You're a Fortune, so no need for politicking. They can think you're weak all they want, and you can have one less vulnerable spot. I, however, need to worry about politics, so I don't give them an excuse to think I'm weak, lest I have them trying to take over my territory."

"Vampires can't be in charge of Fortunes. We'd never allow it."

"Oh, you would if there was no other choice, or you were glamoured, at least until some other witches came in to reclaim the territory. It's happened before."

"Really?" My hands became clammy with just my thinking about it.

"Yup, don't worry, it happened in Utah but only lasted a week before I went in, kicked some ass, and set up a new sheriff."

Strange I'd never heard about this before.

"Of course we lost a few witches in the fray, but it's to be expected."

Now it made sense because she wouldn't want to advertise anyone had been killed on the expedition. Witches looked to her as a protector, not a general. In truth, she needed to be both. I didn't want her job. "I wish our ancestors had wiped them out before we became susceptible to glamour and became mortal."

"You and me both." She nodded vigorously. "They're vicious, hard to kill, and excellent fighters. Still, witches need to understand that we must still stand up for ourselves, even if we can't outright war with them like before."

I nodded in agreement. I didn't want to go to war with vampires, but I could see the likelihood of it. Hopefully, it never came to that. I wished I was braver, but I wasn't.

She stood up then. "Time to get, girl. We need to be there first to make sure no other witches are around."

"You don't want any extra back up?" I frowned.

"Nope, this should be fairly straight forward and civil. I don't want to expose any of my people as future targets."

"Great, just the two of us," I muttered.

"You're already a target thanks to your family's history, living in your aunt's old house, and the fact that you're a Fortune."

"I knew that. I just don't like to dwell on it."

"Hmmph, you don't need to dwell: you just need to be aware." She marched back along the trail at her usual no nonsense pace.

I lengthened my stride to follow. "Oh, I'm plenty aware now."

"Good, now come on, girl. We don't have all day." She gestured for me to pick up my pace. I did.

We took separate cars and arrived at Bump and Grind a half an hour before the scheduled meet. Only one witch lingered in the coffee shop. The others must have gotten the memo that Pammy was having some "me time" when she hadn't appeared earlier in the day. Pammy was brusque with the woman, but as soon as she mentioned vampires, the proverbial fire was lit under the woman's ass, and she rushed to get out of the door.

With nothing left to do but wait, we ordered coffee concoctions and went to sit at Pammy's usual spot. I started to sit in the usual armchair across from her, but she gestured me to a position beside her on the sofa.

"We need to show a united front. You don't want them coming up on your back."

It was reassuring that Pammy was more concerned with my neck, than with seated power plays. It gave me warm fuzzies, until the bell above the door jingled and in strode Fane, with two vampires flanking him. They didn't bother with coffee and headed straight to us.

Fane folded his large body into the armchair and his two friends stood behind him on either side. I recognized one of them as Mr. VIP from the Poppy Den. He didn't say anything, just stared straight ahead like the minion he was. His jaw tight with annoyance. Something told me he'd attack Fane in a hot minute, if he had an opening. For now, the little sidelong glances meant he was biding his time.

Fane crossed his legs and leaned back, his arms draping casually over the armrests. "Ladies, I don't normally like being summoned, but with the promise of two such lovely creatures, I couldn't resist."

"Flattery is not necessary, Fane. The only way you'd ever get a taste of me is from my cold corpse. I know you prefer something a bit warmer." Pammy's gaze fell firmly on Fane's nose. It was still pretty badass.

"Oh, Pammy, don't you worry, I have a microwave, and for your blood I'm okay with reheated."

"You always say the sweetest things, but as that day is not going to be today. Let's move on to the subject at hand." Her voice held no worry. I looked over, and her face remained smooth and relaxed. Pammy was my new hero.

"The day is still young; you never know what kind of meal I might have tonight."

"I know you like to play with your food, but we both know that this is bluster. Peg is charged. I'm charged. You wouldn't stand a chance. If, for some reason, you were able to kill us, what do you think the goblins would do to you?

Peg here is quite cozy with their prince and investigating on his behalf. His mother would be very put out if you upset her boy."

"You ladies seem to keep hiding behind the goblins." He leaned back into the armchair steepling his fingers. "Have old alliances been renewed? I haven't received any declarations."

"No, we're still flying solo, but while Peg is friendly with them, I'd think twice, if I were you." Pammy shrugged.

Pammy was lying through her teeth but managed to brush uncomfortably close to the truth. Deval didn't have any interest in me romantically, but I wondered what my goblin heritage would mean if the vampires killed or hurt me, even after our working relationship was over. I needed to ask Deval, but it felt presumptuous. Would any protection extend to my family? Things to ponder later. I didn't mind letting Pammy run lead because she was, after all, my boss. But I wanted to get this show on the road. "You knew about the curse on Grant Vonn. I need to know if you can see him."

Fane's attention snapped to me, his arctic stare making me wish that I had kept my mouth shut. Still, I held my gaze directly in the middle of his forehead, trying to mimic Pammy's stare.

"The young T.A. I'd nearly forgotten about him."

"How could you have forgotten about him? Why didn't you bring him up when I came into the Poppy Den?"

Pammy leaned back into the couch cushions, letting me take lead with a false nonchalance. A little buzz of electricity popped in the air. If Fane made good on his threats, she was primed for an attack.

"Silly girl, we're not on the same team. Yes, I was fond of Violet. Her blood was exquisite, although I expect yours would be even better. A great insult was placed against us at her murder, and we will take care of it our own way."

"Why didn't you say so?" I asked sarcastically.

Pammy didn't move, but she got back in the swing of the conversation. "She may have been your blood whore, but she was still a witch. We take care of our own, even when they're led astray."

That wasn't entirely true, but Pammy needed to maintain a strong stance.

"Ladies, it's been fun, but I'm feeling peckish. Since you two aren't yet willing to make the offer, I must go to one of the other lovely witches at my beck and call. Good luck finding a man you cannot see. We do not have such a problem. Also, thank you for confirming the curse has held, even after Violet's death." Fane stood up abruptly and headed toward the door, his men following behind him. Once there, he stopped and turned back to us, giving a little finger wave before blowing us a kiss. The gesture was ridiculous but still sent a shiver down my spine.

When the door closed behind them, my muscles turned to jelly and I sunk into the couch.

"Who knew the sociopaths would be so sentimental?" Pammy muttered.

"If they planned on killing Grant anyway, why didn't they say that when I went to the Poppy Den?"

"They like games, Sug. Besides, as much as I want to let them take out the trash, there is still the question of how he stole the chest from the goblins. The goblins are neutral for now, but I don't think their prince will be very happy if he's cut off from the answers as to how the hell that happened."

"Him or his mother."

"Nope, the queen wouldn't like having justice taken from her. We already planned on executing him ourselves since murder trumps theft. But you still need to find out how he got in the goblin's house to steal the safe. Nobody should know where their actual homes are. And no, the high rise he took you to last night doesn't count."

My eyebrows raised. "How did you know it was a high rise?"

"I didn't, you confirmed it. This information is harmless, but you need to learn to watch your responses and reactions."

"Too bad there's not a Fortune boot camp."

"There is actually. It's run freelance and costs a mint, but after you get a few paychecks under your belt, it wouldn't hurt to look into it," she told me helpfully.

"That might have been good information to have before I started working for you."

"You didn't ask, and you can't afford it yet. No need to worry about professional development until you're all in anyway. Though I can see you're getting there, which is why I brought it up."

Before I could respond, my phone went off. Ivy's name popped up on my screen. I looked at Pammy and stood, grabbing my purse. "I need to get moving. I'll keep you updated."

Walking toward the door, I heard her call from behind me, "You better, Sug, and make sure to be careful."

I turned back and gave her a quick nod before walking out the door. Accepting the call, I lifted the phone to my ear.

16

I vy didn't say hello. "Peg, Imogen called. She needs to see you."

"Perfect, I need to see her too." The universe was suddenly on my side again.

"It was weird. She called right after I'd gotten your message. I'm worried she's on something. She keeps talking about murder and ghosts."

"Sounds like she's had rough time of it." I fumbled with my keys to open the Jeep's door, finally getting it open and climbing in. Silence met my comment. Pulling the phone away from my ear, I checked the screen. The call wasn't dropped. I placed it back to my ear. "Ivy, you still there?"

Another brief moment of silence, then Ivy cleared her throat. "Yeah sorry, I expected you to tell me she was being crazy. Not about the murders, but about the ghosts. Good Lord, now I have to worry about ghosts?" She ended the sentence on a decidedly shrill note.

I sighed. "I never said there was such a thing as murdering ghosts."

"I didn't say murdering ghosts. I said regular ghosts. There are murdering ghosts?" If her voice went any higher my windshield would be a goner.

"Ivy, pull it together. I did not say that there were ghosts, let alone murdering ghosts."

"But you're not saying there's not," she accused.

"I will tell you that I've never encountered one."

Apparently I'd given the right answer. "Well, good then. I told Imogen she should speak to you. I thought I'd have to push the issue, but she was downright eager, if nervous, to meet up with a Fortune."

"Great, when and where did she want to meet? Please tell me she's still in the Phoenix area."

"She is. She wants to meet at the old McDonald's off Main Street in Mesa. I think she can be there in half an hour."

"I can do that."

"Just keep my baby sister safe." She hung up.

I can't even keep myself safe, doubt whispered in my ear.

Ideally the meeting would have been in private so we could speak more openly, but Imogen sounded a bit skittish. With the new intel on Grant, it might be safer in a more public place, so there had been no point in arguing. I ended up at a rundown McDonald's on Main Street that had yet to receive a corporate face-lift. The fast food outlet was fairly busy, and the shrieks of small children playing in the ball pit rang through the air. I waited in line and got a large diet soda before taking over a booth as far away from the playground and the other patrons as possible.

The minute she walked in, I recognized her. She looked a lot like Ivy, with her long dark hair and tanned skin. She was wearing a pair of sunglasses. Hopefully, she wore them because of the sun and not because she thought they were a good disguise. She turned her head scanning the restaurant. I gave her a little wave. She tensed, probably taken aback that I easily recognized her. She came to the booth with obvious reluctance, practically dragging her feet. Sitting on the very edge of the bench seat, she was ready to run at a moment's notice.

"Hi there, my name is Peg. I'm guessing you're Imogen?"

The girl took a deep breath before answering, "Yeah, Ivy said you might be able to help me."

"I can certainly try. Do you want to tell me what's going on?"

She took another shuddering breath. "You'll probably think I'm crazy, but there's a ghost following me."

My gut told me I knew who her ghost was. I pointed to myself. "Witch here. It takes a lot for me to think you're crazy."

Her shoulders relaxed. "I was staying with Violet after my fiancé died."

"Your sister mentioned that. I'm sorry for your loss."

She nodded sharply. She tipped her head back, but I saw the trembling lip, and a tear escaped past her sunglasses, which she hastily wiped away. "It was really hard; we'd been together since high school. I needed to get out of Tucson when it happened. Ivy suggested going to stay with Violet for a bit. She wasn't as close with us as she was when we were younger, but we still thought of her as family. So, I called her up. She told me that I could stay with her. I came up, you know, to get away from all of the reminders. It was like suddenly every place I went held a memory of Zack. He was everywhere."

I nodded sympathetically. "I understand."

"It was great, at first. It was like I could pretend it had never happened. I stayed with Violet and went about my business. I had a little bit of money saved up, and Violet didn't charge me anything for rent, so I hung out with friends who were going to ASU. About a week in, Zack came to me."

"What do you mean Zack came to you?" I prodded.

"He spoke to me."

"Where did this happen?"

"In the room I was staying in at Violet's. He came to me and told me he was sorry he had left me and that he was trying to get back to me."

"What did you say to this?" I tried for patience.

"I know it's stupid. The dead can't come back, but here I was, living with a witch, and I started to think it might be possible. At first he was sweet, but different." She stopped talking, twisting a napkin into a crumpled mess.

"Different how?" I prompted.

"His voice was different, but he said it was from crossing over, that it changed him a little, made him a little wiser."

A decent cover story to tell a naive young woman.

"At first it was nice to have Zack back. Then he told me Violet had cursed his motorcycle, causing the accident. He wanted me to watch her. Said she could bring him back, but I couldn't say anything to her. He said she would kill me."

That story should have been a hard sell even for a grieving young woman. "Did he say why Violet would have killed him?"

"He said she was bitter and jealous of our love. In retrospect, that seems kinda silly. I mean, she knew about us from some emails we exchanged. We were friends on Facebook, she saw pictures of us, but she never even met him. Still, I believed him. I started watching her and I suddenly saw how guarded she was. Then there were these patients who came by the house. Some of the men were scary. When they came by, she told me to stay in my room, but I peeked. The ghost said they were part of an evil coven that preyed on the weak, that they stole people's blood under the guise of lab work, to cast evil curses on them."

I worked hard to keep my face sympathetic despite my annoyance at the evil witch doctor stereotype. "Okay, what did he want you to do about it?"

"He said he couldn't watch her all the time and wanted to know when the men came to see her or if I saw anything strange. I told him every time there was a man in the house. Once I started paying attention, I realized they kept a regular schedule. He also told me to look out for anything that she was hiding, so we could blackmail her with it."

"Did you find anything?"

"Just the puzzle box I gave Ivy. She said she'd given it to you."

"Did you know its contents?"

She shook her head. "No I just found it hidden under her bed one night when I was snooping. I couldn't open it." She didn't realize it was magically activated.

"Were you there the night Violet was killed?"

Imogen hung her head down, her long dark hair sheltering her face. "I had gone to stay with another friend for a few days. Zack didn't like that, but I was scared. I decided to go back one more time and, I don't know, spy on Violet? I thought about confronting her. Zack convinced me that Violet was evil, but after he started acting strange, I began to wonder if he was who he said he was. I parked really far away from Violet's and was walking toward her house, but then someone called out to me and chased me. It freaked me out.

Wonderful, I was the great intimidator. "Sorry, Imogen, that was me. I saw you and thought you might have known Violet."

She let out a shuddering breath. "Well, I did know her, and for all I know, I got her killed. I went and hid at a friend's house, but I should have known a ghost would be able to find me." She straightened from her slumped position taking off the sunglasses. They weren't meant as a disguise, they were hiding an angry shiner. The deep-purple coloring her eye spread out into yellows, blues, and greens on her cheekbone. A veritable rainbow of pain.

I hissed in a breath. "Yikes."

"Yeah, but I got away. He was so caring, until I said we should go to the witch sheriff. Violet hadn't always been evil, and if she was up to no good, the other witches could help, and they would punish her. I didn't know what he thought a human or a ghost could do. When I insisted it was the right thing to do, he got really angry and hit me. I left, intending to go to the witches, but the only witch I knew was Violet. I didn't know who or what to believe at that point. I hid until Ivy called and told me Violet was dead. She asked me what the hell was going on. I don't know, but I didn't know what to do. I even went to church and asked a priest about exorcism. He thought I was crazy and suggested I speak with a professional psychologist."

"Have you heard the ghost since you left Violet's?"

"I just told you, he finds me. I was couch surfing at a friend's when he woke me up this morning. He said he was sorry, but I needed to help him complete his mission so he could come back to me. I already knew he wasn't Zack, but I pretended to agree with him. I'm just glad I didn't give him the box."

"What did he want you to do?"

"He wanted me to find you."

I stiffened in my seat, my magic rushing to my palms as I used it to scan the room. It wasn't until I pushed my magic out to the parking lot and not finding any signs of an invisible aura, that I relaxed slightly. "You decided to lead him right to me?" My voice was low.

She flinched. "No, I left where I was staying and called Ivy as soon as I could. It was weird that she told me to talk to you; it's like all connected."

"Okay, well, now you know I'm a witch, and that I work for the sheriff, I can tell you we're already looking into Violet's death. We know about your ghost, but he's not a ghost. He's just a man."

She shook her head. "No, I can't see him at all."

"He was the victim of a curse that makes him invisible to women. Currently, we're looking for him, and we intend to find him. In the meantime, please tell me you have some male friends, or have the means to go home and stay with your father."

She nodded. "Yeah, I have enough money to get back to Tucson. My dad would be happy if I stayed with him."

"Good, now were you supposed to meet with the ghost once you found me?"

"He told me to call a number. I thought it was odd with him being a ghost and all, but he said he could listen to a message if I left one, and then he would come to me."

"Can you give me the number?"

"Of course." She pulled out her phone and a pen, and then wrote the number down on a napkin.

"Perfect. Now, can you call the number and leave a message telling him to meet you at Violet's house at seven tonight?"

Her lip quivered slightly as though Grant could hurt

through the phone, but she did as I asked and called the number and left a message. Her voice shook a little, and I hoped Grant would think it was nerves versus fact that he was being set up. She ended the call and powered her phone off before standing. "Thank you for helping me. I know Fortunes don't usually help humans."

I stood as well and placed a hand on her shoulder. "Sweetie, if you're ever dealing with this kind of issue you can call us. We don't care if you're human or witch; we want to keep the peace." Pulling my hand back, I reached into my purse and took out one of my cards. "You can call me whenever you want. If you're ever in danger and can't reach me, call Bump and Grind in Tempe and ask for Pammy. She's the witch sheriff."

Imogen gave me a watery smile. "Thanks, I knew Pammy was the witch sheriff. I just didn't know how to reach her."

I gave her shoulder another reassuring squeeze. "Promise me you'll head straight to your father's."

"I will, as soon as I stop by a gas station."

"Good, call me if you have any more problems."

She nodded again and put her sunglasses back on before walking out of the fast food restaurant. When a toddler let out an excited shriek near her, she jumped a little. Good, hyper-awareness would keep her alive.

As she walked to her car, I did another aura scan, pushing it in her direction until she was safely inside, engine running. Nothing out of the ordinary. I let out a long breath. I didn't envy her explaining the situation to her family, given its fantastical nature. Hopefully being raised with Violet as a close friend would make it easier. Either way, my gut told me she would be safe in her father's house.

I hit the soda machine for a refill before leaving and

getting into my car and making my next call. Unfortunately, I wasn't able to get ahold of Deval. I left a message. "I don't know why you want updates if you're not even going to bother to pick up your phone when I do call you."

Since it was already six, I didn't have time to wait for Deval, so I called Bruce. If anyone would be able to subdue a murderer, he would.

He was kind enough to answer on the second ring. "Peggy girl!"

"Never call me Peggy."

"Oh, come on, it's cute."

"When I hear Peggy, I see red bouffant hair, stiletto sling backs, and tight leopard print lycra."

"Peg Bundy is a TV legend."

A moment of realization washed over me. "Oh dear gods, you're right. She went by Peg, not Peggy."

"Does that make "Peggy" okay?"

"No, for some reason, it doesn't."

"I still think it's cute."

"Whatever, still not an approved nickname." I said firmly. "More to the point, I need your help, and it could get ugly."

"Uglier than the time Lola had too many Jell-O shots, decided to dance on a bar, and fell off, nearly breaking her neck?"

"Well, this time you won't be fighting off ten drunk guys upset you're taking away their entertainment. But if it goes right, you'll get to beat down one man who wants me dead."

"Oh, honey, that sounds like a fun night, but don't tell me the big bad Fortune can't fight off one measly human."

"If only it were that easy," I muttered.

17

---

 ruce parked next to me around the corner from
Violet's, and we headed to the house. I had been
smart enough to put Violet's keys on my key ring, so I
didn't have to crawl through a pet door this time. There
were some gouge marks around the doorframe that hadn't
been there before. It didn't make me too nervous since
Grant had been getting in and out of Violet's home for a
while without a crowbar. Given Violet's home business, I
had a good idea who had entered the house.

We entered the house quietly, and I headed straight to
the lab. As I suspected, the medical equipment was gone.
The vampires had reclaimed their property. Good, it
meant I no longer needed to worry about another witch
stumbling on the lab and tarnishing Violet's memory.
Though the more I investigated her, the less likely that
appeared to be a possibility. Violet didn't seem to have any
witch friends.

I pushed my magic through the house and found no
issues. "He's not here," I turned to Bruce.

"Might as well take a load off," Bruce advised, heading

back toward the living room where there was a good view of the front door. We would hear if the back door opened. The blinds were closed. We sat on the couch. Bruce sprawled while I perched, nervous and ready. Sitting on the hard cushion, I winced and shared a knowing look with Bruce.

"I will never understand why people choose style over comfort," he mumbled.

"You're preaching to the choir, sugar bear."

"Sugar bear, haha."

We both fell quiet then, not wanting to startle our prey with a masculine voice. After a while sitting on a hard surface would make your ass go numb. We spent time shifting uncomfortably before I stood up and quietly paced behind the sofa. Bruce stubbornly maintained his lounge position. Silence made time stretch, but we somehow managed to remain quiet, aware of every creak and groan the house made. After what felt like an eternity, I checked my phone and saw that it was an hour past seven. "Damn it, he's not coming."

"Do you think he was watching the house?"

"Must have been, that's the only explanation I can think of."

"Thems is the breaks, kid." Bruce finally stood, lifting his arms over his head, and twisting his back from side to side, it audibly cracked.

"You should have stood earlier."

"Nope, I'm way too macho to complain about a hard sofa."

"You just did, an hour ago," I pointed out. "What you are is too stubborn to live."

"And yet I will live on and on," he joked.

"That you will my friend, that you will. Any chance you could walk a vulnerable young lady to her car, kind sir?"

"Vulnerable my ass, but it would be my honor, young lady."

We left together, Bruce watching my back while I locked the door. He walked me to my car and went around the vehicle, looking inside and out to make sure I didn't have a secret passenger. He nodded, giving me the all clear. I opened the door and got in, rolling down the window.

Bruce leaned against the Jeep. "Well, lady, what are you going to do now? I don't like the idea of you going home alone."

My nostrils flared. My inner feminist chafed against the sudden restrictions placed upon me. That gave me an idea though, maybe a way to take back my power. "I'm not going home. I'm going to go ask Alice."

His mouth quirked at my reference. "That woman may be a nut, but she's a smart nut. What are you going to ask her?"

"How to break a curse that survives post mortem."

Bruce chuckled, the sound rumbling deep from his chest. "That would be a challenge even for her, but I wish you luck. If you need company later, to keep the bad guys away, give me a call."

"I appreciate that." I grabbed his hand. "You're a good friend. I hope one day you'll take me to doctor's appointments and call me grandma."

He smiled back, but I saw sadness flash over his eyes. The curse hadn't just hurt the witches, but their friends, too. Until this week I hadn't realized it would be hard for the other races. But with Deval telling me the problems for goblin and witch offspring, and seeing Bruce worrying over my mortality, I understood that it affected everyone.

Bruce pushed past the melancholy and grinned wider. "I'm gonna call you Grandma Peggy."

"Oh, good gods." I rolled my eyes.

I turned on the Jeep, letting the vibrations of its rumbling engine seep into my bones. Pulling away from the curb, I saw Bruce watching me. He didn't get into his truck until I was all the way down the street.

I walked up to Alice's ruin and past the glamour. How she kept this a secret from the government was beyond me. Granted, plain-sight illusions were the best, but still...it was a pretty impressive feat. At the door, I forewent the bell pull and placed my hand on the door, the static pulsing of the powerful ward vibrating under my palm. I released a little of my magic, sending out the standard knock-knock. I didn't wait long. A second later the door opened by itself. I walked in, calling out a cautious, "Hello?"

"Peg, what brings you to my humble abode at this hour?" Her voice came from above me.

Looking to the left of the cavernous entry, I found her standing at the railing of the second-story landing. "I have some questions about a post mortem curse."

"Well, come on up then." She waved me toward the stairs.

At night, it was dark in the ruin. The only lighting flickered from actual candle chandeliers hanging from the ceiling forty feet above. Closing the door, I started up the stairs, the flat beams covered in a thick carpet. With every step I took, the ambiance settled like a shroud. The building had plenty of strange energy during the day, but the late hour magnified it. Alice stood at the top, her lavender hair tamed into some pink sponge rollers. She wore a fuchsia housecoat and honest to gods bunny slippers.

A grin broke across my face. "I like your slippers, Alice."

"Thank you, my dear. They seemed fitting."

Coming to the top of the landing, I was happy to see that her crystal-like gray eyes lacked any cloudiness. I sent up a small prayer of thanks to the gods that be. "Sorry about the late call, but I have a tough one and thought you might know the answer."

"Don't concern yourself, dear. I prefer night to day. The dark brings with it a certain comfort that only hidden, secret things can, and I always love a visitor."

I laughed. "You sound like a character in an old gothic novel."

"My dear, I live in a ruin, I am a little mad on top of it, so I am a caricature of a gothic novel protagonist. Or could I be the antagonist?" She wiggled her eyebrows.

"I suppose it depends on your perspective," I said, smiling. "Better than being the misunderstood monster though."

"That we can agree on. Dr. Frankenstein was a villain, that poor creature."

I nodded my head in agreement.

"What was this question you had about post mortem curses?"

That snapped my back to attention. "Why do they happen? And what can I do to break them?"

"Come sit by the fire. We can discuss theories, and I can tell you what your best chances are."

I followed to the little alcove we met in the last time I visited and sat in the chair next to hers.

"Now for your first question, I know the answer, but I can't give you a direct answer."

"Can't or won't?"

"Since it falls into the realm of self-preservation, I'm going to say both. I would if I could, but the answer wouldn't necessarily help you anyway. On to question two, what was the curse, who cursed whom, and why does it need to be lifted?"

I explained the circumstances behind Violet's death while Alice listened quietly, nodding occasionally.

When I finished explaining, she said, "Well, that's a tough one."

"Tough, how?"

"The theory is, that the dead decide whether to let a curse fade with their death or not, and I can't see why Violet would let the curse fade."

"Because he's a murdering sociopath who can be brought to justice?"

"Punishment is subjective, and Violet doesn't need you to get justice."

Taken aback, I tensed in my seat. "What do you mean by that?"

"Don't get upset, lovey, it's obvious he feels likes he's being punished. Another Fortune, a male one, wouldn't need to break the curse to bring him to justice."

"You know that male witches are somewhat rare. There aren't any male Fortunes within the greater Phoenix area."

"But Pammy could bring one in. Don't want to split your bounty?" Her voice was light and not accusatory.

I bristled anyway. "To be honest, since I'm the one doing all the work, splitting a bounty or possibly losing it, doesn't seem fair, but if that's what you're saying needs to be done, then I'll call Pammy right now."

"It would be a smart choice, but money and smart are not mutually exclusive. As long as you have a male companion with you, it is still very possible that you can do this."

"The patriarchy is alive and well."

She let out a musical titter. "Oh dear, the old boys club will never die, but you're hardly that exposed to it. As you mentioned, male witches are a smidge on the scarce side. We're a matriarchy by default."

"There is power in numbers," I muttered.

"I do understand your conundrum, so I will give you a recipe for a spelled potion that may help you. But like I said, this is an 'if.' There are powers at play that only the scholars understand, and even then, it's very theoretical."

"Alice, you're a scholar. If you know the theory behind the spell, why won't you share it?" My hand flew out as if to underline my point.

"We're back to the first question, which is still in the realm of self-preservation. Besides, wisdom should be gained through study and life experience."

"Aren't scholarly conversations the essence of study and wisdom?" I argued.

"Nice try, but it would be more along the lines of half-assing it. If you want to study, I will be happy to teach, but I doubt you have the time to read a couple dozen books and write an essay." She leaned back in her chair and folded her arms.

"Yeah, not so much, this guy is a ticking time bomb. It's only a matter of time before he kills again. Honestly, I'm surprised he hasn't yet."

"That we can agree on; although he seems to be fixated on Violet, he obviously has issues with witches in general. Let me write this down for you. And, dear, I know you did all the work, but you should give Pammy the heads up that a male witch may be necessary. If this doesn't work, it may piss Grant off, and we can't count on goblins and shifters to fight our battles."

"Because that would make us appear weak?"

"Oh well, that is part of it. Pride is another factor," Alice said.

"Pride is for fools."

She ignored me and reached forward to open a drawer in her side table. She pulled out a note card and a pen and began methodically writing out instructions. We sat in silence, while I felt like a scolded puppy. She finished her writing with a pointed stab of her pen. "Yes, pride is for fools, but sometimes pride may be all you have left to hold onto. Pride is better than meekly accepting circumstances."

I swallowed, she was right, but it still felt foolish. "You're probably right; I've never felt meek in the presence of Deval or Bruce. I consider them allies, but I admit I don't want to step in it with them."

She looked up from the card her eyes lit up. "Bruce? I haven't seen that boy in twenty years. How is he?"

"Oh good, just playing Cowboy Casanova."

A dreamy look crossed Alice's eyes. "Yes, he was always good at that. Tell him to visit me sometime. It would be good to catch up, for old times' sake."

My cheeks flushed at knowing that Bruce had a history of fun with other witches decades before we met. It was an odd contradiction of the young, full-of-life guy I knew. But age was an illusion for some. "I will. I'm sure he'd love to see you."

"Perhaps, old arguments fade with time. At least they should." She passed me the note card.

I studied the ingredients. Except for one particular item, I had most on hand. Death ash, or bone of the witch who cursed. "This may be difficult to get."

"The death token is necessary, call BBTT."

"Is this a necromancy spell?"

"Don't be silly, child, of course it is."

"Are you saying that I can raise the dead? Why didn't

you tell me this was possible when we first met? I could have asked Violet a week ago who killed her."

"Oh my dear, what is possible and what is wise, are two different things. This will not raise Violet's shade, but it may allow you to loosen her ties on the living. This magic is gray at best and takes a very powerful witch. Pammy told me you have a lot of raw magic. You should be fine. If you want to learn the finer points of this craft, we can speak further at another date. Now, please do not share this spell with anyone. It is not good to play in gray areas. It disturbs the order of things and brings with it more problems."

I nodded, gripping the note card a little more tightly, somehow feeling privileged to be given the trust and responsibility to see this through. "Thank you, and, Alice, I would like to study with you, once this guy is brought to justice."

She sat forward, grabbing my free hand and giving it a squeeze. "My dear, it would be wonderful to have a student again." She released my hand.

I stood up giving her a shy smile, pleased at the attention she was giving me. "Thanks again, I'd better get going. I doubt that Grant will do us the favor of offing himself."

She laughed, nodding. "No, he doesn't seem the type, does he?" She pulled her large frame from the chair with some effort and enveloped me in a hug. She smelled like lavender and cinnamon, like some exotic cookie. This woman gave good hugs. Pulling away, she gave me a pat on the back. "Take care of yourself, young lady. I look forward to future adventures with you."

I nodded, reaching down to grab my purse sitting next to the chair, before heading down the stairs. At the front door I turned and gave Alice a wave as she stood at the landing on the top of the stairs. As I walked out the front door, the illusions and wards fell like a curtain behind me.

18

Back in the Jeep, I needed to make two calls. The first was to BBTT, where I learned the ashes had been released this morning to Pammy. My calls went up to three.

She answered on the third ring. "Catch him yet?"

"Nope." I explained the implications of the curse and asked if it was a thing to have another male Fortune on standby.

"Sure thing, Sug, but you're gonna have to give up a hundred bucks to have them travel up here. The closest guy I have is in Tombstone."

"Is there a need for a Fortune in Tombstone?"

"He doesn't do this full time and travels as needed when he's not working on his art."

"Okay, yes, I'll give up part of my fee." Saying the words hurt, but Alice was right.

"You said you need some of Violet's ashes?"

"About a quarter of a cup will do."

"Burnt down, there isn't much left, that's practically a quarter of a body. Wanna ask Dusty first?"

I thought about it for a second. It would be respectful, but I didn't want to burden him until I had good news. "I'm doing a curse to try to break your daughter's curse on her killer" conversation didn't sound like a great conversation. I made the asshole decision. "I'm okay with not asking him, if you are."

Pammy let out a throaty chuckle. It kind of creeped me out, given that I was used to her girlish giggle. "Sounds like someone is becoming more ruthless, good."

I wanted to contradict her, to tell her my reasoning, but it would sound feeble at best and defensive at worst. It didn't really matter what she thought of me. Maybe I'd get more jobs if she thought I was ruthless. "Can you drop it off to me, or do I need to come to you?"

"You planning on doing this spell tonight?"

Checking the time on my phone, I noted it was almost midnight. Yeah, I didn't think I could get a babysitter to watch over me this late. "No, I guess not. I'll work on it tomorrow."

"I'm heading down to Tucson tomorrow around eleven, I can drop it off on the way."

"Thanks, Pammy."

"No need for thanks. I'll call you when I'm on my way in the morning."

"Okay."

Originally, I had planned on calling Deval to have him come over while I worked on the potion. Seeing the time made me yawn in reaction. I should crash for a few hours. I wanted to see Cheddar but didn't feel up to inviting myself to spend the night at Deval's condo, so I called Bruce.

"Peggy girl."

"You're pushing it today," I said, more tired than annoyed.

"I'm all for pushing boundaries. Let me guess, you want to come over and spend the night?"

"Yes, please."

"Well, when a looker calls up and asks nicely to come over at this hour, how can I refuse?"

"So, you'll have the guest bed made up?"

"You're no fun."

I snorted into the phone because we both knew the idea of a physical relationship between us was laughable. The drive to Bruce's took thirty-five minutes. If there had been more than a handful of cars on the road, it would've taken longer. His ranch-style home sat on five acres in Queen Creek. He used to live on the reservation, and I was pretty sure he still owned his home there, but he moved to Queen Creek a decade prior, when some of the non-shifter kids noticed he wasn't aging. There were plenty of shifters in the tribe, but not all of the people knew about them. His plan was to live in Queen Creek another ten years and then either move back to the Res under a different name or move to another Arizona town for ten or twenty years.

He greeted me at the door with a toothbrush, a big T-shirt, and some boxers.

"My hero." I got on my tippy toes and gave him a kiss on the cheek.

He smiled. "You know the lay of the land. Make yourself comfortable."

I walked in, feeling at home. His place looked like a cowboy lived there, which was accurate. Saltillo tile, worn leather sofas, pictures of old West scenes. Out front he even had two old wagon wheels as porch decorations. As I passed the living room on my way toward the spare bathroom, Dolly and Cash, Bruce's Catahoula dogs, barely lifted their eyelids in acknowledgement of me as they rested on their dog beds. They had a sweet deal, and the dogs didn't feel the need to be as protective of their owner when said owner could shift into a bear.

In the bathroom, I got ready for bed. I called out goodnight to Bruce as I made it to the spare bedroom. He groggily responded. I guessed the old bear was tired, too. I tucked myself into a queen-sized pine bed with a worn red quilt. It wasn't a luxurious as the bed at Deval's, but it was plenty comfortable. I fell straight into a deep sleep.

There were worse things to wake up to than the smell of coffee and bacon. The only thing that could make it better would be a large ginger cat sleeping on my ribs. I stood and stretched, grabbing my previous day's clothes and taking them back to the spare bathroom. I brushed my teeth and splashed some water on my face. The curly mop on my head was too tangled to be brushed without looking like I stuck my finger in a socket. Claiming some bobby pins in the bathroom drawer, I twisted it into a knot and secured it. Dressed, I went to the kitchen to enjoy the bounty Bruce provided. "Morning, Bruce."

"Morning, little lady, I've got toast, bacon, and eggs all ready to go. I've got to get a move on. I told a buddy I'd help him with some calves this morning."

I made a face because I'd hoped he'd play bodyguard. "Guess you're unavailable to be my babysitter this morning?"

His face fell. "I should have thought of that. Want me to cancel?"

"Nope, don't worry, I forgot to ask you. I'll force Deval to come over. He actually has a vested interest in this case."

"So do I. There's this girl with un-tamable curls that's like my baby sister."

251

"Damn and I'd thought I tamed them." I smiled over the coffee he poured for me.

"You always think you have. Sorry to break it to you, but your hair has a mind of its own."

"Amen." I dug into the plate he set before me at the breakfast bar.

We ate in companionable silence and then he walked me out. "If Deval can't come over, call me and I'll cancel."

"Thanks, big guy, I will."

He smiled, closing my Jeep door for me. It was ten-thirty when I got on the road. I hoped Pammy wasn't punctual this morning. I called Deval from my car.

He answered on the first ring. "What do you need?"

"You at my house in thirty minutes."

There was a pause on the other end, and I heard him muttering to someone about changing meetings around before he answered, "I can clear my schedule. Are we going to hunt for the thief?"

"Eventually, but in the meantime I need you to watch me."

The phone was silent for a moment before he responded, "Did you have me cancel my afternoon meetings because you need a male companion? Aren't there any other men in your life who could monitor you?"

"If you wanted to know if I was single, you could have just asked."

"That's not what I meant—"

I cut him off before he could put his foot in it any further. "I'm not going home to play dress up and watch TV. I'm working on a spell that may break the curse on the killer."

"Or we could hunt him down."

"Do you want to be able to question him to see how he got your safe?"

"Of course I do, but I don't need you to see him to be able to torture him."

"Yes, but torture doesn't always work, and my magic could come in handy if I were able to use it against him."

He was silent again. "Fine, we'll do this your way."

"You should be happy. No one should have business meetings on a Saturday."

He hung up on me.

He hadn't given me too much grief, but he might be right. Maybe it was silly to go this route when I could hunker down at Bruce's house until the Tombstone Fortune arrived. I shook my head. No need to second guess myself. There wasn't anything wrong with having a plan A and a plan B. Arriving home before Deval or Pammy, I practiced hyper-vigilance as I pulled up to my house. I kept all of my senses open as I approached my front door, but once there, decided against going inside.

I'd begun to think of my foyer as the hallway of doom. Plus, since Pammy hadn't invited me into her home, I didn't feel the need to be a gracious hostess. Wariness was a good survival mechanism. Sitting on the front porch swing, I waited all of about three minutes for Pammy to roll up in an older sedan that she could have gotten from an old police car auction.

I remembered one of the groupies asking her once why she didn't drive something flashier. Her reply had been something along the lines that comfort and reliability over flash should be everyone's priority. She probably didn't approve of my Jeep being painted a bright turquoise. But it had been my father's, and the color reminded me of family. Besides, the color fit the desert quite well.

The amount of effort it took for Pammy to hoist herself out of a seat indicated it must be extra comfortable. She looked over the top of the cruiser and grunted at me in greeting before walking around to the passenger door. I walked down to the sidewalk to meet her. When she opened the passenger door, I saw an urn strapped into the passenger seat.

"It's always nice to have a buddy on a road trip," I quipped.

"Okay, smart ass, you got something for the ashes that you're asking for?" Her tone was gruff, but I caught the corner of her mouth twitch before she turned to undo the seatbelt.

I pulled a plastic baggie out of my back pocket and held it out to her. It was from the stash I now carried in my purse. She took it and carefully opened the bronze container.

She was cautiously pouring some of Violet's ashes into the baggie while I held it open, when a large black SUV pulled into my short driveway behind my Jeep. My driveway length had never felt lacking until there were two overlarge vehicles in it. The driver's side door was on the far side of where we stood. I didn't see Deval until he walked around the hood.

I let out a wolf whistle. "You clean up nice. Hopefully our afternoon will be uneventful; I'd hate to see that suit ruined."

He gave me slight nod, obviously aware of his own devastating effect. "I would willingly see this one covered in the blood of my enemies."

I looked around, suddenly hyper aware we were standing in my neighborhood surrounded by my human neighbors. Thankfully it appeared everyone was too busy to be out enjoying the fall weather. Looking back at him, I said, "As long as you don't charge me for the suit."

"Wouldn't want you to have to put a lien on your

home," he replied before turning to Pammy. "Pammy, a pleasure."

Pammy was busy putting the lid back on the urn. She didn't answer until she set Violet's remains carefully back in the passenger seat and redid the seatbelt. Once finished she turned and gave him a somewhat regal nod. Until now, I hadn't seen her interact with any of the other power players in the magical community that weren't psychopaths. It was interesting. She held herself like a de facto queen. Accurate enough.

"Well, I won't keep you two occupied. I have official business to take care of."

If it had been just the two of us, I was pretty sure she would have been less formal, maybe even elaborated that she had a Big Gulp and a dead girl waiting for her, but Deval's presence took away any hints of her playfulness. The woman was already a hard ass. I would hate to see her like this on a regular basis.

"Safe travel, Pammy. Give Dusty my best."

"Yes, dear, I'm hoping for good news when I get back. By the way, I called Lief in Tombstone. He has an art show today but will come out tomorrow morning if necessary. Please let me know. I called around, but anyone else would take as long to come out."

"Thanks, Pammy."

"I hope he won't have to make the trip."

I swallowed. So did I. I wanted to stop looking at my house as the chamber of doom. She nodded goodbye to Deval and walked around her car, missing the look I gave my home. Apparently Deval hadn't because as he followed me up the pathway to the front door, he leaned in close to my ear, "Don't worry, we'll kill him, and you'll feel safe in your home again soon."

I harrumphed in response. "Yeah, but what about

goblins who like to travel through magic boxes to show up unannounced?" I opened my front door, gesturing for him to enter first. Grant couldn't hurt him, and he might as well start on his duties.

"It's your plane. I can only enter because you allow me to. You must think of me as some sort of protector."

His words struck home, but I didn't want him to know that. I closed the front door and pointed to the kitchen and proceeded to follow him into the room. "More like the bane of my existence."

"The lady doth protest too much."

"Personal friends with a lot of ladies in waiting?" I asked.

"How old do you think I am?"

"Old enough you should probably feel like a creeper for ogling me in my pajamas."

He stared me down. "I do not ogle."

I swatted a hand in the air. "The gentleman doth protest too much."

"I appreciate. Sleeping garments have evolved in my lifetime, and I appreciate that modesty is no longer a prerequisite for a woman's value."

"Of course you do."

"I was raised by a strong female figure. Had she been human, she would have had a wasted life a century ago."

"That's a pretty strong statement. Is motherhood really such a waste of a life?"

"That is not what I said."

I began gathering the tools needed for the spell, taking care to set Violet's remains on a safe spot on the counter. I waved Deval to take a seat at the bar. "Explain what you meant."

"Every woman has different dreams and skills. My mother is an excellent one because she is fulfilled by her duties. Her intelligence, cunning, and diplomacy are her best talents. If she had to stifle them, she would not have been as happy. That would have reflected in my upbringing. There are other women who are complete nurturers and being a stay at home mother would not stymie their life purpose. Still, I would think that it is better to have the choice than not. Luckily, we supernaturals have never been forced to follow their lead."

"Speak for yourself." I added water and herbs to my pot, carefully following Alice's instructions.

"You'll rise again. The powerful can never stay culled."

He said it with such strong conviction I looked up from my pot and met his gaze. Deval's eyes were liquid steel. He meant it. "And here I thought you pegged us for the weak ones, but after four hundred years, I'm not sure that your view is a realistic one."

He shrugged. "Don't give up, or I will think that you're the weak ones. Pammy certainly hasn't given up. She carries herself like queen."

"Caught that, did you?" I studied the recipe while we spoke, measuring every ingredient carefully as I added each to the pot.

"It's her right. She cares for this area, even if it's as a mob boss. She just found the most efficient way to care for her people."

I looked up from the card. "Yeah, I suppose you're right. It seems odd that she has taken the position without anyone's go ahead."

"You have all given her your permission by not opposing her and being unwilling to do the job yourselves. I didn't see anyone else drive up to Utah to kill the vampires who killed your governing body there."

I glared at him. "To be fair, I think I was a teenager at the time." I didn't tell him that I hadn't even known about the attack until recently. I guessed at my age because I hoped that I was only that unaware due to being caught up in hormones and puberty rather than what he was implying about witches as a whole.

"You are not the only witch in area. Pammy will risk her life to see that the population is taken care of. She's a bit of an egotist, which she displays with her minions. She doesn't make the choices I would, but I can't fault the woman for taking care of problems that no one else will."

Damn, he was observant if he knew about Pammy's fan club. I had mixed feelings about Pammy as a leader mainly because I was still getting to know her, but he was right; I wouldn't have gone to Utah. Although I'd like to think that once I had educated myself and had more expe-rience as a Fortune, I would have. "You're right. I'm not sure if I'd be willing. I don't think I could take out Fane, let alone an entire nest."

Deval let out a harsh laugh. "You do realize that Fane is so old, he's bordering on an ancient?"

I dropped the wooden spoon I was using to stir my mixture. "Are you serious?"

"He approaches a millennium: there is a reason not many could take him. My mother could, and with the recent revelation of your heritage, you may even qualify for her protection. Did you ever ask your family about any mysterious distant relatives?"

"Nope, I've been meaning to, if nothing else for curios-ity's sake, but I wouldn't ask for protection."

"Why not?" He sounded baffled.

I picked up the dropped wooden spoon and gave the pot another quick stir before setting the spoon down, gently this time, and placing the lid on the pot and reducing the heat. The herbs needed to simmer for ten minutes. I turned to him. "It would feel like I was turning my back on the community that raised me, my heritage."

"That's ridiculous. Technically speaking, goblins are also your heritage."

"So we suspect. I still need to check on that."

"There would be no other way for you to claim a plane. Enter, yes, if you used strong magic, though the stories I have heard have all said that it took the trespassers years of preparation for even the one visit."

"Okay, I'm part goblin, but until a week ago I didn't know that. You guys wouldn't even let me have a sleepover with my friend because I was an outsider."

"We are protective of our community."

"As you should be, you guys have a good thing going, but I don't belong with your people. It would be wrong to expect protection from the goblins, when I feel no loyalty to you."

"You may change your mind."

I nodded. "I might. You know, I've always hated the phrase 'waffler.' It came up in an election a few years ago."

"Huh?" His brows drew together.

"It was a big deal because a candidate changed his position on some issues. Here's the thing though, I think it's worse to keep a death grip on your policies. People should evolve and new knowledge that contradicts your previous beliefs should make you change them. There's nothing wrong with learning. I can't respect people who are adamant that they will never change their minds. I prefer when people have closely held beliefs but believe there is a possibility they may be wrong and if given more knowledge, admit it."

"You may not be as naive as I thought you were, which makes me surprised you aren't taking me up on my offer.

In your current position, you could use all the protection you can get."

He leaned forward in his seat. "You're not wrong, but I'm not sure if mixed loyalties would be a good look on a Fortune. Pammy might not even accept it."

"What Pammy doesn't know, won't hurt her."

"Pammy would find out eventually, she trades in secrets as well as bounties, and when she did find out, things would be worse because I didn't tell her. I'm not even sure if I want to tell her anything. It's not like I could tell her about the plane anyway, without you guys killing me."

"Since we're being honest, that is a possibility. Though I would be incredibly surprised if Pammy did not already know."

"Why the secrecy?"

"Pammy is smart enough to keep her mouth closed. We only kill the stupid."

It sounded like a joke, but he was dead serious. I made a lot of stupid mistakes; not claiming my goblin heritage was probably for the best. "I'd be dead within a month."

His eyebrows drew together. "Are you calling yourself stupid?"

"Nope, but I've been known to learn via mistakes. If a mistake equals death, I'll be totally screwed."

"I think you're overanalyzing this. People die from mistakes every day, regardless of intelligence; it's a willful stupidity when a people believe they can outsmart the law."

"No one can beat the law and topple the queen?"

"I would suggest you did not repeat that sentiment, and yes they can, but if they are smart enough to do it, then they deserve to lead."

"Many people vying for the throne these days?"

"You haven't met my family." He shook his head as though he was surprised he'd said that.

"This is one of those times that a smart person would ignore your last comment, right?"

"That would be wise." He closed his eyes and pinched the bridge of his nose.

The timer on the microwave beeped. "Would you mind going over to sit at the far side of the table?" I turned back to him and pointing to the chair at the far side of the kitchen. He quirked an eyebrow but dutifully rose and walked over to the chair, settling in with his legs stretched out, crossed at the ankles, and his arms folded on his chest.

Huh, he could do what I asked without arguing. Who'd have thunk it. The stare he gave me, however, implied he wanted an explanation. I'd started to grow used to his looks now. A week ago it might have made me want to pee my pants, so win for me. "I want to be in your eyesight while I power the spell because I will be too preoccupied to scan for the empty soul that is the murdering T.A."

"And I need to be over here why?"

"State secrets," I answered smartly. I didn't feel like sharing witch spells with a goblin. Besides the natural resistance to witch magic would allow him not to be harmed by the power I was using. It would probably make his skin itch, though, and since he was being nice, I didn't feel the need to make him uncomfortable.

He laughed, apparently amused by my answer and returning to his usual smug self. "Proceed then, witch."

Right, like it was his idea. Taking Violet's ashes, I poured half of them into the simmering mixture on the stove. I whispered a command to the mixture, and it began to stir itself. While it stirred, I moved my face into the steam of potion and waved it closer with my hands, inhaling until my lungs were uncomfortably full. I held my breath and the magic, focusing on my power, letting it infuse the steam. Traces of Violet's magic fused with my own. Startled, I almost let the steam out before it was ready. Something to ask Alice about later.

Re-focusing, I held the steam in, feeding it my power, wrapping it around the already spelled essence. A minute in, when pricks of light stabbed at my vision, I forced the spelled steam from my lungs into the potion whispering, "*Ex propositoque*" with the last of my breath. I took in a deep breath as the spell's power flowed across the kitchen like a blast, tickling my skin and invading my senses. A burst of blood-red steam erupted from the potion. I wasn't sure if that was a good thing but hoped it boded well for my first necromancy spell.

Turning off the stove's heat, I needed to let the mixture cool before putting it into the thin glass jars I used for defensive potions. They broke more easily when being thrown at an enemy, but they also broke when scalding liquid was poured in them.

I walked over to the table on shaky legs but made the effort to sit in the chair like my legs weren't spaghetti. Deval uncrossed his ankles and sat forward, studying me. His predatory look made me glad I'd put in the effort to not look like prey.

"Again you surprise me," he said.

It took effort to not just lay my head on the table for a nap let alone play verbal acrobatics with a goblin, but when you invited help, you invited questions. "What was it this time? That I can hold my breath for a full minute?" I leaned back in my chair, trying to appear flippant.

"No, I keep thinking I have figured out your power level, and then you do some other powerful thing. I think in a year, you would be willing to go to Utah to go toe to toe with a vampire clan."

A shaky laugh escaped. Little did he know, I was always

a powerhouse, but the plane he accidentally gifted me with increased my potential. "Well, thank you, I think."

"You need to learn to take a compliment."

I said nothing for a moment, letting the silence stretch between us.

He broke it first. "Are you still feeling the cold?" He said it casually, but it seemed like a test.

I did a full body check before answering, "No, the cold is gone. If you could gift me with another plane in July, I might even thank you for it."

"You should thank me for the one I already gifted you." He smiled.

I think I passed the test. "Perhaps one day I will."

"I look forward to that." He took my hand, and his eyes met mine. His crinkled in the corner and may have even held a spark of affection.

Unsure if it was the type of affection someone paid a younger sister or something more, I felt heat rising to my cheeks. Next would come the nervous sweat. I hastily pulled my hand away. "Can I get you some iced tea?"

Just like that, the affection disappeared, and his eyes became shuttered. "That would be nice. I had begun to think that you had no skills as a hostess."

My laugh was forced, but it broke the tension. "Yeah, my house is more self-service." I stood and hastened over to where the potion was cooling and after stirring it a few times, decided it was ready to go into its containers. First, the prince's beverage. I took out two large tumblers and filled them to the brim with ice before pulling the pitcher of Earl Grey out of the fridge. "It's unsweetened, but I can get some sugar if you prefer it sweet."

"Sweet is overrated."

The double meaning made me a nervous as I handed him his glass. Thank the gods I didn't drop it in his lap. He took it with a small smile, and I turned back to pour the potion. The small bottles made it necessary to use a funnel. I concentrated on filling them, not bothering to make small talk. The only noise was the ice cubes hitting the plastic of the glass while Deval drank his tea. Five minutes later, I had five full bottles.

I spilled a few drops. I glared at the liquid. The amount of my essence poured into the potion was a lot of work. I shook it off.

"Need a refill?" I turned back to Deval. He opened his mouth, but before he could answer, his phone started chirping a generic ring tone. He probably disapproved of my customized ring tones.

He grunted before answering his phone with a curt, "Yes." The chill he delivered with that one word made me glad I wasn't on the other end of that phone call.

The pitcher was still on the counter, and I grabbed it to refill his tea, but he held up his hand rejecting the offer. "I'll be right there. If you have allowed this to happen on your watch, you had better be prepared to suffer the consequences." His voice was so low I could barely make out his words. He ended the call and stood abruptly. "Get your purse."

"Huh, why?"

"I need to drop you off with another male. I have to go."

"You don't have to drop me off, let me grab my potions. I'm perfectly capable of driving myself somewhere else. If you could just walk me to my Jeep and verify that no cursed men are hiding in the backseat."

He nodded, obviously distracted by his phone call. I rushed to grab my purse and wrap my potion bottles in a kitchen towel before carefully placing them into my purse. He hurried me out the door and did a thorough check of my Jeep before holding the door open for me. "Go straight to a man."

"If this was any other situation, this would be the time I would tell you to go fuck yourself."

He grinned. "I hope that you would." With that he closed my door.

I started my Jeep and watched him start his own SUV from my rearview mirror. He pulled out of the driveway with a controlled recklessness.

Alone, I felt exposed. Following his lead, I pulled out of my driveway one handed, fishing in my purse for my phone to call Bruce. I found it because it started to go off with Fleetwood Mac's "You Can Go Your Own Way," Alice's newly programmed ring tone.

My hand hit pay dirt, and I pulled it out. "Hey, Alice, I just finished the potion. Fingers crossed it will break the curse."

"It better, bitch, if you want this abomination to live."

19

Cold washed down my spine. I recognized the voice from the attacks.

"What do you want, Grant?"

"I hope for her sake that your little bodyguard is gone."

"And if he's not?"

"I'll slit her throat right now." A muffled cry sounded through the phone.

"There's no need for that. He's gone. I don't think he'll like that you called him little or my bodyguard."

A grunt sounded through the phone followed by a scream. "Still feeling brave, bitch?"

I cringed. I wanted to say yes, but I wasn't at his mercy, and Alice hadn't asked to be brought into this. "What do you want?"

"Come to the church, alone. Your spell better work, or you're going to wish you had never been born." He hung up.

In a daze, I stared at my phone for a moment before a honk rudely reminded me I had stopped at a stop sign to take the call. They screeched around me, flipping me off for their trouble, but I didn't care. I needed to save Alice although I was very aware that Grant planned to kill us both once I arrived. The sense of impending doom lingered, but I pulled the Jeep over a couple of feet hoping to avoid other angry drivers. My fingers shook as I scrolled through my recent calls. I hit send, calling Deval. He didn't answer the first, second or third time. "Deval, I don't know what you're doing, but your thief is holding Alice hostage. You need to meet me at the First Baptist Church in Phoenix."

I didn't have the time to sit on the corner. I pulled into traffic, calling Bruce, Deval, and Pammy on a repeat cycle. No one answered. Before I knew it, I had pulled onto the street the church stood on. I was on my own. Oddly, I realized that the only thing in my favor was if the potion worked, which was exactly what the murderer wanted. If the curse lifted, Grant would be susceptible to my magic, and I'd be able to see him. Alice made no guarantees about the potion, I didn't have a ton of hope, but I clung to what I could.

I reached for my power. Despite it being depleted an hour ago, I had a decent reserve. If I'd had any idea I would be going into battle, I would have made Deval come into the plane and ask him about decorating tips, just to recharge my batteries. At least I still retained some juice. I needed to throw the potion on Grant, and when it worked, subdue him. That was my grand plan. Nothing fancy, and I hoped it would work because plans B, C, and D hadn't answered their phones. Unwilling to announce my arrival, I parked down the block. Taking a deep breath, I opened the Jeep door.

The walk to the ruin was the longest of my life. I counted out the steps, a nervous habit I'd picked up years ago. One hundred and fifty-two brisk strides later, I passed through Alice's wards. What was the proper hostage situation etiquette? If I were visiting, I would knock. If I were some military commando, I'd scale a wall or rappel in, breaking a window with flying glass surrounding me in a hail of badassery.

Before I could ponder on the various ways the movies told me I should enter a hostage situation, a voice called out from behind the door. It was faint, but I heard "come in, bitch," loud and clear. He needed to expand his vocabulary. At this point, hearing "see you next Tuesday" would at least show variety. My power rushed to my wrists at my sudden flood of adrenaline. If my body was choosing fight over flight, that was a good thing, right? Maybe I would pull this off.

I opened the door with force, courtesy of my newfound bravado. There was no sign of Alice or the invisible man in the entry. I walked past the white adobe walls and looked up to the landing. Alice stood frozen at the top of the steps, her eyes wildly darting around her. Her purple and lime green muumuu was stained around the neck. It looked like blood, which brought me to the floating knife at her throat. "I'm here. I have your potion. Let Alice go. She has nothing to with this."

"All of you whores of Satan have something to do with this."

"Yeah, but you chose to sleep with a whore of Satan. What does that say about you?" I regretted the words immediately as the knife pressed into the abused flesh at Alice's throat.

Alice let out a small whimper.

I winced. "Sorry, I'm sure she tricked you."

"As if you stupid bitches could trick me. I gave that whore what she wanted. I just didn't want to play house afterward."

"Sorry, my mistake."

He grunted, temporarily appeased. If I could see him, I'd bet he would be sporting a look of self-righteous indignation.

"Can I come up?" I wanted to get this show on the road before I lost my nerve.

"Walk to the top of the stairs and roll the potion to me. Try anything at all, and I'll slit her throat."

No need to throw it at him then. I'd wasted the thinner bottles for nothing. It sounded like he would happily shower in it. As I walked up the stairs, I couldn't help but remember how I used to find the thick carpet comforting. Right now the sensation reminded me of quicksand. I climbed anyway, counting again in sets of three. One, two, three, one, two, three. My eyes never leaving the knife as I watched for any twitch. Countless sets of three later, I stood on the top step.

"Now, let me see the potion."

I reached into my purse and pulled one from the kitchen towel. "Do you want me to roll it?"

"That's what I said, right?" His voice oozed condescension.

My brow creased in annoyance, but I bent over, eyes still on the knife and gave a surprisingly good roll. It still didn't exactly go to Alice, but we were dealing with a lopsided bottle and thick carpeting. Apparently universal physical laws were my fault as well.

"Stupid witch." Alice jerked like a rag doll a foot to her left as Grant went after the bottle. He had to be a big guy if he was able to pull her around like that.

Alice fell to her knees as the bottle was picked up, floating in the air like the knife.

"Do I drink it?"

"Uh, I think you can just pour it on yourself."

"You're not sure? What are you an amateur?"

"Witchcraft is not a science. I've never had to cure the invisible man."

He let out a harsh laugh. The stopper came out of the bottle and the liquid poured out. This was where I needed to get ready. My adrenaline-fueled magic was primed. I directed it toward my palms and waited. Nothing happened.

"You lied. Guess that means you both die," he said, his voice was flat.

Alice's head snapped back as he pulled her hair. "Try drinking it," she said her voice suddenly calm and authoritative. Lucid Alice joined the party.

"Are you trying to poison me, cow?"

Alice grunted which increased the trickle of blood running down her neck. "Like she said. Some of magic is trial and error. If you want to stay stuck like that, suit yourself." Her voice was softer this time, she seemed to be trying to avoid further damage from the knife.

"Well, bitch, do you have any more?"

I nodded and reached into my pocket, wishing I had a vial of poison instead. This time when I rolled the vial, it managed a wobbly path right to him, and it was scooped right up, uncorked, and I assumed, devoured. With Alice on her knees and knowing where his head was I had the perfect opening. I swallowed my nerves and let my magic loose. I hoped for a scream that never came. Maybe I hadn't actually hit him? He remained invisible and my magic passed straight through where I thought he was.

He laughed. "Stupid bitch, didn't you realize? I'm immune to your shit now, which means you can't see me still. I thought you bitches would be useful. Guess I was wrong." The knife quivered for a moment.

Suddenly Alice reached up and scratched at the hand

holding the knife with her nails. There was a yowl of pain, and the knife fell. Alice ducked and began to crawl away, but then I heard an oomph, and she went sprawling across the carpet.

I rushed forward without thinking, I needed to save my friend who was curled in a ball clutching at her ribs. I tackled the space above her, satisfied to hear another. With no formal fight training, I tried to punch, bite, and claw my opponent to submission.

He let a few grunts and a laugh. "Really think you can win this? Why couldn't you just do what I asked? I'm going to make you hurt."

His first punch landed, hitting me right on my cheek-bone, snapping my head to the side. The floor seemed to rise up to meet me. There was no time to react before kicks hit me in a relentless staccato. I wanted to fight back, but blinding pain shot through me. The darkness began to close in when I heard Alice. Her voice acted like a beacon, allowing me to hold on to consciousness a bit longer.

"You idiot, the spirits have spoken, and they are unwilling to release you. Do you think killing their kin will convince them to grant you mercy?"

I had no idea what she was talking about, but it kept the darkness at bay for the moment. I wanted to give into the pain, but letting the darkness in meant death.

"What are you talking about?" He asked, pausing his assault.

"Just what I said. We gave you the tools to free yourself. You did not seek forgiveness. You sought justification of your supposed wrongs. Well, death does not agree with your self-righteousness."

Suddenly a hand grabbed my hair, pulling my head up at a sharp angle. "Hear that, bitch? Your friend bought you a few extra minutes." Hot breath hit my ear.

My head was thrust back down and hit the carpet with enough force cause the shadows to return for a moment as the air above me shifted, and he kicked me again. My entire body was in agony, but the kicks brought fresh jolts of pain to my system.

"Come on, boy, kill me. Your curse will only be ten times worse." Alice said laughing as Grant turned his attention to her.

I clung to her words and tried to sit up. My body revolted. I could hear him begin to start punching and kicking Alice. She was a stronger person than I and didn't make a single sound. Inside my head, I was screaming in fury as the sounds of cracking bones and a wet noise that sounded like blood being drawn filled the air. I couldn't lie here. Pain engulfed me, as I found the will to roll over. I needed to help my friend. The knife was on the floor since he decided beating us to death would be more satisfactory. It was there, out of reach, taunting me.

I dragged my body forward inch by excruciating inch. My fingers found the hilt, but they didn't seem to want to grip the hilt. Something was wrong with my arm. I gritted my teeth and forced my fingers to cooperate. Knife in hand, I slashed blindly and hit something. I heard a yowl of pain, and a body fell to the floor. Hopefully it was Grant. Maybe I managed to hamstring him, but there was no way of knowing.

My pain suddenly stopped, as my power realized this was my last opportunity for survival and rushed through my body, giving me one last burst of adrenaline to hide the pain and the willpower to keep fighting. I crawled forward until I felt the hard body of a large man. I began stabbing indiscriminately. He punched me some more, yanked at my hair, getting in any blow he could. I kept stabbing. His blood was visible when it left his body, and I had never seen anything more beautiful.

A punch to my ribs brought the pain rushing back as the magic powering my brief recovery left as quickly as it came. Pushed onto my back, I felt strong hands encircle my neck. I tried to stab him again, but all the blood coating my fingers made the knife slippery. It fell from my numb hand. I didn't even have the satisfaction of looking in my killer's eyes. Needle points of light invaded my vision, as I feebly clawed at the hands, not wanting to give up.

Just as the darkness was going to win, the weight crushing my throat was gone. Sucking in a sharp breath, my lungs burned. My fractured ribs protested. Blinking, I managed to clear my vision, expecting to see Deval or Bruce. Instead another danger appeared. Fane Dimir was smiling down at me. My mother was going to be so pissed that the vampires got me in the end.

"Peg, you look good enough to eat."

I was sure he was referring to the fact I was covered in blood, but he would say that even if I weren't. He turned his attention back to Grant, whom he could apparently see.

"You thought to take my property, did you, you stupid little mortal?"

"Stupid fucking witch, I didn't take your property. That bitch belonged to me."

Fane's laugh sent shivers up my spine. "Is that what Violet told you—that I'm a witch? You are too stupid to live. Witches are nothing compared to my race. Violet was always mine." His razor-sharp fangs extended two inches from his extra set of upper and lower canines.

Grant screamed in terror.

Fane looked down at me, his ice-blue eyes glowing. He winked, and my body shuddered involuntarily bringing a fresh wave of pain. I wanted to scream, too, but could barely breathe. There might have been a lung punctured.

"What a lovely sound, don't you think, darling?"

I stared back transfixed, unable to say anything.

He laughed and turned back to his first prey. The sounds of wet popping and torn flesh filled the air. Grant's screams continued for a moment, before turning to gurgles followed by a deafening silence. I turned my head to the right. Alice looked back at me. She was bruised and bloody but breathing. Her eyes were open, but they held that glossed-over look. I thought that it was either shock or that she'd checked out again, possibly both. Suddenly there was a thud, and I was looking into the eyes of a dead man. *Hello, Grant.* He really was handsome; too bad he was evil.

I didn't want to look, but realizing Fane was being very quiet, I didn't have a choice. Death stared back. It was the first time I had ever met and held a vampire's gaze. Well, I got my wish. I would be able to look my killer in the eyes.

He got down on the floor, crawling over me, careful not to touch my injured body. I was surprised he wasn't deliberately manipulating my injuries. Oh right, he was going for mental torture. He straddled me but didn't touch as he studied me. With an injured woman under him, and Grant's corpse practically touching him, he was in psychopath heaven. He continued to stare silently.

"Kill me already."

He laughed softly and placed his face in between my breasts, inhaling as he moved his head up my chest to my neck. "Killing you sounds fun, but I wouldn't want to deny myself your particular vintage in the future. Just a taste I think. I want to savor your blood, your fear, your body." He spoke in my ear, like a lover. Then he bent back to the top of my breast and took a light nip, licking the fresh blood before dragging his tongue back up my neck and to my ear, where he took another quick bite.

Fear induced shivers wracked my body, but I locked my jaw, refusing to beg or scream.

The sound of a door being slammed open downstairs was the most beautiful thing I'd ever heard.

"Peg! Alice!"

It was Deval, thank the gods.

"Well, my sweet, looks like our time is up for now. I will dream of you tonight, I think. Dream of me as well." He dragged a fang along my lower lip and licked my mouth before standing up with unimaginable speed. He looked to Alice. "I heard your secrets, witch. With the goblins here, you have a brief respite, but I will come for it. You ladies have brought so many interesting new games into my life."

I could hear Deval pounding up the stairs and felt strangely safe, even with an ancient vampire standing over me with a proverbial hard-on. Darkness finally won.

EPILOGUE

Another day, another bouquet. As per usual, they were gorgeous. Today's bunch was two dozen roses, a deep crimson and a purple so dark they were almost black, arranged into a heart shape. I should be thrilled with the expensive flowers filling my home, but they all came with simple white card that simply read *Fane*.

As with this one, not all of the arrangements came with a vase. The few vases that I already owned were full, so I grabbed a large mason jar, which had held marinara in a previous life, to support and contain the heavy arrangement. The flowers settled, and I set them on the table in the kitchen. There were already two arrangements on the table. I'd figure out a place to put the new ones later.

A sturdy knock sounded on my front door. Checking the peephole, I my breath quickened when I saw Deval. I opened the door and gestured him in. "This is a surprise."

"I wanted to come and check on you."

I did a little twirl, ending in a bow. "Nothing a talented witch practitioner couldn't heal."

He gave me a hard look, apparently unamused, and

bypassed me to make himself comfortable in my living room. I shrugged and followed. He took a seat, and I picked one on the love seat opposite from the couch he chose. "You were very close to death when I saw you. I'm surprised you're moving about."

He didn't need to know the first thing I did upon arriving home was take a sleeping bag to my plane and sleep for ten hours straight. "Yes, I've been very fortunate."

"How is Alice?"

"Sore and shook up, but she's doing better. She's offered to train me. I have a lesson with her later tonight."

He nodded in approval. "You couldn't ask for a better teacher. Even my mother speaks highly of her."

"Are they friends?" I asked.

"More like friendly acquaintances. They respect one another." He looked around and suddenly noticed the multiple vases around the room. "You certainly have a lot of people wishing you a speedy recovery, or an admirer perhaps?" He quirked an inquisitive brow.

"Yeah, he's tall, blond, and a psychopath. Every girl's dream. Still, he does seem to have good taste in flowers." I surveyed the various arrangements throughout the room.

"Fane has been sending you flowers?" His body tensed as he leaned forward and inspected each bouquet as if they were a ticking time bomb.

"Yup, he's taken quite a shine to me."

"You're being a little blasé about this. Why are you keeping the arrangements?"

"It's not the flowers' fault that they were bought by a man who wants to eat, torture, and rape me. They're beautiful."

"One would think that you wouldn't want the reminder."

"The reminder is good. I need to step up my game.

He's fixated on me, pretending he doesn't exist isn't going to help me. I want the reminder so that every day I spend getting strong enough magically and physically will allow me to be the one who kills him."

He nodded. "I'll have a talk with him."

A week ago I told Deval that I hadn't wanted him to intervene on my behalf because I didn't want mixed loyalties. After nearly dying, I was more pragmatic. I wasn't ready to out myself as part goblin, but I also wouldn't turn down the offer. "I'd appreciate it, but I don't think it will hold him at bay forever."

"You'd be surprised."

Maybe I would, but I wouldn't count on it. "Perhaps I will, but apparently I'm a special vintage."

"Yes, I imagine you would be. Mixed heritage has become rare. He probably hasn't tasted a goblin-witch mix in several hundred years. Even if your goblin heritage is small."

"I'm not sure if he realized what he tasted."

He shook his head. "He at least suspected. I'm afraid my talk with him will confirm those suspicions. Yet, even the implied relation should keep him from acting on his promises."

"We'll see. Did he say anything to you that day at Alice's?"

"Just that I could thank him for saving my friends. He was trying to imply I owed him a debt."

"I'm guessing you told him otherwise." I laughed.

"Yes, I was angry he had killed my prey."

"Can't say I feel the same way."

"Understandable, but that means I still need to find out how he did it."

I nodded. If his property had been stolen once, it could

happen again. There was no way that Grant didn't have inside help. Deval had a traitor among his people. "If you need my assistance, I'll cut you a fair deal."

His lips twitched. "You would charge a friend?"

"Are we friends?" I asked, tilting my head.

"We could be. Maybe more than friends."

My cheeks flamed. "Oh, really? That's presumptuous."

"We'll see." He stood abruptly and walked purposefully toward me.

I scrambled out of my seat, rising to meet him and feeling a bit like a rabbit ready to flee. He stopped, leaving an inch between our bodies. He gave me a smoldering look before his face broke into a grin. Reaching up to tuck my hair behind my ear, he leaned in and closed my eyes. He didn't kiss me but placed his cheek against mine. The feel of his stubble against my cheek was strangely erotic. I inhaled sharply.

He spoke softly in my ear. "We could have a lot of fun. Next time I tie you up, you'll enjoy it."

I leaned into him enjoying the sensation of his hands cupping my face and was a little disappointed when he dropped a hand. Then it was at my breast. The sound of rustling paper made me open my eyes as I realized he wasn't copping a feel but putting something into the pocket of my button up shirt.

"Don't argue about this. It's a reward. I will not be indebted to you."

With that, his hand dropped, and he pulled his face back to look into my eyes. "Yes, this is going to be fun." He turned and walked out my front door.

Well, damn. My dance card was filling up, though I shouldn't consider Fane a suitor since he took "until death do us part" too far, in my opinion. I pulled the paper out of my pocket and sat down my legs turning to jelly. A check for five grand. Add that to the three grand I'd gotten as a Fortune, and I didn't need to take any Fortune gigs for a while. I would though. Every job meant more experience, which might just keep death at bay a little longer.

ABOUT THE AUTHOR

 Originally from Arizona, I'm currently residing in Chicago, having traded an oven for a freezer. I write Urban Fantasy because I like spooky things. I have a degree in English Literature from Arizona State University and the typical laundry list of jobs that goes with it. When I'm not working the day job or writing, I enjoy eating, reading, watching TV, pretending to be an elf (RPG), coding, and spoiling my cats.

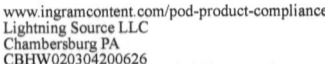